THREE WISHES

SERESSIA GLASS

Genesis Press, Inc.

Indigo Love Stories

An imprint of Genesis Press, Inc.
Publishing Company

Genesis Press, Inc.
P.O. Box 101
Columbus, MS 39703

ISBN-13: 978-1-58571-278-6
ISBN-10: 1-58571-278-7
Manufactured in the United States of America

First Edition 2003
Second Edition 2008

Visit us at www.genesis-press.com or call at 1-888-Indigo-1

DEDICATION

—*To my friends, who understand and leave me alone when I get writer's face.*
—*To my brothers and sisters, who don't mind when I forget to call.*

I'd love to hear from you. Feel free to visit my website at:
http://www.seressia.com
—*and to drop me an email at* **write-me@seressia.com**.

ONE

Everything changed the day little Taylor Whitfield got locked out of her house.

Maya had driven home slowly, wipers flashing frantically in the pounding rain. As she pulled into the driveway of her Grant Park home, she noticed a dark form huddled on the porch of her neighbor's house. She parked and shut off the car, then managed the awkward maneuver of exiting the car, opening the umbrella and grabbing her briefcase.

The little girl sat in the swing on her neighbor's porch. She looked to be no more than seven or eight. What was the family's name? They'd moved in about six months ago, she recalled, the little girl and her father. Maya had never seen a woman at the house, except for an older woman who left when the father came home.

Why in the world was the child sitting on the porch? She looked soaked to the bone; April rains were chilly, even here in Atlanta. Maya told herself it wasn't her problem as she unlocked her door and dumped her wet belongings on the parquet floor of her foyer. She shouldn't get involved. She had enough problems of her own

With a sigh, she reopened her large umbrella and dashed across the short distance to her neighbor's house. The child was soaked to the bone, her dark hair plastered to her skull, her blue eyes large as she watched Maya approach.

"Hi," Maya said, stepping onto the porch. "Are you locked out?"

The girl looked at her but didn't answer.

"I'm Maya Hughes," she tried again, keeping her voice soft. "What's your name?"

"My daddy told me not to talk to strangers," the child said, her voice barely coherent through her chattering teeth.

"Your daddy's right," Maya said, wondering where in the world he was and why he'd left his daughter on the porch. "But we're neighbors and we met before, do you remember?" The little girl nodded. "So that hardly makes us strangers."

She seemed to think about that for a moment. "I'm T-Taylor," she finally said. "I'm locked out. Nana Henderson should be here, but she's not."

Maya came to a decision. "Then you're coming home with me. We'll get you dried off and you can wait for your father."

Taylor shook her head. "I should talk to Daddy."

"Good idea," Maya agreed, reaching into her pocket for her cell phone. "What's your father's phone number?"

Taylor gave her the number, adding, "My daddy's a doctor. That's the answering service."

Maya bit off the "You've got to be kidding me" she was about to say. *God, the man's daughter has to call an answering service just to talk to him? What kind of father is he?* The service answered on the second ring. "Hello, I need to speak to Dr. Whitfield."

"I'm sorry, ma'am, but Dr. Whitfield is in surgery for the next two hours. Would you care to leave a message?"

She fought her temper down, fearful of frightening the little girl. "This is Maya Hughes, Dr. Whitfield's next-door neighbor. Please inform him that his daughter was locked out of their house, and I am taking her next door. He can pick her up there." She rattled off her cell and home phone numbers, then disconnected.

"Your father's going to call us soon," she informed Taylor. "In the meantime, we'll go over to my house and I'll introduce you to Hamlet and Horatio." She held out her hand.

"Who're Hamlet and Hor-Horror Show?" Taylor asked, slipping her hand into Maya's.

She held the umbrella over them both, making her way carefully across the flanking driveways. The little girl's hand was small and trusting in hers. "Hamlet is my dog, and Horatio is a cat that thinks he's a dog."

Taylor laughed. "Cats don't think they're dogs."

"This one does. The lady I got them from told me that Horatio just showed up in the litter of pups, about two weeks after the puppies were born. He was newborn himself. The mama dog let him stay and nursed him too. Since then, he's thought of himself as a puppy."

Maya opened the door and immediately heard the scratching sound of claws gaining purchase on the hardwood floor. "Stay behind me, Taylor," she warned. "My boys can get a little excited."

The little girl dutifully stepped behind her as Maya's "boys" scrambled into view, vying for attention. "This is Hamlet," Maya said, pointing to the beagle that thought he was a greyhound. She turned to an overweight calico that bounced around her ankles with the same exuberance the beagle possessed. "And this is Horatio. Don't say the C-A-T word to him, or he'll get offended."

Taylor giggled. "They look like little fat hot dogs. Can I pet them?"

"Of course you can," Maya said, shutting and locking the door. "Why don't you give me your coat? Then I'll find something dry for you to change into."

"Kay." Taylor slipped out of her soaking wet jacket. Her jeans were also drenched from the knees down. Apparently being soaked was the least of her concerns because she simply flopped on the floor and into a barking, meowing, giggling bundle of child, cat, and dog.

Maya dropped her briefcase on the couch, then took the soaked outerwear to the laundry room. She'd toss it into the dryer with the jeans after she got something for Taylor to wear. As she climbed the stairs to the guest room her nieces used, she tried to keep her anger in check. Where in the world was Taylor's housekeeper? Since Maya often worked out of her home, she knew the Whitfield's housekeeper arrived around noon and stayed until Taylor's father came home. If something had happened to her, why didn't Taylor have a key? And why didn't her father have an emergency number? Maya didn't care that he was in surgery—if she had a child, there was no way—Her hands froze on the wardrobe handles as the old regret surfaced. She didn't have a child. Seven years of trying to get pregnant and one year of blame and anger equaled eight painful years of marriage that ended in an acrimonious divorce. No, she didn't have a child of her own, but if she finally decided to adopt, there was no way she'd ever let her child come home alone, soaked and locked out of the house.

She retrieved a change of clothing for Taylor and retreated downstairs. The sound of delighted laughter stopped her in her tracks. Her heart leapt in her chest.

How often had she dreamed about her child's laughter filling the emptiness of her home, her heart? Too long.

She entered the living room to see Ham and Harry vying for who could get the most licks on Taylor's face. "Taylor, here's some dry clothes for you to change into. There's a bathroom just down the hall you can use."

Taylor got to her feet. "You have a little girl, too?"

"Ah…no, I don't."

"Why not?"

Maya suppressed a groan. How could she have forgotten how inquisitive seven-year-olds could be? "Maybe I will one day, but right now I've got my hands full with Ham and Harry, and I have a couple of nieces your age, and a nephew to keep me busy."

"Do you think I can play with them sometime?" Taylor asked, lifting her pale face to Maya. She had creamy skin like a doll's, and wide blue eyes framed by thick dark lashes. Definitely destined to be a heart-breaker one day. "If they like me, that is. Do you think they'll like me?"

The wistfulness in the child's voice was obvious. Despite herself, Maya reached out and stroked the girl's damp locks. "We'll have to ask your father first, but Leila and Tamera like to make new friends. They'll be over this weekend, so we'll see, all right?"

Taylor beamed at her. "'Kay."

Maya felt ridiculously pleased at having made Taylor smile. "Why don't you get out of those wet clothes and dry off while I fix you a snack?"

"Do you have peanut butter?"

Maya smiled. "Of course."

—◆—

Nick Whitfield pushed open the door leading from the scrub room, emotionally and physically exhausted. Mrs. Bowerman's surgery had taken three excruciating hours, but it had been successful. He gave her relatives the good news and continued on his way to the break room to snag a cup of coffee before heading home. With any luck, he'd beat Taylor home and be there to help her with her homework.

He glanced up at the clock, surprised to find that it was already after five. Why hadn't Taylor called as soon as she got home? Squelching the momentary worry, he made his way over to the nurses' station, deliberately ignoring the friendly smile from the pretty brunette behind the counter. "Hi, Ms. Reeves. Let me see the phone for a minute, will you?"

"Of course, doctor," the nurse said, giving him a larger smile as she handed the receiver over. "Is there anything else I can get for you?"

"No, this is it, thanks." He punched in his home number. It was possible that time had slipped away from Taylor, but his daughter knew that checking in when she got home was a rule he never wanted broken, for any reason.

The answering machine picked up. He disconnected with a frown. Perhaps Mrs. Henderson had needed to run an errand and had taken Taylor with her. Even so, the housekeeper knew to call in. Ignoring the niggling feeling of trepidation on the back of his neck, he placed a second call, to his answering service.

"Oh, Dr. Whitfield, we've been trying to reach you!"

"You have? My pager didn't go off." He unclipped it from his belt. "Oh, looks like the batteries went out."

"You have two messages, sir. One from a Robert Henderson, saying that his mother had an accident and had to be rushed to the hospital."

Oh God. "When was this?" he demanded, gripping the receiver tight. "Where's my daughter?"

"The message came in about 2:30 this afternoon, sir," the voice on the other end of the line said. "I don't know any other details. But I do have another message for you."

"What is it?"

"Your daughter is with your next-door neighbor, Maya Hughes."

Maya Hughes? He struggled to recall the faces of the neighbors flanking him, people he hadn't bothered getting to know since he'd bought the house six months ago, an oversight he definitely planned to remedy. An older white couple in their 50s…Jacobson was their name. On the other side…

His stressed memory called up an image of a black woman with a complexion somewhere between cream and honey-tan, with shoulder-length ebony hair. She'd brought them a damned good casserole when they first moved in—something he hadn't thought people did anymore, but was glad she had. Maybe she wasn't a child molester, but how was he to know? He'd never considered his neighbors when planning for emergencies with Taylor.

"Did Mrs. Hughes leave her number?" he asked, trying to keep his voice even. Hell, he didn't even know if she was married, if she had kids, or bred pitbulls in her backyard. His little girl could be in serious trouble, all because he didn't plan, he didn't think things through. He wouldn't lose her like he lost her mother. He couldn't.

The attendant gave him two numbers. He thanked her, then disconnected. His fingers trembled as he dialed the home number, and he forced himself to calm down. Child molesters wouldn't leave home and cell phone numbers, would they? Everything would be fine. So his daughter had been in a stranger's house for the last two and a half hours without his knowledge.

Nothing had happened, nothing was wrong—
"Hello?"

The voice that answered the phone was warm, feminine. "Where's my daughter?"

Silence. Then, "You must be Dr. Whitfield." The voice had changed from honey to ice in two seconds. "Let me get Taylor for you."

There was a scuffling noise, then the sweetest sound he'd ever heard. "Hi, Daddy."

"Taylor." Nick closed his eyes in silent thanks. She sounded okay. "Are you all right? You're not hurt or anything?"

"I'm fine, Daddy. I got real wet in the rain and I don't know where Nana Henderson is. But Maya said I could stay here and wait for you. She said we weren't strangers because we're neighbors and we met before."

"Oh she did, did she?" Nick gripped the receiver tighter. His trusting little girl. He'd brought her here to have a normal life, to be safe. Fear snaked in his gut. She could have been hurt—

"We had lots of fun. We had peanut butter sandwiches and I played with Hammy and Horror-Show. Then Maya helped me with my homework. She's real nice, Daddy."

The fear receded some. No one with evil intent would help a child with homework, would they?

"Who are Hammy and Horror Show?" he asked, dreading the answer.

"Hammy is a dog and Harry is a big fat cat," his daughter explained. He heard something like a meow-bark in the background. "I'm sorry, Harry thinks he's a dog, but really he's a c-a-t," his daughter said in a whisper. "He actually barks like a dog, too."

Good grief, his daughter was alone with a strange woman and her psychotic pets. "Let me speak to...Maya again, cupcake. I'll be home as soon as I find out what happened to Mrs. Henderson."

"Yes?" The cool voice came back on the line.

"Maya. Mrs. Hughes. Thank you for looking after my daughter for me."

"Well, I couldn't leave her on the porch, soaked to the bone," she said. "Locked out of her own home."

Her barbs struck the sensitive part of him rubbed raw by fear. "I just found out through my service that Mrs. Henderson had some sort of accident. My pager ran out of power."

"Then I suggest you invest in some batteries, doctor." There was actually a hint of humor beneath the coolness. "Do you know what happened to Mrs. Henderson?"

"No. I'm going to check with admissions here, then call a couple of other hospitals if I come up Empty. Can I impose on you for another hour?"

"Taylor isn't an imposition," she answered, her voice flowing like honey again, soothing his frazzled nerves. "My dog and cat enjoy the company, and so do I."

She lived alone? He'd never paid attention before, but he'd just assumed that a beautiful young woman in a neighborhood like theirs was there to raise a family. "I really appreciate you looking out for Taylor for me. S-she's all I have."

"I understand," she said, her voice soft. "Would you like to speak to her again?"

"Thank you." He waited until he heard his daughter's voice again. "Cupcake, I'm going to find out where Nana Henderson is. I want you to be a good girl and I'll be there as soon as I can, okay?"

"Okay, Daddy, I love you, bye!"

Nick stared at the receiver. It was the first time his daughter had ever rushed him off the phone. Because of Maya Hughes.

Who was this woman?

TWO

"Are you married?"

Maya looked up from her laptop. Taylor sat on the floor in front of the TV, watching Cartoon Network, with Hamlet and Horatio tucked close on either side of her. "Uhm, no. I'm not married anymore."

"My daddy isn't either," the little girl announced.

"Really?" Maya kept her voice non-committal since she had no idea where this conversation was heading. Besides, she didn't want get involved in her neighbors' lives, no matter how unpopulated her own.

"Yeah." Taylor pulled both pets into her lap. "My mom died when I was born."

"Oh, no." At a loss for words, Maya placed her laptop on the couch and moved to sit beside the little girl.

Taylor turned to face her. "Daddy said she got sick and had to go to heaven. I talk to her all the time. Do you think she hears me?"

"I'm sure she does," Maya answered, her heart twisting for the little girl. "When you talk to her, don't you feel better, and all warm inside?"

When Taylor nodded, Maya added, "That warm feeling is your mother letting you know that she's listening to you and that she loves you."

"That's what Daddy said." Taylor smiled as Hamlet licked her cheek and Horatio, not to be outdone, patted a paw against the other cheek. "He doesn't talk about Mommy, but I think he gets lonely sometimes. Do you get lonely, too?"

Maya blinked at the blunt change of topic. "Hamlet and Horatio keep me company, and my family visits all the time." She didn't answer the question, but how could her loneliness matter when she'd just learned that Taylor never knew her mother?

"We don't have pets, and Grandma and Grandpa live in Florida," Taylor confessed. "I have a picture of my mommy beside my bed. Sometimes when Daddy comes to tuck me in, he'll look at Mommy's picture but he doesn't smile."

"I'm sure he misses your mother as much as you do," Maya said softly.

"Yeah." Taylor looked up at her, and Maya realized the child had brilliant sapphire-colored eyes. "Can I come back sometimes, and play with Hamlet and Horror-Show?"

Maya couldn't help herself. She reached out, touching the little girl's sable curls. "I'm sure they'd like that, but we'd better get your father's permission first."

Taylor thought about it for a moment, her dark brows knotted in concentration. "He'll say yes," she announced. "Especially if you let him play with them, too. You will, won't you? He's very nice, and he saves people, so I'm sure he'll like them."

How could she deny the child anything, especially when Taylor looked at her with such longing in those huge blue eyes? "I'll talk to your father when he gets here," she promised. "Now what do you say to helping me make dinner?"

Taylor's eyes grew round. "Can I really?"

Maya laughed. "Of course you can. Go wash your hands and we'll get started."

Dinner preparations passed in a blur of activity and laughter and talking. Maya told herself not to get used to it, even as she relished the presence of a child in her home. Taylor displayed intelligence and humor far beyond her years, but childish innocence still shone through. It was easy to give in to the fantasy of mother and daughter preparing dinner, sharing the events of the day and debating which boy band was the cutest.

Just as they put the finishing touches on dinner, the doorbell rang. "That's probably your father," Maya said unnecessarily, wiping her hands before heading for the door. Taylor followed suit, the animals already scrambling to accompany her. Maya shooed everyone back, then peeped through the viewer. She got a glimpse of dark hair and a tanned jaw before a fist beating on the door blocked her view. Promising silently not to give the man a piece of her mind, Maya unbolted the door and opened it.

"Daddy! Daddy!" Taylor leapt into the man's arms. Hamlet barked boisterously with Horatio doing his best imitation.

"Hey, pumpkin, I'm sorry you got locked out," the man said, clutching Taylor like a lifeline. A lump formed in Maya's throat, an old pain. She backed away, calling her pets to her with a soft word.

Taylor's father slowly eased his grip on the girl. "How are you, honey? Are you all right?"

"I'm fine, Daddy. Maya and I had a snack, and she gave me some clothes to wear, and helped with me my homework and I played with Hammy and Harry and helped with dinner! She said she was my friend. It's all right if we're friends, isn't it? You can be her friend, too."

"Really?" He set Taylor down, then rose, and Maya got her first good look at Dr. Nicolas Whitfield. He was just under six feet, with russet highlights gleaming in his thick, dark hair. Stunning sky-blue eyes framed by thick lashes regarded her, wide set below thick brows, and a strong nose sloped down to hard, thin lips. Not what she would call gorgeous, but definitely easy on the eyes.

And then he smiled. *Whoa, Nelly.*

"Mrs. Hughes, thank you so much for looking after Taylor for me," he said, extending a hand. "I'm so sorry to impose on your family."

"Like I said before, it was hardly an imposition," Maya said, taking his hand. Long, strong fingers gripped hers warmly. "Besides, my family enjoyed the company." She pointed to her pets with her free hand. "And I'm a 'Ms.' now, but you can call me Maya."

"Maya. Call me Nick." His fingers tightened around hers. "Whether it was an imposition or not, I'm grateful you were here."

"It was my pleasure, really. Taylor and I had a fun couple of hours together. Did you find Mrs. Henderson?"

"I did." He finally seemed to remember that he held her hand, and let go. "She slipped on the porch and broke her hip. She's staying in the hospital tonight, but it looks like she'll be home on bed rest for the next several weeks."

"But she's okay, isn't she?" Taylor asked, her eyes glittering with sudden tears.

"Of course she is," Nick said, rubbing his daughter's back in reassurance. "I saw her just before I came home. She's in pain and exhausted, but in good spirits, and she's sorry that she missed you today. I'll take you to see her tomorrow, okay?"

"Okay. But who's gonna take care of me until Nana Henderson gets better?"

Nick was clearly at a loss for words. "I-I'll figure something out, pumpkin. I'll change my schedule around tomorrow and Friday so I can pick you up from school. Then I'll try to make other arrangements over the weekend."

"Why can't I stay with Maya?"

Maya watched Nick's gorgeous eyes widen with surprise as his daughter stepped away from him to stand beside her. *Oh Lord, that's not gonna go over good.*

"Sweetheart, I'm sure Maya is a very busy lady, and we wouldn't want to take up more of her time. Mrs. Henderson can probably recommend someone to temporarily replace her."

"You don't have to do that." Maya's insides tightened as Nick focused on her again. She plowed ahead. "I design educational software for children, and I do most of my work from here. Since I go into the office only a couple of times a week, I can certainly pick Taylor up from school tomorrow and Friday and watch her until you get home."

Taylor obviously thought it a wonderful idea, because she grabbed her father's hand and held on for dear life. "Please, Daddy, can I? Please?"

"I don't want to inconvenience you," he said, an unmistakable hesitation coloring his words.

"I understand. You don't know enough about me to leave your daughter here, right?" Maya smiled to take the bite out of her words.

He had the grace to look sheepish. "Yeah, I guess you could say that."

"I'll tell you what. Why don't you actually come inside so I can shut the door?" He quickly stepped over the threshold, giving Maya the opportunity to close and lock the door. "Now, Taylor and I have already fixed dinner. Let's all sit down and you can ask me just about anything you want. We're neighbors, after all. We should know each other better."

Know each other better. Nick knew Maya meant nothing suggestive by the comment, but his mind immediately headed for the basement. He couldn't help it. He looked at her and immediately thought of food, a sensual buffet created for pleasure. Her skin was dusky butter and honey, smooth and unblemished. Eyes the color of expensive cognac flecked with gold sloped upwards at the outer corners, giving her an Asian look. A round nose perched above lips that looked as if they'd been eating berries. Her hair reminded him of melted chocolate, thick, completely sinful, and begging to be dived into. Her body was slim, but not to the point of seeming fragile. Hunger claimed him, a hunger he hadn't felt in years.

He blinked, wondering at his reaction. Sure, it had been a long time since he'd had a relationship, but he was surrounded by women at the hospital. No one else had reminded him of a sensual smorgasbord. Maya Hughes definitely reminded him of food, the kind of food you crave even though you know it's bad for you.

"Nick?"

Maya called his name, and he was sure it hadn't been the first time. He began to answer her with an extremely elegant "huh" when she touched his hand. His mind instantly went blank again.

"Shall I stroke it for you?"

"What?" He couldn't have heard her right.

She looked at him as if he'd grown an extra head. "I asked if beef stroganoff is all right with you?"

On cue, his stomach stirred to life. It wasn't the only thing stirring. He needed to get away from her, if for no other than reason than to ensure that some blood remained in his brain instead of rushing south. "No, thanks. I really should get Taylor home." His stomach rumbled again.

Even as Taylor chimed in with "Please, Daddy?" Maya laughed at him, a light and musical sound. "Stop trying to be polite, especially with your stomach growling like the MGM lion."

"All right," he capitulated, enjoying the fact that he'd made her laugh. He didn't attempt to retract his hand. He might have been incoherent, but he wasn't stupid. "I felt I had to make a token protest, though."

"Token protest noted." She gathered Taylor with her free hand and guided them into the dining room. "But since I'm interviewing to care for Taylor after school, you should at least see me in my natural habitat."

Nick almost tripped over his own feet. Natural habitat. That brought up an image so overtly erotic that parts of him sprang to attention. He could imagine her spread in welcome on a bed, her skin glistening with excitement as she waited for him to join her, his body sliding over hers, breathing in her scent, entering her dark, hot body…

"Daddy, you can sit here."

Looking into his daughter's eager face cooled his blood as his own will could not. It had been too long since he'd had a woman. Maya had offered to take care of Taylor, not him. And she was his next-door neighbor, for chrissakes! He couldn't think of her as a potential bed partner no matter how long it had been or convenient it could be. Then there was the big point of her being black, or at least black mixed with something. She probably would never consider seeing a white man, and he certainly wouldn't broach the subject.

He removed his jacket and took the seat his daughter pointed him to, then watched as she followed Maya to what he assumed was the kitchen. They should have done this months ago, he thought, the whole getting to know each other better. After the welcome-to-the-neighborhood casserole she'd given them, they'd seen each other coming or going on occasion, but not done anything more than nod or briefly say hi. He'd been too absorbed in getting Taylor settled and finding a sitter she liked to take note.

Nick took note now, watching his beaming daughter precede Maya, bearing a big bowl of salad. Taylor carefully placed the wooden bowl on the lace-draped walnut table, her tongue sticking out with the effort to take care. It was already set with nice gold and blue place settings, candles, and real napkins. Just for them?

Maya caught his curious glance as she set a bowl of pasta on the table. "I come from a big family. We were always going off in different directions, but Mom made sure we gathered for meals. She'd always use her best china, saying the good china wasn't doing much good being used twice a year." She smiled at the memory, teasing him with the fleeting glimpse of a dimple in her right cheek. "So meal time is always a big production. It's a hard habit to break, even though it's usually just me and the two boys."

Her expression darkened for a moment, then cleared. "Anyway, having next-door neighbors over for the first time is reason enough to celebrate, don't you think?"

Any reason was a good reason to celebrate, Nick thought, especially if it meant that he'd get to have whatever smelled so good. "What do you need me to do?"

"Sit there and prepare to get your eat on, as my brothers would say. And what would you like to drink with dinner? I have milk, water, Kool-Aid, and red wine."

Nick's gaze went again to his daughter, who had scampered back to the kitchen and returned with a basket of dinner rolls. Did she help out like this at home? For some reason he couldn't remember, and it bothered him.

"Since it's a celebration like you said, I think Taylor can have Kool-Aid instead of milk. And since I don't have any surgeries scheduled tomorrow, I'll take a glass of that wine."

"Coming right up." She walked back into the kitchen while he watched the swing of her hips every step of the way.

"I like her," Taylor said in a child's whisper that probably carried to the kitchen. "She's very nice. Don't you like her, Daddy?"

"Honey, I just met her," Nick said, even though he thought Maya Hughes very nice indeed.

"She said I could come over and play with Hamlet and Horatio anytime I want—if you say yes," she added. "You will say yes, won't you?"

"I'll think about it," he answered, not quite ready to relinquish his daughter to Maya just yet.

"Maya also said her nieces are gonna be here this weekend, and I can come over and play with them. They're my age, and Maya said they like making new friends, and they're gonna go to the movies and do other things. They're gonna have a lot of fun."

The wistfulness in his daughter's voice tugged at Nick's heart. Even though he had his younger sister growing up, he understood how Taylor could feel lonely at times. His parents had lavished him with attention for the most part, but they couldn't be there all the time, and it just wasn't the same as having other boys to play with. He'd promised himself that when he became a father he wouldn't subject his child to that. Now here he was perpetuating the cycle, all because Jessica—

"Pumpkin, Maya and I will talk after dinner. She's a very considerate person, but we don't want to take advantage of her, do we?"

Taylor pouted. "I guess not."

Nick sighed. He tried desperately to balance his daughter's happiness with the need to make a living and pad her college fund. Sometimes he was painfully aware of how inadequate he was as a single parent, how lonely his daughter was. He knew she wanted a mother, but he'd hoped that Nana Henderson would assuage some of that need. The alternative would be to get married again. The very thought caused his heart to seize up.

"Here we are." Maya's voice jerked him from his thoughts. She'd rolled a cart in loaded with the remaining necessities for the meal, including a pitcher of Kool-Aid and the bottle of wine. She placed glasses in front of each setting, and put the steaming platter of beef stroganoff in the center of the table. "Would you like to say grace, Nick, or do you want me to do it?"

Say grace? When was the last time that he'd done that? He reached for Taylor's hand, then Maya's. Her fingers gripped his with warm assurance, and somehow he managed to stumble through an appropriate blessing.

The meal was beyond good. It bordered on orgasmic. Maybe it was because they were in a new setting, maybe it was the company, but Nick couldn't remember a meal that tasted so good. And considering the way Taylor cleaned her plate and asked for seconds, his daughter felt the same.

Maya couldn't help a smile of pleasure as Taylor and her father enjoyed their meal. She took as much enjoyment from watching them polish their plates as she did making an algorithm go right. Maybe more. Taylor brightened up any room with her presence, and Nick obviously doted on her. Why in the world hadn't he married again? It wasn't her business, of course, and certainly not a question she wanted to ask. Remembering how painful her divorce was made her sympathetic. She'd thought she and Russell would be together forever. It was difficult to imagine how it would be to lose a spouse to death. If she didn't want to get married again, she could certainly understand why Nick had chosen not to.

She looked up to find him studying her. "How's the meal?"

"Best I've had since I last visited my parents," he said, patting his stomach in appreciation. "But don't tell Mrs. Henderson that."

"Your secret's safe with me." She grinned with pleasure. "Do you think you have room for dessert?"

His expression grew uncomfortable. "Don't even tempt me. I don't think I can even blink, so I know I can't eat another bite."

"I like hearing that people enjoy my cooking," she said, "something I learned from my mother. If you want, I'll be more than happy to get some leftovers together for you."

Nick looked at his daughter. "Taylor, we moved in next to an angel and didn't even know it."

Taylor laughed. "She's not an angel, Daddy. Is she?"

"Of course I'm not," Maya laughed, enjoying the teasing. "I'm just a woman who learned to cook before I learned to walk."

"Not that I'm able to have dessert," Nick said, "but hypothetically, if I did have room, what would it be?"

"Apple pie with vanilla ice cream, but I can't claim the recipe. I'll put some in a container for you to take home anyway."

Nick groaned. "I'm out of token protests, and greedy enough to say yes, and thank you very much. Can I at least help you with the dishes?"

"No, I'll take care of them after you've gone."

Nick looked at his daughter. "Taylor, what do you say?"

"Thank you for dinner, Maya," Taylor said. "It was really good."

"You're welcome. Why don't you go watch TV while your father and I talk?"

"Okay." She slid off her chair and went into the living room, the pets following behind.

"Put it on Nickelodeon only," Nick called after Taylor, then turned to Maya. "Is there a female version of knight in shining armor?"

"Does this mean that I passed muster?" Maya asked.

"You did more than pass." Blue eyes darkened with seriousness as he reached for her hand. He seemed to be as much of a natural toucher as she was. "Are you sure you want to do this?"

Sure? Logically, she wasn't sure. Emotionally, she was already attached to the motherless little girl. Her hand grew warm in his, driven by the thought that his question held more than one meaning. He had the most amazing eyes, and they seemed to delve inside her, making promises she couldn't translate. Somehow she remembered how to take a deep breath. "I'm very sure."

Nick sighed with apparent relief, then smiled, and again his face went from ordinary to wow. "I really appreciate this, Maya."

"No problem," she said again, extracting her hand from his with a gentle tug. "I'm sure it can't be easy for you, being a surgeon and a single parent."

"No it's not," he agreed, "but I wouldn't trade it for anything in the world."

Don't be jealous, she thought to herself. *Don't be jealous of this man and his daughter, don't be jealous of what you don't have.*

She pushed to her feet. "I'm sure you need to get Taylor ready for tomorrow, so why don't I put the left-overs together for you while you gather her things? Taylor's clothes and jacket are in the laundry room, just past the guest bathroom on the other side of the living room."

"All right." He slid to his feet with an easy grace. "Sure you don't need help cleaning up? It's the least I can do."

"No, I'll be fine." She gathered up a few of the dishes and retreated to the kitchen. Alone, she leaned against the counter and closed her eyes. What in the world was she getting herself into? It had taken her a long time to recover from her divorce, to attempt to make peace with her apparent barrenness. It had taken even longer to watch parents with their children and not be consumed by jealousy and depression. Her emotional walls had been firmly in place until she saw Taylor sitting all wet and bedraggled on her porch. Maya knew, she just knew, that taking care of Taylor had the potential to be absolutely wonderful—and absolutely heartbreaking.

THREE

After emailing project updates to her boss, Maya spent the early part of Friday afternoon scouring the house and shopping. Having her sisters and nieces come over for the weekend always guaranteed a hilarious time, but she wanted it to be extra special since Taylor would be joining them for the first time.

Just before leaving Wednesday night, Nick had told her that he would put her on the approved list to get Taylor from school. She'd picked Taylor up with little fanfare yesterday. Today, Nick planned to drop Taylor off after they'd gone to see Mrs. Henderson. Maya probably had an hour to break the news to her sisters and nieces that Taylor would be joining them.

She found it hard to contain her nervous energy. She wanted the weekend to go well for her relatives and for Taylor. She had the feeling that Taylor hadn't had much in the way of parties or sleepovers, and she wanted to give the little girl a weekend she'd never forget.

At five-thirty, her sisters and nieces showed up. "Hey girl," Nadine said, giving Maya a hug as her two daughters pushed past her. "Are you ready for the weekend?"

"Most definitely," Maya said, returning the hug before turning to hug her younger sister, Jasmine. "How 'bout you, Jas? You're not getting too old for this, are you?"

Twenty-three-year-old Jasmine threw her silky-straight black hair over her shoulder with a laugh. "Come on, if I spent every weekend with Kyle, he'd start expecting it. Have to keep him on his toes, you know."

"You're sounding way too much like Mom," Nadine said, "but I agree with you."

They filed into the living room. "Hey everybody," Maya called. "I wanted to let you know that we'll have a guest spending the weekend with us."

Her nieces, Leila and Tamera, stopped playing with the pets. "Is it another girl?" Leila asked.

"Sure is," Maya confirmed. "Her name is Taylor, and she's my next-door neighbor's daughter. She's your age, Leila, but I think both of you will like her."

"Taylor's a boy's name," Leila said.

"It's a special name for a special girl, just like yours is," Nadine told her oldest daughter. "So don't make fun of her."

Tamera looked up at Maya with serious eyes. "We'll have to give her a princess name then, won't we?"

"I didn't think about that, but you're right." One weekend they'd gotten the brilliant idea to give each other princess code names. Nadine, the psychologist in the family, decided that it would help reinforce positive attitudes about being a girl. Their princesses weren't the waiting in the ivory tower kind, but were the kick-butt-and-take-names Power Puff Girls variety.

"Okay, we'll go look for princess gear after we go out to dinner," Maya said. "Why don't you take your stuff up to your room and start thinking up names while we wait for Taylor to get here?"

"I think it's time for some tea," Jasmine announced, heading for the kitchen. Maya and Nadine followed.

"Why did you invite your neighbor's daughter over here out of the blue?" Nadine wondered, following Maya into the kitchen.

"It wasn't out of the blue," Maya said, opening a cabinet for cups while Jasmine put the kettle on to boil.

"You've never talked about your neighbors before, so it seems surprising that their daughter is spending the weekend," Jasmine said.

Maya sighed. She should have known she'd be double-teamed by her sisters. But then two were always ganging-up on one. "Long story short, I'm looking after her until her nanny's broken hip heals, and I thought it would be good to have her over for the weekend."

Nadine opened the fridge. "And why do you have to take care of her?" she asked with her head stuck inside.

"I don't have to, I want to." Maya set places at the breakfast nook. "Her father's a single parent and a doctor. As far as I know, he doesn't have anyone else to look after her."

Maya related the events of the previous two days. Nadine closed the fridge with her hip, carrying a bowl of fruit and a coffeecake to the table. Jasmine added loose tea to the teapot, then joined her sisters. "I'll admit, I wouldn't leave the poor child on the porch either. But did you have to step in with the whole baby sitting thing?"

"He wasn't going to find a sitter on such short notice, and I don't go near the office on Thursdays or Fridays. It was a perfect fit."

"A little too perfect if you ask me." Nadine's knife punctuated her words as she sliced melon.

"Dina, stop trying to psychoanalyze me." Maya knew once her older sister got started, there would be no stopping.

"I'm not trying to get into your business," Nadine said, her black curls moving as she shook her head. "I just don't want to see you get hurt."

Maya lifted a slice of coffee cake onto her plate. "Look, I'm not some fragile doll. I'm doing a favor for a neighbor. I'm certainly not going to flip out over this."

"Of course not," Jasmine replied, her dark eyes filled with concern. "You know we can't help worrying about you."

Maya quelled a sigh of frustration. Of course the family worried about her. Being the product of a mixed marriage made Maya and her six siblings extremely protective of each other. Other kids had learned quick enough that you only picked on a Hughes once, and if you picked on one, you picked on them all. No one had picked on Maya and her sisters during high school—especially with four Hughes brothers the size of linebackers. It was easier to become friends with the Hughes clan, and those friends never regretted it.

All the siblings had retained their closeness even when college and careers took them in separate directions. The whole family had gathered around Maya during her fruitless attempts to conceive and the acrimonious divorce that followed. Her ex-husband had even arrived at one of their dissolution meetings with a black eye, though none of her brothers ever owned up to it. Her father had merely smiled when she'd asked him about it.

"Dina, Jas, I appreciate you worrying about me, but I'm fine." She poured a drop of tea into her cup to test its readiness. "This is just temporary, and we all know that."

"Okay, okay, I'll stop bugging you," Nadine said, picking up the tray and heading for the sunroom just beyond the kitchen. "Let me check on the girls and I'll be right back."

Maya breathed a sigh of relief as her older sister slipped away. In the two years since Maya's divorce, Nadine had never missed an opportunity to make sure that Maya's mind remained on an even keel. She was also the family spy, reporting back to their mother and ex-military dad any and everything that happened with the siblings. Sometimes she wanted to freak out just to make her family stop worrying.

"You know she means well," Jas said, as if reading Maya's thoughts.

"I know. I guess it comes with the territory of being the oldest sister.

"So, is he cute?" Nadine returned, plopping into the padded chair with a sigh.

"Is who cute?" Maya asked over her tea.

Her sister rolled her eyes. "Your single doctor neighbor, of course!" She turned to face Maya, her smoky eyes alight in her pale tan face. "Well? Is he?"

"Oh, for goodness sakes!" Maya turned her gaze out the window. No evidence of yesterday's storm remained except the streaks of florescent green pollen that lined the streets and drainage. The Friday late-afternoon sun streaked the few clouds with reds and purples above the houses across the street. She'd tried not to think about Nicolas Whitfield in any way other than as her neighbor.

It hadn't been easy. Long after he and Taylor had left, Maya had thought about Nick, the highlights in his hair that reminded her of mink, the brilliant blue of his eyes, the way his entire face went from cold to ka-boom when he smiled. She remembered the warmth in his hands, the ease with which he reached out to touch her. No, it hadn't been easy to think about Nick as just her neighbor. Not easy at all.

Tapping brought her attention back to her sister. Nadine looked at her expectantly, one peach-colored nail tapping the rim of her teacup. "I'm waiting."

"You're impossible, you know that?" Besides inheriting more of their mother's features, Nadine had also inherited Loan Hughes' penchant for matchmaking. Jasmine had their mother's backbone, and Maya, it seemed, had inherited the nurturing instinct. So far only one of the brothers had succumbed to Nadine's efforts, but Maya knew she didn't want to up her sister's average.

"I suppose he's all right looking," Maya said grudgingly. "He's actually very ordinary looking. But when he smiles, his whole face lights up, and this little dimple appears in his right cheek."

"Really?" This from Jasmine, who rested her chin on the back of her hand. "Do tell."

"Well, there's really nothing else to say. We all had dinner together Wednesday night—"

"Whoa. You just met him and you're already going out to dinner?"

Maya narrowed her eyes at her older sister. "Do you want to hear this or not?"

Nadine sat back in her chair, lifting her teacup. "Do go on," she commanded.

With a roll of her eyes, Maya continued. "I had already started dinner here. It was a simple thing to get Taylor to help me, and even simpler for Nick to agree to stay, since he'd gotten home late and Taylor needed to eat."

"Nick, huh?" Both sisters' eyes glowed with pure mischief.

"I am this close to tossing you two out of my house!" Maya pinched her thumb and forefinger together. "And I don't think I want to talk about this anymore."

"I'm sorry, sis, go on. I swear we won't interrupt anymore." Nadine's expression veered so close to her youngest daughter's that Maya gave in.

"I figured that since I'd offered to look after Taylor, he should get to know me better. It makes perfect sense. We talked some over dinner. He's very person-able, and he obviously loves Taylor a great deal."

"That's it?" Jasmine asked when Maya reached for a piece of fruit. "That's all you have to tell us?"

"There's nothing else to tell."

"But you can't expect me to go home with just that little bit of information to give Mom!" her younger sister wailed.

"I don't want you to go to Mom at all. She'll have Nadine psychoanalyzing me and our brothers snooping around." The idea of their four brothers ganging up on Nick made her stomach roil. "And there's no telling what Dad will do." Their father and brothers weren't exactly happy with her ex-husband, and they'd made sure he knew it. Russell eventually moved out of state. Not that she minded, but Maya didn't want Nick to get grilled because of her. Especially since they weren't even seeing each other.

"It won't be that bad," Nadine said.

Maya rolled her eyes. "Have you forgotten how they treated Kevin when you first started dating?"

"Oh." Nadine's pale face grew paler. "You have a point."

"I know." Maya poured herself another cup of tea. "Besides, there's nothing going on with Nick and me. Last night was the most that we've interacted since they moved next door six months ago. I'm looking after his daughter for a couple of weeks, that's all."

"Okay, okay." Jasmine held up her hands in surrender. "I get the point. No running to Mom with all the gory details about your new man, I swear."

"Thank you. And he's not my new man."

———◆———

Nick rang the doorbell, then stuck his hand in his pocket, wondering why he felt nervous. Probably had something to do with the big bouquet tucked under his other arm, and the helium "Thank You!" balloon grasped in Taylor's hand. He'd wanted to give Maya some token of appreciation and couldn't think of anything other than flowers. Now he wondered if he should have thought harder. What would Maya think about the flowers? Would she think he was being too forward? At least Taylor had thought to add the balloon. Maybe Maya wouldn't think too much of it.

The door jerked open, and an Asian woman with gray eyes and short black hair curling about her face stared back at him. "Why, hello there. You must be Dr. Whitfield."

The gleam in the woman's eyes made Nick suddenly feel like a lobster in a choosing tank. "Uh, yes I am. And you are?"

"Nadine. Maya's older sister." She stuck out a hand. Nick juggled the bouquet and finally managed to shake Nadine's hand. She looked down at Taylor.

"And you must be Taylor. What a beautiful girl you are."

Taylor moved behind Nick. "Hi."

"I think my daughters are going to enjoying meeting a new friend," she said with a smile, her eyes crinkling up at the corners. She had a slight resemblance to Maya, but Nick couldn't help wondering if one of them had been adopted or had a different parent.

Nadine stepped back, opening the door wider. "Come in. Pretty bouquet, by the way. Maya loves flowers."

Reassured somewhat, Nick stepped into the foyer, Taylor pressing close behind him. "Is she here?"

"Of course. She's just—indisposed at the moment." After shutting the door, Nadine grabbed his wrist and led him and Taylor into the living room. "This is our youngest sister, Jasmine. We were just finishing our tea, but I can make some for you, if you like." She pushed him onto the sofa.

"Er, no, but thanks." Nick fell against the dark blue cushions, turning to find the younger woman sitting beside him on the couch. "Hi, I'm Nick."

"Pleased to meet you," she said, a smile splitting her honey-colored face. "We've heard wonderful things about you and your daughter."

"Really?" Nick found it difficult to keep his equilibrium. Were all the women in Maya's family this beautiful? Jasmine looked more like Maya than Nadine did, though Jasmine's hair fell in a straight cut past her shoulders. Yet as pretty as they were, they weren't Maya.

His thoughts were interrupted when a dog, a huge cat, and two little girls entered the room. He got to his feet, leaving the bouquet on the couch. Taylor stood next to him, slipping her hand into his.

The older woman crossed to the two girls. "Girls, I want you guys to meet someone." She led them forward with a hand on each girl's back. "This is Aunt Maya's next door neighbor, Taylor Whitfield."

All three girls stared at one another with huge eyes and awkward silence. Nadine put her hand on the tallest girl's shoulder, whose dark brown hair was pulled into two pigtails. "This is Leila. She's seven. And her little sister is Tamera. I'm assuming you met Hamlet and Horatio already?"

Nick and Taylor nodded. The oldest girl stepped forward. "We have to tell you about being a princess, so you can decide your name."

"I like my own name," Taylor said. Her hand squeezed Nick's tighter, and he suppressed a groan, Maybe this wasn't such a good idea after all.

"You get to keep your own name," Leila said with a sigh of impatience. "Your princess name is just what you use when you're here."

Maya chose that moment to enter the living room, tucking her shirt into the waistband of her jeans. "Did I hear the doorbell?" She stopped short when she saw Nick. He took that as his cue to say something and searched for elegant and appropriate words to say. He settled for "Hi."

"Hi yourself," she replied, coming towards him with a soft smile. "Did everyone meet everyone?"

"We did," he answered. "I just hope there's not a pop quiz later."

"We'll give you a pass this time," Jasmine said, rising to her feet. With all three women standing together, Nick could see the family resemblance.

Jasmine's movement caused the balloon to float into view. "Oh wow, are those for me?"

"They are." Nick lifted the bouquet from the couch and thrust it towards her. "They're just, you know, a way of saying thank you from Taylor and me."

Maya's eyes lit up as she reached for the bouquet. "Oh, wow, Nick," she breathed. "They're beautiful. Thank you." She tucked the bouquet into the crook of her left arm and reached to hug him.

Surprised by the gesture, Nick instinctively wrapped both arms around her, pulling her close. The spicy scent of her skin combined with the flowers in an intoxicating fragrance. The feel of her slender body pressed against his, however briefly, made him feel as if he'd just been electrocuted. When Maya stepped away he felt bereft, his palms itching with the need to hold her close again.

"Why don't you let me put those in water for you?" Nadine asked with a knowing grin.

"Thanks, Dina," Maya said, passing her sister the bouquet so that she could hug Taylor. "Thank you, Taylor. Did you pick out the balloon?"

"Sure did. I told Daddy you'd like the flowers."

"Well, you were right." She ruffled Taylor's hair. The look of pleasure on his daughter's face squeezed Nick's heart tight.

He cleared his throat. "Hey, give your old man a goodbye hug before he leaves?"

"You're not that old, Daddy," Taylor laughed, giving Nick an exuberant hug. "Eskimo kiss!"

Nick rubbed his nose against his daughter's, suddenly not wanting to let her go. Aside from a visit to his parents during summer, Taylor was always with him. "Have fun, pumpkin," he said tightly. "And make sure you mind Ms. Maya and her sisters."

"I will, Daddy."

Leila's younger sister stepped forward. "Do you know how to play jacks?" she asked in a quiet voice. When Taylor nodded, Tamera took her by the hand and led her off into Maya's office, which had a wood floor perfect for bouncing balls.

"That went well," Jasmine said, her sigh blowing her bangs up. "I'll take Taylor's bag upstairs for you." She slung the backpack over her shoulder and headed for the stairs. They were suddenly alone.

Maya gave Nick a grin. "My sisters didn't grill you too much, did they?"

"No," he admitted. He had a feeling he'd escaped a firing squad.

"That's because we didn't have enough time," Nadine said, sweeping back into the room. "We can start now, if you like."

"Nadine." Nick heard the warning in Maya's voice loud and clear. Still, he couldn't help smiling. Maya had talked to her sisters about him. That was a good sign, wasn't it?

"Nick, would you like something before you go? We were just finishing a pot of tea."

What he wanted would probably get him slapped if he'd asked for it. "No, thanks. I just wanted to drop the flowers off and see Taylor before Girls Weekend officially starts. What's this about princess names?"

"I'm afraid that's confidential information," Maya said, "seeing as how you're not a girl and all."

"Definitely not a girl," Jasmine as she reentered the room. Maya cut her a look that Nick didn't miss, and he hid a smile. "Can you tell me anything about what's going to happen this weekend?"

"It's like an all-girls weekend. My sisters and I take the kids out for really bad food and a movie, or we'll rent a couple of videos and bring them home. We have a big slumber party in the living room. Sometimes we read books and the kids act out the parts. Tomorrow we all fix a big breakfast, then all go shopping—have to start training early for that, you know. By Sunday, the energy's hopefully winding down. That's usually art day."

"Wow." Nick shook his head. "That sounds more like summer camp than a weekend. And you want Taylor to stay for all of it?"

"Of course. She'll have a good time. And you'll get to do whatever you want to do."

"Like what?" Nick had no idea what to do with an entire weekend without his daughter.

"I'll tell you what my husband is doing," Nadine volunteered. "Tonight, it's bowling with co-workers. Tomorrow afternoon, they'll sit around someone's house drinking beer, watching sports and fixing cars. They'll end the night with poker, during which my dear husband will smoke a cigar. He'll then spend Sunday morning trying to destroy the evidence of smoking said cigar by doing laundry."

"Do you sic a private detective on him or something?" Nick asked.

"I don't have to," Nadine said with a smile. "We've been together for twelve years, married for ten. It's almost like I have eyes in the back of my head."

"Why don't you make him quit smoking the cigars?"

"Are you kidding? Sunday is the only day I get a break from laundry."

They all shared a laugh. "Well, I do the weekend laundry and I don't smoke cigars or bowl," Nick admitted. "I'm still clueless about what I should do with all this free time."

"Visit some friends. Go on a date. Have a few beers and watch whatever sports event is on TV." Maya gave him a grin. "I'm sure you'll think of something."

FOUR

Think of something. Nick wandered through his silent house fifteen minutes later, still clueless about what to do with his new-found freedom. He wasn't used to the house being so quiet this early in the evening. Flipping on the TV brought in noise, but it didn't provide entertainment. Between raising Taylor and his physician duties, he had no idea what adult shows were on anymore. Besides, if he sat and stared at the television, all he'd do was wonder how Taylor and Maya were doing.

He needed to get out. Maya had given him the perfect opportunity. What had she told him? "Go on a date." Yeah, like he could call up a woman out of the blue and ask her out. Sure, he'd waded into the dating pool, but the scant relationships he'd attempted over the last few years hadn't been more than a string of one night stands that occurred when Taylor went to Florida to visit his parents. Not exactly what enduring relationships were made of.

He dug his organizer out of his pocket, turned it on, and scrolled through his contacts until he found the name he wanted. Lifting the cordless handset, he punched in the numbers then waited for the call to be answered.

"Galindo."

"Hey, A.J. This is Nick."

"No."

"No? You don't even know what I'm about to ask," Nick pointed out.

"If it has anything to do with covering a shift for you, the answer is no," his best friend said.

"I don't want you to cover a shift for me. I was wondering what you're doing tonight."

"Tonight?" Nick could hear the excitement in A.J.'s voice. "You mean you want to go out?"

"You don't have to sound so surprised," Nick muttered.

"Nick Whitfield, wanting to hang out on a Friday night." A.J.'s disbelief rang through the phone. "Hey, do you hear that sound? I think that's hell freezing over."

"Come on, man," Nick complained. "It's not that bad."

"I guess not. Though I think the last time you went out was sometime in the last Ice Age. Where's my little god-daughter, since I'm assuming she's not there?"

"My next door neighbor is having a sleepover with her nieces, and Taylor's staying the weekend."

"All weekend?" A.J.'s voice climbed again. "Who are you and what have you done with my best friend?

The Nick Whitfield I know wouldn't let his daughter out of his sight for an entire weekend, not even next door."

"Maya's a nice woman. She's looking after Taylor in the afternoon until Mrs. Henderson gets better."

"She must be a saint then," A.J. said, "else you wouldn't let her near Taylor."

Nick had no intention of discussing Maya with A.J. "Blackbook" Galindo any time soon. Probably ever. "Hey, do you wanna hang out tonight or what?"

"I'll see you in thirty. And I'm bringing clothes with me. Everything in your closet is probably out of style."

An hour later, Nick leaned over a pool table in a Buckhead bar, trying to remember how to look cool.

A.J. chalked his cue. "Okay. Who is she?"

"Who is who?"

"The woman on your mind."

Nick felt a flush creep up his neck. "I don't have a woman on my mind."

"Who you think you talking to?" A.J. said, signaling the waitress for a drink. "I've seen that look before, and it says woman with a capital 'Whoa!' "

Nick concentrated on lining up his shot, the better not to meet his friend's all-too-knowing gaze. "You've known me for three years, A.J. What makes you think I've got a woman on my mind all of a sudden?"

The look A.J. gave him was definitely of the you've-got-to-be-kidding-me variety. "Well, now, could it be that you've been hugging the pool table all night without noticing any of the hotties walking by? Could it be that you had that pretty blonde ready to climb into your pocket and you just brushed her off? Only two reasons for that, my man: either there's a woman, or you're dead. And it's my expert medical opinion that you're not dead."

The cue ball careened off the corner pocket, totally missing the nine ball. Nick stifled a curse. "Couldn't it just be that I'm concerned about my daughter spending the weekend over Maya's house?" He frowned as A.J. grinned. "What are you laughing at?"

"I told you there was a woman involved." A.J. took his place at the table, chalking his cue. "So, it's just Maya, huh? No 'Mrs.' attached to that?"

"Not any more," Nick said, not really liking his friend's tone of voice. He'd had enough people wanting to grill him today. Hell, even Mrs. Henderson had asked him about Maya.

A.J. sank his shot then moved around the table looking for another. "Is she a hottie?"

"Excuse me?"

"Your single next-door neighbor," A.J. said, leaning over the table. "Is she hot?"

Nick took a sip of his drink so that he wouldn't hit his best friend over the head. "Your definition of hot and mine are probably diametrically opposed. If you mean beer-tub girl hot, then the answer is no." Thank God.

A.J., certified single and loving it, wouldn't understand what drew Nick to Maya. Hell, he couldn't understand it himself. She unsettled him and put him at ease at the same time. Her smile made him feel good and made him want to be very, very bad. Three hours in her company, and all he knew about Maya Hughes was that he really wanted to see her again.

"Hey, are you in there?" A.J. snapped his fingers before Nick's eyes.

"What?"

A.J.'s grin widened in his olive face. "Wherever you went, it sure made you happy. I think I want to see this woman."

"I don't think so." No way in hell was he putting Maya in the same room with A.J. Alejandro Jesus Galindo knew he had *International Male* good looks and he used them to his best advantage. A self-proclaimed connoisseur of the female form, A.J. had never met a woman that his libido didn't like. "Look, man, she's my next door neighbor. She's just helping me out with Taylor until Mrs. Henderson gets better."

"Uh-hhm," A.J. said, sinking another shot. "Methinks the man doth protest too much."

Uh-oh. When A.J. started quoting literature, Nick knew he was in trouble. "Seriously, Wednesday was the most time we'd spent together since I moved in next door. I don't know if she's seeing anyone and I don't care." Okay, that was a lie. "All that matters is that she's a decent woman, she takes good care of my daughter, and Taylor likes her. That's it."

Nick lined up his shot, then proceeded to clear the rest the table. "Now, what's the next stop on the Nick Freedom Tour?"

A.J. finished his drink, then racked his cue. "Are you sure you're up for this? And your lady won't mind?"

"Absolutely. And she's not my lady."

A.J. gave him a grin that was downright evil. "Remember you said that."

—⁕—

"The Hall of Princesses is ready," Jasmine called from the sun-room.

Maya looked down at the girl beside her. She'd braided Taylor's dark hair into two French braids before dusting her with glitter. Dozens of fake baubles hung around her neck and graced her fingers. A dark purple cape trimmed with imitation white feathers hung from her thin shoulders. "Are you ready?"

"I think so," Taylor whispered, her hand clutching at Maya's. "You look really pretty."

Maya wore a ruby-colored silk kimono embroidered with golden dragons and ivory lilies. Her mother would roll her eyes, but Maya liked it, and it was perfect for the princess ceremony. "Thank you. You look pretty too."

"What if they don't want me to be part of the Secret Princess Club?" Taylor asked, her face scrunched up with worry.

"They will," Maya attempted to reassure her.

"But what if they don't?"

"Well then, it's my house, so I have final say. And I say you will be a princess." She gave the girl's hand an encouraging squeeze. "Let's go."

Hand in hand, they walked through the living room, past the formal dining room to the sunroom. Candles glowed on every available surface. Her sisters and nieces knelt in a semi-circle on a blanket, facing them. All of them wore tiaras like Maya's although they dressed differently, running the gamut from a Disney princess dress to an Indian sari. On a plush burgundy pillow sat a tiara and scepter.

"Our princesses are different shapes and shades," Nadine said in a solemn tone of voice. "To be a princess here is to accept the other princesses as they are, to always believe in yourself and stand up for yourself. It means respecting others, helping others, and never being mean or cruel to other people. But most of all, being a princess means having fun." She looked at Taylor. "Do you understand?"

Taylor nodded. "And do you want to be a member of the Secret Princess Club?"

Again Taylor nodded, "All right, then. Now the princesses need to vote."

Maya put an arm around Taylor's back "I, Princess Golden Lily, vote yes."

Tamera went next. "I, Princess Merry Weather, vote yes."

Jasmine. "I, Princess Moonbeam, vote yes."

Leila. "I, Princess Honey Blossom, vote yes."

Nadine smiled down at Taylor. "And I, Princess Karaoke, vote yes." She lifted the tiara from the cushion. "The Secret Princess Club hereby welcomes you, and gives you the name Princess Mistletoe."

Taylor leaned into Maya. "What's missestoe?"

"It's a good luck flower that's usually around at Christmas time."

Nadine placed the tiara on Taylor's head, then handed her the scepter. "Welcome to the Secret Princess Club, Princess Mistletoe!" Everyone started clapping, cheering and tossing glittery confetti.

Taylor beamed and blushed as Maya's sisters and nieces made a big production of leading the newest member of the club into the dining room to build sundaes. Maya had snapped pictures throughout the initiation, and snapped even more. She couldn't stop beaming herself, and wondered if she'd go through more rolls of film before the weekend was over. Probably.

Taylor came up to her as she entered the dining room. "Thank you, Maya, for letting me come over this weekend."

"You're welcome. How do you like being a princess?"

"It's great. I don't feel bad anymore."

Maya knelt in front of her. "Why would you feel bad?"

"Because Leila and Tamera have a mommy, and I don't."

"Taylor." Not knowing what else to do, Maya wrapped the little girl in a hug. "It will be all right, I promise." She didn't have a clue as to how to keep that promise, but she'd try.

"Can I come over whenever Leila and Tamera are here?" Taylor asked in her ear.

"Of course you can," Maya said. "They're your friends, and they'll want to see you."

Little arms tightened around her neck "Are you my friend, too?"

Maya closed her eyes against an unexpected rush of emotion. "Of course I am."

"Does this mean friends forever?" Taylor whispered.

"It most certainly does," Maya whispered back. "Friends forever."

FIVE

The remainder of the weekend passed in a flurry of activity, fun, and laughter. By the time Sunday afternoon arrived, Taylor, Leila and Tamera were inseparable and Jasmine, Maya, and Nadine were a few hundred dollars poorer. Not that they minded, at least Maya didn't. Hopefully Taylor had gotten a sense of family that she hadn't had before, even if it happened to be temporary. One thing for sure, the little girl had made friends and memories to last her a lifetime, and Maya was glad to give them to her.

Nick arrived less than five minutes after her sisters and nieces left. Maya opened the front door before he could even ring the bell. "Hey there," she said with a grin, taking in the pale blue polo shirt tucked into well-worn and fitted jeans. The casual clothes showed off his lean physique to the best advantage, and the colors made the blue of his eyes stand out with devastating effect. How had she not noticed how handsome her neighbor was? "Come on in, we've been expecting you."

"Daddy!" Taylor ran full tilt into her father. Nick scooped her up, hugging her as if he never wanted to let her go. Maya ignored the twinge of jealousy that always surfaced whenever she saw parents and their kids. There had to come a time when she would be used to it, wouldn't there?

"Hey, Pumpkin, did you have fun?"

"Sure did!" Maya shut the door and trailed after them into the living room, listening to Taylor's exuberant recitation of the weekend's events. "I got a new princess name and we went to the movies and Leila got sick on too much popcorn and we played dress up and painted stuff and went to the IMAX movie—"

"Slow down, Speedy Gonzales," Nick laughed. Something in Maya's gut clenched tight at the sight of that smile. "I want to make sure I hear every word of this fantastic weekend you guys had. How about over dinner?"

"Okay, but can Maya come, too?" Taylor asked, turning in her father's arms to face Maya.

Maya debated for half a second. There were tons of things to do around the house to get ready for the work week ahead, and she could certainly use some down time…

"What about it, Maya?" Nick asked. "Dinner at Chez Whitfield. I owe you a meal anyway."

"I'm going to have to take a rain check," Maya said reluctantly. "I've got a lot to do to get ready for work tomorrow, and I'm sure you've got a lot to do to get ready for your week, too." She turned to Taylor. "I'll see you tomorrow afternoon, okay?"

"Okay."

Taylor's crestfallen expression was enough to almost make Maya change her mind. Of course she wanted to have dinner with them, but Nick hadn't seen his daughter all weekend, and he deserved some alone time with Taylor. "Don't forget to show your father the pictures."

"Oh yeah." The seven-year-old instantly brightened and squirmed out of her father's arms. "We took lots of pictures, Daddy. Wait 'til you see!"

Nick sobered as Taylor scampered into the living room. "She wasn't too much of a handful, was she?"

"Of course not. She and my nieces became fast friends." Maya grinned as Taylor returned with her gear. "Don't be surprised if she doesn't make it to her bedtime." She bent over, tucking a dark curl behind Taylor's ear. "Remember to be a good princess at school tomorrow, all right?"

"Okay." She threw her arms around Maya's neck. "This was the best weekend ever!"

Maya gave Taylor a light hug before setting her away. "I think so, too. See you guys tomorrow."

Nick gave her a grateful smile, though his eyes seemed to hold a wealth of meaning she couldn't translate. "I'll hold you to that dinner."

"I fully expect you to," she answered, leaning against the door. "See you tomorrow."

She watched father and daughter walk across the driveway to their house, then shut the door. She leaned against the cool wood for a moment, feeling the silence of the house wrap around her. The weekend had been successful in many ways. Taylor and her nieces had gotten along so well, they'd invited Taylor to spend the night at their house one weekend soon.

That did nothing for Maya and her quiet house. She pushed away from the door and headed into her office. Sitting at her desk, she picked up a green file folder that was never far away. The folder contained all the information on the Georgia adoption process that she'd gleaned over the last few months.

Maya opened the folder slowly, not really looking at the documents inside. She'd gotten to the point where she could consider adoption, but it had been an arduous process. She and her ex-husband, Russell, had met doing volunteer work. It had been love at first sight, but they'd waited until after graduating from college to get married. Russell had been welcomed into Maya's large family, and his dysfunctional background made him determined to have and keep a family. Maya had learned from her mother how to balance career and family, and her instinctive desire to nurture made her a perfect fit with her husband.

They'd tried for two years before Maya began to suspect that something was wrong. She'd gone to fertility specialists, internists, taken drugs, eaten strange food and herbs, done everything everyone had told her to do, including standing on her head. Nothing had worked, and the doctors couldn't find anything wrong. They just made vague pronouncements about the mysteries of the female body.

Russell had gone from supportive to accusatory. He kept wondering what was wrong with her, and accused her of trapping him into marriage when she knew she was messed up on the inside. When she'd angrily suggested that he go get checked, he'd dropped the bombshell that he knew he was fine because he already had a son by another woman. He'd moved out that night and filed for divorce the next day.

Maya sighed, replacing the folder in her desk drawer. She spent the next hour restoring her house to order, using the process of cleaning to cleanse her thoughts. It didn't do to dwell on the past, but the dream of having a family full of love and laughter like her parents had been a hard dream to let go of. And the way that Russell had treated her still smarted. She had no desire to go through that again.

After spending some time storyboarding her new software idea, she retreated upstairs to her bedroom, pulling off clothes along the way. She changed into pajamas and completed her bedtime ritual before settling into bed with a book, Hamlet and Horatio stationed in their usual places at the foot of the bed. Her pets seemed as out of sorts as she did, looking around as if expecting someone else to come careening into the room and leap onto the bed in a fit of giggles.

"You guys are missing all the excitement too, aren't you?" Maya asked, tossing her book onto the nightstand and picking up the packet of photos instead. Her boys crawled up on either side of her as she settled back against the headboard. "We had a lot of fun, didn't we?"

She flipped through the pictures, copies of the set she'd given Taylor. Every shot had captured a moment of pure fun: beauty time with all of them in robes, mud masks, and rollers; the food fight that had erupted when Horatio accidentally knocked over a bowl of M&Ms when they were baking cookies; she and Taylor mugging for the camera, looking like Elton John wannabes in their IMAX 3D glasses; and an official portrait of them all in their princess gear.

Longing pulled at her. It had been a fantasy weekend, a fantasy in which she'd pretended she had a daughter and that daughter was Taylor. Taylor must have picked up on it, because the child had been constantly at Maya's side at every outing, and whenever Leila and Tamera had gone to their mother for something, Taylor had imitated them. That had been reason enough for Maya not to join them for dinner tonight. The fantasy was just that, a fantasy. Real life was that she wasn't Taylor's mother and Nick wasn't her husband.

The thought bought instant heat to her cheeks. She remembered how he'd looked in his jeans and shirt, how the cloth had molded to the muscles in his arms and legs. He certainly hadn't looked like a doctor then—okay, maybe a TV doctor, but not a real doctor. He'd looked like what her friend from Texas called a "long tall drink of water." And Maya had wanted very much to put her hands around that drink of water and gulp down every drop.

––≈––

Nick lay sprawled on his bed, going through the photos Taylor had brought home. Maya had been right; Taylor didn't make it ten minutes past dinner. The couple of hours before then, she'd regaled him with exciting tales of "Ms. Maya did this, Ms. Maya said that."

The sparkle in his daughter's eyes warmed his heart. The move from Virginia hadn't been an easy one, but the only thing keeping his parents from retiring to Florida was the responsibility they felt to help him take care of Taylor. He'd relied on them long enough during the last seven years. At thirty-five, he'd accepted his mentor's offer to move to Atlanta and help in a semi-private practice, in order to abandon the brutal hospital schedule and spend more time with Taylor. He'd thought Taylor had adjusted well, but seeing these pictures, he realized just how desperately she needed a female presence in her life.

He paused at a picture of Maya and Taylor beaming into the camera. His daughter was dressed like a princess, complete with purple cape and silver tiara. Maya looked stunning in a scarlet kimono and gold crown. They had their arms wrapped around each other as if they'd known each other for years.

Nick stared silently at the picture. It amazed him how happy his daughter looked. And how much older. He still pictured Taylor as a toddler sometimes, or even as a snaggle-toothed five-year-old. Now he was suddenly aware of the years that had passed by, the years Taylor had spent without a mother. There would soon come a time when she'd need the presence of a mother figure, when she'd want to talk to a woman before she'd want to talk to him.

Taylor needed a mother.

The thought had been haunting him for a while. He'd done his best to avoid facing it. Even after all these years, the fact that Jessica was gone still hurt. And on top of the hurt were guilt and anger. Anger that he'd been left with a newborn and a brutal medical residency. Guilt that he had ignored the signs, that he'd been unable to prevent anything. Almost eight years later, he still didn't want to get back out there, didn't want to jump through the hoops required for finding someone remotely compatible. But he couldn't think of himself, he had to think of Taylor.

He stared down at the picture, eyes drawn to Maya's smiling face. The attraction that he'd felt since Wednesday flowed over him again. If he could afford to be selfish, he'd do something about the attraction he felt, or at least make the attempt. But with his daughter involved…Would it be a bad thing to allow Taylor to become attached to Maya? They'd obviously had a terrific weekend, and Maya seemed just as taken with Taylor as Taylor was with her. Maybe Maya could be taken with him as well. She hadn't said she was interested in him, but she hadn't said she wasn't interested either.

Stretching across the bed, he picked up the receiver and dialed Maya's home number. It took two rings for her to answer. "Hello?"

Her voice was soft and warm. "It's Nick. I didn't wake you, did I?"

"No, I was just lying here looking at the pictures from the weekend."

So was she lying on the couch or in bed? Nick tried to imagine her in a bedroom he hadn't seen. What did she sleep in? Did she sleep in anything at all? "So am I," he said, his voice husky. "I don't think I've ever seen my girl this happy."

"She really enjoyed herself. So did everyone else." He could almost feel her smile through the line. "And how was your weekend? Did you go on a date or anything?"

"Who, me?" Nick snorted. "I've been out of the dating pool for so long, I'm dehydrated. I played pool with my friend A.J. on Friday and spent the rest of the weekend playing handyman around the house. I think I can be officially declared a geek."

Maya laughed into the phone, a laugh as soft and intimate as a whisper. "Hey, I design software. That makes me a geek, too. We'll just have to be geeks together."

A huge grin stretched his face. "Thanks for that. But when you consider that I spent the weekend being jealous of all the fun my daughter obviously had, I think that qualifies."

"Oh Nick, I'm sorry," she said with remorse. "I didn't think you'd be bothered with having Taylor away all weekend. You could have come over at any time, you know."

"Don't apologize," he said, feeling bad for making her feel bad. "Taylor hasn't had that much fun in a while, and I didn't want to ruin it for her."

There was a pause on the other end, and Nick wondered if he'd offended her. Then she said, "Taylor told me about losing her mother. I'm sorry."

Nick winced. Of course Taylor would share that with Maya. "I'm sorry, too. Taylor's a good kid, she deserves a loving mother."

"I'm sure you're doing a wonderful job in both roles."

"I don't know," he sighed, rubbing his free hand across his forehead. "Taylor's getting to that age when she needs a mother to confide in, when Mrs. Henderson won't be enough. But the thought of putting myself back out there and dating again…" He shivered. "I'd rather have my teeth pulled. Without Novocain."

"I understand," she said, her voice quiet on the other end of the line. "My divorce was two years ago, and believe me, I'm in no hurry to get back on that horse."

"Do you and your husband have children?" he asked.

Another long pause, and Nick mentally kicked himself again. He didn't have the right to pry into her life. He just had a burning need to know more about his beautiful next-door neighbor.

"No," she finally said, her words tight. "I don't have children."

Something in her voice caught his attention, but he decided to let it pass. He had no intention to push her further. He gave a rueful laugh. "Listen to us. The way we're talking, we should have razor wire and attacks dogs around our houses."

"And armed guards and sensor alarms," Maya agreed. "You know, I'm by no means an expert, but if Taylor should want to talk to me about anything, something that she may feel uncomfortable discussing with you or Mrs. Henderson, do you want me to do it? Nadine's a family therapist, and I can always go to her for advice."

"As long as it's not about the birds and bees," Nick said, feeling his chest tighten. "She can't get that talk until I buy my shotgun and rocking chair to sit on the porch."

Maya laughed again. "Nadine's husband already did that. My nieces are seven and five, but you'd think they were ten years older."

"You said you have a big family?" Nick rolled onto his back, propping himself against the pillows.

"Yes. You met my two sisters, and we have four brothers. Another reason that I cook big dinners is because they all have a tendency to drop in unannounced. It's either come to Maya's or go to Mom's, and they know I won't be nearly as nosy as my mother is." She chuckled. "And if you tell her I said that, I'll have to kill you."

"Scout's honor." Nick crossed his heart, even though she couldn't see it. "Speaking of dinner, I still owe you one. Why don't Taylor and I take you out sometime this week?"

"You don't have to do that, you know."

Damn. Maybe he was pushing his luck. "I know, but I want to." He swallowed. "We want to. So what do you say?"

Just when he thought he'd have to play it off somehow, she said, "I say that sounds like a great idea."

Nick let out a breath. "Terrific. Which day would be best for you?"

They decided on a day, and Nick decided to quit while he was ahead. "All right then, I guess I'll see you tomorrow when I'm done with work. And if I haven't said it before, thanks for giving Taylor such a wonderful weekend."

"You're welcome," she said softly, and he could almost feel her breath breezing over his skin, tightening parts of him to painful awareness. "Good night, Nick."

"Good night, Maya." He hung up the receiver, then lay back, letting out a slow breath. What a week. He wondered if years from now, he'd look back over his life and realize that this was the moment his life irrevocably changed.

He had a feeling that he would.

SIX

"Maya, I'm going to be late tonight."

"How late is late?" she asked, cradling the phone against her shoulder.

Nick's sigh was audible through the phone line. "I don't know. Maybe nine, probably closer to ten."

"That is late. Is anything wrong?"

"I hate to do this to you," he said, his agitation clear. "I have an emergency surgery coming in in half an hour, and it's going to take a while."

"Well, you couldn't foresee something like that. Do you want me to take Taylor back to your house and watch her there?"

"That would be great! If I'm not home in time, her bedtime is eight-thirty." He paused. When he spoke again, his voice was lower, warmer. "You're an amazing woman, Maya Hughes. I don't know what I would have done if I hadn't met you."

Maya felt a blush creep up her cheeks as she grinned like an idiot into the phone. "Thank you, Nick." She cleared her throat. "Do you want to speak to Taylor?"

He did, and she gave father and daughter a few moments of privacy before Taylor called her back to the phone. "Don't worry, Taylor and I will be fine. And I promise not to rummage through your medicine cabinet."

"You can rummage through whatever you want," Nick said with a laugh. "Though I have to warn you, my closet's pretty scary."

"I consider myself warned. We'll head over now, so if you need us, we'll be next door."

"Okay. I'll be home as soon as I can."

Maya said goodbye and disconnected, staring at the phone. Whether he meant to or not, she liked the casual way he'd included her when he said home. Of course, she'd been included in more and more Whitfield events in the past two weeks, including a couple of dinners out and grilling on Nick and Taylor's deck. As much as she outwardly resisted becoming used to being a part of their lives, Maya found herself looking forward to the time she spent with her widowed neighbor and his precious daughter.

Maya gathered Taylor, the dog and cat, then trooped next door. The Whitfield house possessed the same layout as hers, but boasted more traditional furnishings than Maya's eclectic tastes. Dark navy and hunter green swirled in a muted pattern on the couch and matching loveseat. A cream-colored throw on the back of the couch and rug brightened the space. The other parts of the house that she'd seen carried the same sense of traditional style, from the colonial dining room to the country-styled kitchen.

"Taylor, why don't you put your things in your room and I'll see what we can have for dinner," Maya suggested, locking the door behind them. She went ahead and flipped on the porch light for Nick.

"Can we have pizza?"

"No, we cannot have pizza," Maya retorted with a smile in her voice. "Just because your dad's working late doesn't mean we're not going to have a healthy dinner."

"But pizza's healthy," Taylor argued. "Isn't it?"

"Depends on who you ask, I suppose. Let's save pizza for Friday night, okay?"

"Oh, okay." Taylor pouted, but Maya knew she wasn't seriously upset. It was natural for a child to see what they could get away with when their parents weren't around. Maya knew that from experience. And with six siblings, she had a wealth of experience.

While Taylor dragged her backpack upstairs, Maya entered the kitchen. She stood in the middle of the floor, suppressing a sigh. Country kitchen was not her first choice for decorating. Heck, it wasn't her second or third choice either. Then again, it wasn't her kitchen. But if she had her way, pale blue chicks and geese wallpaper would be declared illegal.

She was rummaging through the side-by-side refrigerator when Taylor returned. "What if we have Chinese food?" the seven-year-old offered.

Maya straightened, her arms full of ingredients. "What if we eat some of the food your dad bought before it all goes bad?"

Taylor rolled her eyes with a sigh, acting as if Maya had just asked her to find the Holy Grail. "Oh, all right."

Maya didn't let the theatrics get to her, especially since Taylor gobbled down every bit of the shrimp and broccoli pasta alfredo on her plate. Afterwards, Taylor helped her clean up, and then she helped the little girl pick out clothes for school.

"Okay, now it's time to get ready for bed."

"Do I have to?" Taylor whined. "Daddy lets me stay up until nine."

"Don't even try it," Maya said with mock severity. "You know your father told me eight-thirty."

"Oh, all right." Taylor sighed dramatically. "Will you read to me after I take my bath?"

"Only if you brush your teeth real good."

"And will you braid my hair-like you did for the Secret Princess Club?"

"Of course I will."

She did, and afterwards, Maya followed her into a bedroom that was probably every little girl's dream. Decorated in sunshine yellow and white, the room boasted a white canopy bed dressed in yellow gingham, matching white wicker furniture and bright yellow walls.

"Did you have a story in mind?" Maya asked, looking at the plethora of titles jammed into the bookcase.

"Whichever you want," the seven-year-old replied magnanimously, slipping into the lemon and custard confection of her bed.

Maya chose a brightly-colored story about a bear that wanted to be a ballerina. She crossed to the rocking chair beside the bed. "I didn't hear you say your prayers."

"Oh, I forgot!" Taylor scrambled back out of bed and to the floor, her Powerpuff Girls nightgown tangled about her knees. She folded her hands together, closed her eyes and began. "God, watch over my daddy, especially since he's working late. And please help Nana Henderson get better, even though I really like Maya taking care of me. Bless all the princesses in the Secret Princess Club, and I'm sorry for getting mad at Billy Petersen today because it really wasn't a princess thing to do, even though he pulled my hair."

She leaned back, turning her head to Maya. "Do you think it's okay to make a secret wish to God?" she whispered, her eyes still closed.

Maya couldn't hide her smile. "Of course it is. Even if you wish it in your mind, God can hear it."

Taylor turned back to the bed, scrunching her eyes tight. "Okay, God, I hope you heard my wish, and I hope Mommy doesn't mind. And bless Maya too, because she's really, really fun and I like her a whole lot. Amen."

Fighting the sudden lump in her throat, Maya managed a whispered "Amen," then waited until Taylor was back in bed before trying to speak. "Thanks for adding me to your prayers."

"I pray about you every night," Taylor confessed. "You don't mind, do you?"

"Of course not," Maya said quickly. "In fact, it makes me feel good, knowing that you're praying for me."

Taylor gave her a wide, gap-toothed grin that made Maya feel ridiculously pleased. "Why don't I start on this book now?"

"Will you tell me about your family?"

"My family?" Maya asked, perplexed. "What do you want to know about my family?"

Taylor fidgeted with the coverlet. "What's it like having a sister?"

Maya closed the book. "Well, I suppose it was pretty cool and pretty bad at the same time," she said. "Nadine's three years older than me, so she bossed me around all the time. I was nine when Jasmine was born. We fought and argued like a lot of sisters do, especially when Nadine and I were in elementary school."

"Do you have brothers?"

"Sure do," Maya grinned. "I have four brothers. Three of them are older than me."

"So that means," Taylor looked down at her fingers, "there are seven of you?"

"Yep."

"What's it like, having that many brothers and sisters?" Taylor asked, her eyes wide.

"Loud," Maya answered, her voice soft with fond memories. "The only time the house was quiet was when we went to sleep. Despite the fights we had, we were all very close."

Taylor snuggled down under the covers. "Are you adopted?"

"No. Why?"

"Because you don't like your sisters."

Ah, the bluntness of children. Maya put the book on the floor beside the rocker, trying to frame her thoughts. It wasn't that she intended to hide her dual heritage from Taylor, she just wasn't sure how to explain in a way that the seven-year-old could understand. How in the world did you talk to children about race?

"Well, do you know how people are different colors and come from different places?" Maya asked.

Taylor nodded. "My teacher, Ms. Clark, her skin's your color but she talks different. She says she's from the Bahamas. And my friend Michelle, she talks like you and me, but she's darker."

"So your teacher would have an accent, because she's not originally from here, and you and I and Michelle are," Maya said. "My father's from here, too, but my mother is from Vietnam."

The round porcelain-like face scrunched in confusion. "Where's Veternam?"

Maya smiled. "Vietnam. It's a country in Asia, on the other side of the world. My dad met my mom when he had to, uhm, do some work over there." It wasn't her place to explain the Vietnam War to Taylor, though technically Maya's father, as part of the Army Corps of Engineers, did actually work in Vietnam, building roads still in use today.

"Is that close to China?"

"Round about there," Maya said, promising to consult a map first thing in the morning. "Anyway, all the kids look like my mom and dad mixed together, but some look more like my dad and some look more like my mother."

Taylor stifled a yawn. "Well, your sisters are pretty, just like you, so your mom must be pretty, too."

"I think she is."

The blue eyes opened to stare up at her. "So your mom's still alive?"

"Yes, she is," Maya whispered. "I'll show you pictures of my family tomorrow, okay?"

"Kay." Taylor blinked slowly, sliding into the bliss of sleep. "I wish I still had a mom."

"I know you do, sweetheart," Maya said softly, reaching out to touch the girl's cheek. "I know."

After Taylor fell asleep, Maya wandered through the house, touching things she had no right to. Despite the fact that a child called the house a home, the rooms seemed to lack vitality. It was as if Nick and Taylor were so busy living their lives they didn't have time to gather any mementos. Only the places Taylor used showed some form of life, as if Nick cared for nothing but ensuring his daughter's happiness.

Perhaps that was all that he wanted, she thought, remembering their conversations about marriage and dating. Losing a spouse to death had to be a devastating event, something that would take a while to get over. While it seemed that Nick had persevered for his daughter's sake, Maya could certainly understand why he'd never want to go down that path again.

She paused at the door to Nick's bedroom. Curiosity battled manners. Her mother would kill her if she knew what Maya planned to do. But Loan Hughes would probably go right on in even after she sent her daughter scurrying away. Holding her breath, Maya pushed open the door.

Her first thought was that it was definitely a man's room. The bed, with its simple dark wood headboard, sat in a jumble of navy and gray plaid bedclothes. The nightstand on the left boasted a picture of a gap-toothed Taylor smiling up from a sandcastle in progress. The other nightstand held a book, lamp, and the alarm clock. A chest of drawers of the same dark wood sat opposite the bed.

Maya crossed to the bed, hesitating a moment before sitting down. Jealousy and an old ache gnawed at her, and she let it in. She had no reason to be jealous of Nick, but she was. He had a beautiful daughter that thought the world of him, and vice versa. He had a purpose, a reason for getting out of bed each morning.

She bit back a sigh. Ever since her divorce, she had felt herself floundering. The role she'd blithely assumed would be hers had been denied. Yes, she had a terrific career, yes, she had a large and loving family, but they couldn't replace the aching emptiness of not having children of her own, a family of her own. Nothing ever would, unless she adopted.

Or married a man who already had children.

The thought had her jerking with surprise. An image of her in Nick's arms flashed through her mind. Her stomach jumped, and she hurriedly thought of something, anything else. A blush crawled up her cheeks, heightened by the realization that she sat on Nick's bed.

Almost dizzy with embarrassment, she left the room and retreated to the relative safety of the living room. Grabbing the remote, she flicked on the television, then flopped on the couch, hoping something would play that would beat back the thoughts and images that assaulted her mind.

Watching TV proved a useless effort. Try as she might, she couldn't extract the idea from her mind. Oh, there were thousands of rational reasons why she shouldn't even entertain the idea of making a family with Nick and Taylor. First there was the fact that she'd only known them for a couple of weeks, not exactly long enough to make a relationship.

There was also the fact that father and daughter were very much white and she very much wasn't. She had no idea what Nick thought about dating interracially, not to mention marrying that way. Sure, it was the new millennium, but people still faced the same kind of harassment her parents had. She'd never thought about it much one way or another, thanks to the balance that her parents had provided of both cultures. Her ex was black, but she'd dated across races during college, simply going out with men who interested her.

She had no idea if Nick was interested in her that way. They were neighbors, and over the course of the past few weeks had become friends, but he probably still thought of her as the nice neighbor lady looking after his daughter.

Even if he was interested, even if the possibility was as distant as a star on the horizon, there was still the specter of her infertility. Nick was a young, healthy guy. If he thought about marrying again, he was sure to want more children, especially a son. Whatever else Maya could give him, that was the one thing she couldn't do.

Sighing, Maya kicked off her shoes and stretched out on the couch, pulling the afghan over her. She was just the neighbor lady, taking care of her neighbor's daughter. It was best to just remember that, and not think of irrational wishes that could never come true.

~~~

Nick pulled into his driveway, shut off the engine, and leaned his head against the headrest. Exhaustion pulled at him. He'd almost stripped the gears on the way home; he was that tired. But the light on the porch beckoned him, as did the thought of Maya in his house, waiting for him.

Of course, she wasn't waiting for him the way he wanted. More than likely she sat on his couch in a cloud of impatience, ready to get back to her house and her life. Not that he could blame her. He'd definitely taken up more and more of her time in the past two weeks. He was beginning to think that Maya saw his daughter more than he did. Taylor had blossomed under Maya's care; she continually wowed him with stories of "Maya said this" or "Maya does that." Taylor was getting too attached to their neighbor, and the longer it continued, the harder it would be for Taylor to adjust to Mrs. Henderson's return.

Of course, Taylor wasn't the only one getting too attached to Maya. Nick found himself looking forward to coming home, to knocking on her door and being greeted by her crazy pets. To smelling the aroma of a home cooked meal as opposed to canned ravioli. To seeing Maya's face light up in a fantastic smile as she let him in.

Longing tugged at Nick as he left the car. What a great fantasy it would be, to come home on a night like this, a night when he'd lost the fight with mortality, a night when he became all too aware of his shortcomings, and be able to curl up in bed with an understanding woman. A woman who looked, laughed, and cared like Maya.

He unlocked the front door and stepped into the foyer. Hamlet and Horatio lumbered around the corner to greet him. Nick dropped to one knee to scratch both behind their ears. *This is why Maya has pets,* he thought to himself. *So that when you have a day when you felt like the crap at the bottom of a sewer, someone will always be home to lick your face.*

Rising to his feet, he followed the low murmur of the television to the living room. Maya lay curled on her side, afghan pulled over her, fast asleep. The utter peace and vulnerability of her expression stole into him. Had he ever slept like that?

He dropped to his knees in front of her, drinking in the sight. Normally on a night like this, when he felt beaten up and completely useless, he would sit in the rocker beside Taylor's bed and stare at his daughter for hours. Just watching her breathe, watching her sleep, watching her wrapped in innocence and wishing, wishing, wishing he could have some of that innocence back.

Now, as he watched Maya sleep, a different kind of wishing gripped him. He wished that he could slip onto the couch beside her, pull her close, and bury his face into the soft curve of her neck. He wished that she would open her arms and her body in welcome. He wished that she would let him in, let him dive into her softness, let him find the succor only she could provide for him.

Two weeks. In just two weeks Maya had become as necessary a component of his life as anyone ever could. He never would have thought that he'd let another woman so close to him and his daughter. Yet here she was, and the thought that she might not be there one day caused his heart to tighten with panic. How could he go back to just thinking of her as his next-door neighbor, someone to occasionally wave to but not be involved with? How could Taylor?

His hand reached out—to touch her cheek, to pull the afghan away, he didn't know. Instead, he settled it dangerously on the curve of her hip. "Maya, wake up."

"Nick?" Maya blinked slowly. "I'm sorry, I must have dozed off. Have you been here long?"

"Not long." He could feel his hand growing warm on her hip, and wondered when she would sit up and move away from him. "Did Taylor give you much trouble?"

"No, she was a sweetheart." She slid into a sitting position that put her mere inches from his face. "After she pulled the old 'Daddy said I could stay up later' trick, she took a bath, brushed her teeth, and I told her stories until she fell asleep."

"That's good." He sat back slightly, wanting to give her a little space while staying close. She'd moved the afghan aside as she sat up, and he noticed she wore faded jeans and a soft pink top that hugged her curves. Sleepiness gave her an air of warm, fuzzy softness, like a blanket to wrap around yourself on a chilly night.

Nick's fingers clenched against the urge to lay his head in her lap and spill his guts. He knew he walked a dangerous line, and it took everything in him not to cross it. "Maya, I really don't know how I'm going to repay you for everything you've done for me and Taylor. You won't take money, and flowers and a few dinners here and there just don't seem like enough."

She shook her head. "You don't have to do anything, Nick. I don't mind."

"Well, I do." His hands flanked her knees. He didn't even remember moving them. "I'm taking up too much of your life, and you deserve to have it back."

"Nick?" She touched his arm, a light touch that sent a bolt of need shooting through him. "What's wrong?"

"Nothing." He shook his head to clear his dark mood. "I'm just your neighbor, Maya. You don't have any responsibility toward me and my daughter. You shouldn't feel like you have to keep doing this."

"I don't feel that way." She leaned forward slightly so that their eyes were level. "And I'd like to think that we've become friends as well as neighbors."

The concern in her eyes threatened to do him in. "Even friends have their limits," he said, his voice wound tight. "And I'm not gonna keep taking advantage of you. I have some temporary replacements for Mrs. Henderson lined up that I've been putting off talking to. I'll find time to talk to them tomorrow."

She sat back and lowered her eyes. "Oh. I understand."

He'd hurt her feelings. That knowledge deepened the guilt he already choked on, driving him to his feet. "Maya, I'm sorry." He shoved his hands in his hair. "I'm not saying that I don't want you looking after Taylor. I'm sure she'd love for you to keep on doing that. But it's not fair to you. You've got your own life, and we've taken up too much of it."

"Shouldn't I be the one to decide if too much of my life is taken up?" she asked, rising to her feet. "Shouldn't I decide what's fair for me?"

"Maybe you're too nice to tell me," he said, his voice harsh with the effort to stay low. "Maybe you just feel sorry for me and my little girl."

Most women would have instantly denied his words, or retreated into a shell of hurt feelings. Maya did neither. Instead, she folded her arms across her chest and said, "Maybe I did feel that way when I came home and saw Taylor sitting in the rain. But I sure didn't feel that way by the time the day was over. And I certainly don't feel that way now."

She stared at him with wide soft eyes. "Sure, I've got a busy life. But I always have room in it for more friends."

The warmth she radiated threatened the tenuous hold he had on his composure. Why he was more affected tonight by losing someone, he had no idea. Maybe it was because he'd been examining his life of late, thinking about his own mortality and Taylor's future. Still, that didn't mean that he had to burden his neighbor with his mood.

Gathering his composure, he turned to face her. "Okay then, if you say that I'm not taking advantage of you or being unfair to you in any way, then I believe you. But I want you to know, Maya, that whatever you want, if there's anything you need, anything at all, tell me. I'll do whatever I can to get it for you."

The look she gave him held such anguish he almost couldn't believe it. Then she gave him a minimal smile shaded with sadness. "You're not a genie or an angel, Nick. Sometimes miracles just don't happen."

Her words kicked him in the gut. "You're right. Sometimes, no matter what you do, you don't get that miracle. Sometimes, no matter how hard you try, failure kicks you in the teeth."

She blinked as if looking at him for the first time. Her arm stretched between them, her hand reaching out to him. "Something's wrong. Don't tell me there isn't. You look like you've lost your best friend."

Nick gave up, letting his shoulders slump. "No, not my best friend. I just…I lost my patient tonight."

"Oh, Nick." Suddenly she was there, with her sweet scent and warm body, hugging and comforting him. "I'm so sorry"

He held her close, held on for dear life, breathing in the scent that was hers alone. Losing someone in the O.R. was always hard. Before, he would just suck it in, come home, and stare at Taylor for hours as she slept. Now, he wanted someone to listen, someone to understand, someone to hold. He wanted that someone to be Maya.

"Do you want to talk about it?" she asked, her breath brushing against his ear.

"Yes." He couldn't be polite and try to beg off. Tonight he needed to talk, and he needed to be listened to even more.

They retreated to the living room couch. Once seated, Nick hardly knew where to begin. Maya faced him, one leg tucked under her. She squeezed his hand once in understanding, giving him the silence and the contact he so desperately needed.

Like a faucet twisted to full strength, the story spilled from him in detail as he examined everything he'd done, every decision, every order he'd given during the time leading up to the patient's crash. Through it all Maya sat quietly, gripping his hands between hers, silently offering support.

"I'm not an expert, but it doesn't sound like you did anything wrong," she said when he finished.

"I know," he sighed, feeling drained. "But it doesn't stop me from beating myself up about it, and it doesn't stop his family from blaming me either."

Her fingers tightened. "How can they blame you?"

"It's a natural reaction when you lose someone," he managed to say, his throat tight. "You look for someone to blame, someone to pour your anger and grief out on, even when it's no one's fault."

"What happens now?"

Nick loosened his fingers to rub his forehead. "There'll be an inquiry, of course, to see if there was any wrongdoing. And an autopsy will be performed on my patient to see if there was any pre-existing condition I overlooked. If the family decides to attempt legal action, then the hospitals lawyers will get involved. No matter what the outcome is, my malpractice carrier will probably decide to raise my already astronomical premiums."

"Has this happened to you before?"

"Losing a patient?" He leaned back against the couch, closing his eyes against the memories assaulting him. "During my residency, when I had to do an ER rotation. Car accidents, domestic abuse, gang hits—you begin to lose your faith in humanity after a while. I would come home and just hold Taylor and wonder what in the hell was I thinking to bring a child into this insane world. Then the next day I'd push it away and keep on going."

"It must be horrible to have to deal with that alone," Maya said, her voice hushed with sorrow.

Nick opened his eyes to find Maya staring at him with tears shimmering in her eyes. Remorse filled him. He hadn't intended to make her feel bad, or sorry for him. "I've gotten better at dealing with it over the years," he said, trying for a lighter mood. "It's just some days it seems to hit harder than others."

He glanced at his watch. "I think I've kept you long enough," he said, rising to his feet. "Why don't I walk you to your door?"

"You can just watch me walk across the yard; that'll be enough," she said, slipping on her sneakers before climbing to her feet. "That way you don't have to leave Taylor alone."

"Good idea." He led her to the front door, barely avoiding tripping over her pets. Before opening the door, he turned to face her. "It looks like I have to thank you once again."

Maya smiled. "You could try not thanking me for a while, and I can stop being embarrassed each time you do."

"Does it really embarrass you?" he asked, incredulous.

She shrugged her shoulders. Nick felt his pulse jump as his eyes automatically dropped to her chest. "When I do things for people, I'm not looking for thanks. I do it to make them feel better, not to get a pat on the back."

"Well, I do feel better, and I have you to thank for it." He held up a hand to stifle her protest. "Not that I'm gonna say it or anything. But I do want to say that I'm extremely lucky and glad that you're my friend and neighbor."

She dipped her head, and he could tell by the way she shuffled her feet that he'd embarrassed her. He thought it was the cutest thing he'd ever seen. "Maya?"

"Yes?"

Before he could change his mind, Nick leaned forward and kissed her. She stood frozen for a moment, her hands automatically at his shoulders. Just when he thought he'd made a huge mistake and decided to move away, Maya tightened her arms around his neck and kissed him back. Her lips were full, sensuous, sweet. His hands crept to her waist, drawing her closer with a soft subtle movement.

The kiss deepened as need flared inside him. Tossing subtlety aside, he pressed against her, slanting his lips across hers. Her lips parted and his tongue swept inside to taste her fully, completely. He grew hard, his erection straining against his trousers, blindly seeking relief.

Nick ended the kiss with reluctance, resting his forehead against hers. "Maya—"

"Shut up," she whispered, putting a finger to his lips. "Don't ruin the moment."

He did as ordered, standing still and enjoying the touch of her fingertips along his jaw, the weight of her body against his. If the feel of his arousal pressed against her stomach bothered her, she gave no sign. Instead, she rose to kiss him again, leaving no mistake in his mind that she'd wanted it as much as he had. Finally she sighed. "I guess I better go."

"Yeah, you should," he agreed roughly, wanting nothing more than to take her upstairs. The thought was enough to allow sanity to return. He certainly could *not* take her upstairs, not with his daughter sleeping blissfully down the hall. "Goodnight, Maya."

"Goodnight, Nick." She stepped out onto the porch, her pets at her heels. Nick watched her walk across the yard to her front door. He watched her until she gave him a final wave and entered her house, and then he slowly closed and locked the door.

He trudged upstairs, checked on his sleeping daughter, then retreated to his bedroom. The digital clock on his nightstand showed one-thirty. He knew he needed to get to sleep, but he also knew that sleep was an impossibility.

He wanted Maya. Badly. He could no longer pretend that he didn't, that she was just his neighbor helping him out. He'd crossed a line tonight by kissing her. The feel of her lips still tingled against his. Yeah, he'd crossed a line, and it scared him.

Damned if he knew what to do about it.

SEVEN

Nick pushed a cart through the superstore, wondering why in the world he thought this was a great idea. One-stop shopping that took twice as long as going to two or three different stores. He'd been duped, along with the rest of America.

"Daddy, can I have a new doll? I know just what kind I want."

"Sure, pumpkin. I think we've got everything we need from the grocery side anyway."

They passed through the clothing department on their way to the other side of the store. Families, singles, and little old ladies crowded the path, as if after-church social time had begun. Men clutched pails of paint or armfuls of tube-socks, looking straight ahead, fearful of being stripped of their manhood for not being in a home improvement store.

Nick narrowly avoided colliding with a sizeable older woman who stopped in the middle of the aisle for no apparent reason. She shot him a dirty look, which he ignored for his daughter's sake. He moved his cart around her and right into a display of condoms.

Several boxes fell off the flimsy hook, landing atop the Alpha Bits. Taylor, of course, noticed.

"Hey, Daddy, what's a Tro-jan?" she asked, reaching for a box.

Nick snatched it from her curious grasp. "Nothing you need to worry about for the next twenty years," he said quickly, shoving the errant boxes back onto the hook. The idea of talking to his little girl about condoms and their use made him want to hurl.

He breathed a sigh of relief as they made it to the relative safety of the toy department. "What kind of doll do you want?"

Taylor walked down the row of brightly colored boxes. "I want a doll that looks like Maya, but none of these match," she said, her eyebrows knitting together in consternation.

Nick parked the cart and went to stand beside his daughter. True enough, none of the dolls looked like Maya. "Everybody looks different, pumpkin, so you won't find a doll that looks just like Maya." He reached for an African-America doll. "How about this one?"

"Okay, but I need that one, too," she said, pointing to an Asian doll.

"Why do you think you need both?" Nick asked, thinking she was trying to scam another doll out of him. Not that he'd refuse her, but it was the principle of the thing.

"Because Maya isn't black." Taylor rolled her eyes, as if the answer was obvious. "She's Veteranese."

"She's what?"

"She showed me pictures. Her dad is the same color as my friend Michelle and her mother is from a place called Vetenam or something. Anyway, she looks Chinese. That's why her eyes look like that."

God help him. Nick closed his eyes. At the rate Taylor continued to surprise him, he'd be white-haired in five years. "I think you mean Vietnamese, and her mother's from Vietnam."

"Yep, that's it."

That explained Maya's exotic looks, Nick thought, trying to assimilate the information Taylor had given him. Still it seemed strange that Maya would tell his daughter before she told him. Had she intended to keep it secret? Surely she knew that Taylor would tell him eventually.

"All right, you can have both dolls," Nick said at last, putting the African-American doll in the cart and telling himself he wasn't really bribing his daughter. Taylor put the Asian doll in, then insisted on buying clothes for the new dolls and their blonde "sister" at home. The equivalent of an entire department store later, they made it through checkout and to the car.

"When did Maya tell you about her family?" Nick asked, starting the car after making sure Taylor had buckled herself in properly.

"When you had to work late," his daughter replied. "She was going to read me a bedtime story, but I wanted to know about her family."

Taylor didn't have a shy bone in her body. Of course she'd ask Maya about her family. But more than that, Nick knew his daughter had a keen interest in other people's families. Particularly families with both parents and more than one child.

"She has a big family," Taylor continued, her voice wistful. "She's got two sisters *and* four brothers. She said they got in a lot of fights but they had a lot of fun, too. And it was always loud, too." She paused. "Our house is kinda quiet."

Nick stopped at the traffic light, gripping the steering wheel in suddenly trembling hands. He had to swallow several times before he could speak. "Okay then. If it's too quiet for you, I could start snoring really loudly, like this." He made a noise that sounded like a donkey undergoing a very painful operation.

Taylor burst into giggles, as he'd hoped she would. "Daddy!"

"Or I could stomp around the house instead of walking, and sing the 'Jolly Green Giant' song at the top of my lungs." He started to sing, loudly and deliberately off-key.

"That's awful!" She slapped her hands over her ears, still laughing.

"I know!" Nick exclaimed, on a roll. "I could pretend I'm auditioning for New Backstreet Kids on the A-town Block!" He started singing the words to the latest boy-band song, using his free hand to gesture while the other remained firmly on the wheel. "Throw yo' hands up in the a-yare! Party hearty like you just don't ca-yare!"

By the time they pulled into their driveway, they were both singing at the top of their lungs, then dancing as they unloaded the car. Mr. Jacobson was mowing his front yard and gave them an odd look. "Get jiggy wi'it, Mr. Jacobson!" Nick yelled, sending Taylor into another fit of giggles and bringing Mrs. Jacobson to the front door. He didn't care if his neighbors thought he'd gone off his rocker, as long as his little girl kept laughing.

They took their purchases into the house. Taylor immediately went for the dolls as Nick opened one of the bags. "Hey, aren't you going to help your old man with this stuff?"

"Can't I go play now?" she asked. "And you're not old."

Nick laughed. "Nice try with the butter-up," he said, looking down into the bag. Blue cardboard snagged his attention. "On second thought, I can handle this. Go on and take your stuff upstairs. But I expect to see a fashion show later!"

"Kay!" Not needing to be told twice, Taylor grabbed two bags of toys and accessories and ran upstairs.

Once he was certain his daughter had left, Nick pulled the box of condoms out of the bag. How in the world did they get there? He was sure that he'd gotten every last box out of his cart. Obviously he hadn't. That meant another trek to the superstore—without Taylor in tow—to return them.

Or he could keep them, just in case.

The thought made him bark with dry laughter. Who was he kidding? He was a single father who performed surgeries every other day amongst making patient rounds, then he came home to play dolls with his daughter. Every second of free time he possessed he spent with Taylor, and he wouldn't have it any other way. But sometimes...

Sometimes he fantasized about being washed up on a tropical island with a beautiful woman and MacGyver's know-how. With no sign of rescue in sight, he'd build a palace for himself and his island lover, and they'd spend lazy days making love on the beach, in the water, in the trees, with nothing to worry about but sunburn in sensitive places.

That wasn't reality though. Reality was, he'd probably not get the chance or desire to date until Taylor went to high school, and then he'd have to find a woman who wouldn't mind him calling his daughter every ten minutes to make sure she wasn't getting into trouble.

Maya would understand. She had a greater compassion than some nurses he knew. She had some sort of eternal joy that he wished he could bottle up and carry with him wherever he went. Memory took him back to the night he'd lost his patient, when Maya had quickly and freely offered the comfort of her arms. And more.

They hadn't discussed the kisses they'd shared that night in the days since, and Nick wondered if he should even bother to bring it up. Maybe Maya had only felt sorry him, or been as driven by the need to give comfort as he'd been by the need to take it. Maybe she'd wanted to kiss him as much as he'd wanted to kiss Her. After all, she was the one who had initiated the second kiss.

There was one sure way to find out. One sure way to act on his fascination with his next-door neighbor. He'd call her up and ask her out on a date. If she said no, that would be that. And if she said yes…well, he'd cross that bridge when he got to it.

First, though, there was the Taylor bridge to cross.

Resolved, Nick unpacked the remainder of his purchases, then took the box of condoms and other toiletries up to his bathroom. Afterwards, he found Taylor in her room, splayed across her bed with Barbie accessories spread around her.

"Hey, pumpkin, how's the fashion show going?"

"Good." She pointed to the dolls lined up against the pillows. "I decided to let them join the Secret Princess Club."

"Secret Princess Club?"

"Yeah, it's a club that Maya—" she broke off, turning to look at him. "If I tell you, it's not a secret anymore."

His little girl was getting pretty good at the daddy-you're-an-idiot look, Nick thought to himself. Just another sign of how fast she was growing up.

"Taylor, honey, I want to talk to you for a minute."

"Sure, Daddy." She slid over to make room on the bed. "Did I do something wrong?"

"What makes you think you did something wrong?" he asked, sitting down beside her.

"Because you're wearing the serious look, and you only do that when I do something wrong."

She had him there. He made a mental note to practice his poker face. "A couple of months ago, we talked about getting a pet." Her eyes grew round. "I'm not saying we're going to get one tomorrow, but if you can prove to me that you're responsible, we'll go get one."

Taylor sat up, bouncing up and down with excitement. "I want a dog and a fat cat, just like Maya has," she announced.

Of course she did, Nick thought. "Honey, we need to see if you can handle one pet before we think about two."

"I can handle them," she said stubbornly. "Maya lets me feed Ham and Harry, and we take them for a walk when I get out of school. Maya lets me hold the leashes and everything."

News to him. Add one more thing to the list of what he needed to talk to Maya about.

"Okay, we'll see." He held up a hand. "I'm not making any promises just yet. I want to talk to Maya and see how you've been handling her pets, and I want to see it for myself. Then we'll talk about what kind of pet to get. Deal?" He held out his hand.

"Deal." Taylor slapped his palm with her own.

"Ouch!" Nick waved his palm to take away the sting. "Have you been lifting weights or something?"

"Daddy." Taylor sighed and rolled her eyes.

"All right. There's something else I want to talk to you about." He reached out to lift one of her pigtails. "You like Maya, don't you?"

"I think she's awesome." Taylor stared at him with wide blue eyes. "She's not going away, is she?"

"No, of course not," he assured her, then paused, unsure of how to continue the conversation. Might as well just come right out with it. "I was wondering, what do you think about me asking Maya out on a date?"

"Just the two of you?"

"Yeah."

"I think you should take her somewhere pretty where you have to dress up," she announced. "I saw something on TV where the man and the lady went to a nice place and they got to dance and everything."

He shouldn't have been surprised by Taylor's answer, but he was. "Thought about this before, have you?"

Taylor nodded. "Can I tell you a secret?"

Nick felt his stomach jump. What kind of secret did his daughter have, and did it concern Maya? "What is it, sweetheart?"

She fidgeted with her dolls for a moment. "When I say my prayers, I ask God if He'll let Maya be my mommy."

Whoa. "You do what?" He could hardly get the words out.

"Yeah. Is that wrong?"

Wrong? Asking God for a mother wasn't wrong. But asking for Maya? "You didn't tell Maya this, did you?" Oh God, how would he get out of that mess?

"No. Can I?"

Acid bubbled in Nick's stomach, and he put his head in his heads. "No, sweetheart, we should keep this between us and God for right now," he replied, forcing calm into his voice. "Would you mind telling me why you want Maya to be your mother?"

"I like her. She helps me with my homework, and lets me help her cook, and braids my hair all pretty. And she's really pretty, too, and she was really nice to me when I felt bad about Leila and Tamera having a mother and I didn't."

God. He hadn't even thought about that when he'd agreed to let Taylor spend the weekend with them. He gave his daughter a gentle hug. "I'm sorry, pumpkin."

"It's all right. Maya made me feel better."

"And how did she do that?"

"She told me that since my mommy was in heaven, she was with me all the time," Taylor explained. "Maya said I could talk to Mommy any time I wanted because God would make sure that she heard me."

Wow. Maya had held some deep conversations with his daughter. Was this yet another sign how of desperately Taylor needed a mother, needed someone to confide things in, things she obviously didn't want to tell him? Nick couldn't remember the last time he and Taylor had discussed her mother. It was a subject that he avoided if he could. Obviously his daughter knew that, and had decided to share that subject with their neighbor instead.

"You know you can talk to me any time, about any thing," he said finally, tugging on one of her braids. "Even if you think I don't want to hear it, you can tell me, okay?"

"I know," his daughter said. "Anyway, I just want you to know that I like her, and I want you to like her, too."

"I do like her, sweetheart, but I don't want you to get your hopes up," he cautioned. "Grownups have to go through a bunch of steps before they can decide things."

"Why?"

"Well…" Nick floundered, not really sure if he wanted to have a grown-up conversation with his seven-year-old daughter. "It's just something grown-ups do."

"That's weird."

"Maya might not even like me the way I like her."

"She will," Taylor said, brimming with confidence. "I think she already does."

That was certainly news. Still, he curbed the urge to jump up and down and pump his fist in the air. "Okay, pumpkin. We'll see what happens."

"Okay. When I say my prayers tonight, I'll ask God to make Maya say yes."

Nick spent the rest of the evening playing garden party with Taylor and thinking of Maya. After he put his daughter to bed, he placed a call to A.J. "Hey, I need your help," he said when his friend answered the other line.

"I'm not trading a shift with you," A.J. said. "Besides, you get the sweet rotations anyway."

"This isn't about work, though I'll remember you said that when you want something," Nick replied. "I was wondering if you knew a great place to take someone on a first date."

"First date, huh?" Nick would swear he could hear his friend grinning through the line. "I suppose this is the same woman who's been on your mind since we hung out?"

"Yeah it is. You know a place or what?"

"Hey, don't get testy with the maestro," A.J. retorted. "What are you looking for? Something entertaining where you don't have to do much talking or something to blow her skirt up?"

Nick didn't think there was a right answer to A.J.'s question. "How about some place where the food is terrific and there's some soft music to dance to?"

"Oh, that kind of date," A.J. said with a suggestive laugh. "My man Nick, jumping into the dating pool headfirst."

"Maya deserves this," Nick said, even though he knew it would be pointless to argue. "It's a first date and a thank you for all the help she's given me and Taylor."

"Geesh. Wonder what you'll do when you're really grateful."

"You know, sticking tongue depressors under my fingernails would be less painful than this."

"Okay, I'll let up. But this is gonna cost you, you know." Nick closed his eyes. "What do you want?"

"Every single detail of your big night on the town."

"You're kidding me, right?"

"Do I sound like I'm kidding?" A.J. asked.

"No, but why should I tell you what happens? That creeps me out, man."

"Hey, it's purely for referral purposes only," A.J. explained. "Another happy customer to add to A.J.'s book on wowing the ladies."

Nick laughed. "You're one sick puppy, you know that?"

"I know it, and so do half the single women of Atlanta. And trust me when I say they ain't complaining."

There were days when Nick wondered how he and A.J. remained good friends. This was one of those days. Nick had never been the kind to play the field. He'd taken relationships as seriously as his desire to become a doctor. A.J. had never had a serious relationship in his life-unless you counted the relationship he had with the men's store at Macy's.

"One day you're gonna meet your match," he warned his friend. "I hope like hell I'm there when it happens."

"Don't even wish that on me," A.J. choked. "I plan to be single and loving life when I'm ninety."

"There are some benefits to giving up the single life," Nick felt compelled to say.

"Sure, and I guess you're the expert on that."

Nick felt as if his best friend had just sucker-punched him. He heard A.J. groan, then say, "Aw, man, I'm sorry. That was a low blow."

"Yes, it was."

"Hell." A.J. sighed. "Sometimes my mouth works before my brain does."

"How did you even become a doctor?" Nick joked, wanting to get the awkwardness over.

"Good looks and lonely lady professors," A.J. said with a laugh. Nick of course knew it wasn't true, having gone through medical school with A.J.

"I've got the number for Amora's right here," A.J. said. He rattled off the number for Nick. "When you call, ask for Henry. He'll get you in."

"Cool. Thanks, man."

"No prob. I hope she's worth it."

"I think she is."

Nick stared at the phone for a long time after talking with A.J. He was definitely no expert on marriage or committed relationships; he'd never claimed to be. Hell, he was probably the worst candidate, thanks to his last marriage. He probably shouldn't waste Maya's time…

"It's just a date," he muttered to himself, reaching for the phone. Just a chance to go to dinner and dance with a lovely woman. A chance to get out and have fun. That's all it was. He certainly wasn't ready to make it more than that.

"Hi, Maya. It's Nick."

"Hey, what's going on?"

He relaxed, hearing the pleasantness of her voice. "Just getting ready for the week. How about you?"

"The same," she answered. "Oh, that's right, Mrs. Henderson's replacement is supposed to start tomorrow, right?"

"Yeah." He cradled the phone closer. "Her name's Yolanda. I'm going to pick Taylor up from school tomorrow and introduce them. If you're going to be home, I'd love to introduce you to her."

"Really?"

"Of course," Nick said. "Taylor's going to want to see you still, and you have an open invitation to our house anytime. So you should meet her."

"That's a good idea. I'm sure I'll be back home by then. I hope everything works out."

"Me, too," Nick admitted. "I know it's going to be hard, having Taylor adjust to another caretaker. But Mrs. Henderson shouldn't be out for too much longer."

"That's good. Taylor talks about Mrs. Henderson all the time."

"Not as much as she talks about you," Nick said. "She thinks you can do no wrong."

Maya's laughter floated over the wire. "I can do plenty wrong. I just don't leave witnesses."

"I'll store that away for future reference," Nick said with a laugh of his own. "By the way, what are you doing Friday night?"

"What?"

He hadn't meant to make it a sneak attack, the invite just came out on its own. He cleared his throat. "I was wondering if you'd go out with me on Friday night."

"Just you and me?"

Surprise came through loud and clear on the line. Why would it surprise her that he wanted to spent time alone with her? "Yes, just the two of us."

"Like a date?"

Should he have hired a skywriter instead? "Yes, like a date, except it will be a date. Dinner and dancing at Amora's Retreat."

"Wow."

"Is that a good wow or a bad wow?" Nick asked, half-teasing. "I promise to have you back before curfew."

"I'm sorry, Nick. You just caught me by surprise. I didn't expect—yes, of course I'm free Friday night."

"Are you sure?" he asked, not wanting her to feel pressured into accepting. "It's no big deal if you can't go." Even though it was.

"No, no," she said quickly. He heard her take a deep breath. "I would love to go out with you Friday night. What time should I be ready?"

"Uuhm…" Good Lord, he hadn't thought that far ahead. "How about seven?"

"Seven is fine," she replied, her voice warm and pleased. At least he hoped that's what she felt. "I guess I'll see you then. But I'll see you before that, won't I?"

"Of course. You know Taylor and I can't resist Home-Cooking Wednesdays."

"You'd better not," she chided him playfully. "It's officially a tradition now. And we can't go against tradition."

"God forbid I should be the one to break tradition," Nick grinned into the phone. "My little girl would draw and quarter me."

"Oh, I don't think so," Maya said. "Any father who can stand in the middle of his driveway singing at the top of his lungs can do no wrong in his daughter's eyes."

Heat crept up Nick's neck. "You heard that, huh?"

"I think Cincinnati heard that," she joked. "I thought it was the cutest thing I've ever seen."

"Gee, thanks," Nick said sheepishly, slumping down in the chair.

"Hey, if you weren't embarrassed standing in the middle of the neighborhood, you can't be embarrassed now," Maya pointed out. "I mean it. I thought it was terrific of you to do that with Taylor."

"What can I say? If my girl's feeling down, it's my duty to cheer her up."

"What happened?"

"She's starting to feel the pinch of being an only child of a single parent," Nick explained. "She said the house is too quiet, and she wants to get a pet."

"Oh, poor thing," she murmured, sympathy filling her voice. "If my opinion means anything, I can tell you that she's great with Hamlet and Horatio. She walks them with me, feeds them, and basically asks all kinds of questions. 'Course, that could just mean that she plans to be a veterinarian when she grows up."

"Either way, whatever makes my little girl happy is all right with me. And your opinion means a lot. Maybe you'd like to go to the shelter with us next weekend, help us pick out an appropriate pet?"

"I'd love to," she said, "as long as you make sure I don't leave with another one."

"I think I can help you with that," Nick said. "It will be my pleasure."

"I'll hold you to it," she answered, her voice low. "By the way, I'm really looking forward to Friday night." She disconnected.

Nick stared at the phone for a long moment. Friday suddenly couldn't come fast enough.

EIGHT

"Jas, I need your help."

"Maya? What's up?"

"Can you come over?"

"When?"

Maya looked at her watch. "Right now."

"Maya, what's going on?" Jasmine's concern rang through the phone.

"I'll explain when you get here," Maya said. "And don't tell anyone in the family, all right?"

"Is this a break every traffic law thing, or a get there as soon and safely as you can type thing?" Jasmine asked.

"It's a fashion disaster waiting to happen type thing," Maya replied, surveying her wrecked room.

"Oh, that's serious. I'll be right over." The line went dead.

The doorbell rang twenty minutes later. "Thank God," Maya said, flinging open the door and all but dragging her sister inside. Whenever there was a fashion emergency, Jasmine served as 9-1-1. Jasmine had an innate ability to dress to the nines, even when it was ninety-nine outside.

Jasmine set a silver case on the foot of the stairs. "Okay, what's the situation?"

"First date," Maya answered.

Jasmine raised an eyebrow at that, but kept going. "Where to?"

"Amora's Retreat. I've never heard of it."

"I have. What kind of reaction do you want?"

"Reaction?" Maya asked.

"Do you want to leave him breathless, leave him wanting more, or leave him horny?"

Maya choked on a cough. "Leave him wanting more?"

Jas nodded. "That's probably a good idea, though I don't think you'll have to work too hard for Nick."

"Did I say I have a date with Nick?"

Placing a hand on her hip, Jasmine shot Maya a you've-got-to-be-kidding-me look. "Don't tell me you don't notice the way he looks at you?"

"I don't really try to look at him looking at me," Maya said, her blush deepening. "I mean, he never even said anything after we kissed."

"You haven't been on a date yet, but you've already kissed?" Jas asked. "Wait until I tell Momma!"

"You tell Mom about any of this and I'll personally hold you down and give you a bikini wax," Maya threatened. "Let me at least get through the date first."

"Is he a good kisser, at least?"

Maya thought back. "Oh, yeah."

"Hhm. I'm thinking all-out assault on the poor man." She pulled her microscopic cell phone out of her back pocket and pressed a single button. After listening for a few seconds, she hit another button, then pocketed the tiny phone. "Okay, there's no rain in the forecast tonight, and the temperature's going to stay warm. Let's see what you pulled out of your closet."

After waiting for Jasmine to pick up her case, Maya led the way upstairs. Her bedroom looked as if the proverbial tornado had struck it. She wasn't as conservative as Nadine, but she wasn't as daring as Jasmine or her mother either. Still, she knew what colors made her look good and what styles brought out her best features. Tonight, though, she wanted to be stunning, and stunning was definitely her younger sister's department.

"I thought I'd just go with something black, so I could be sure to fit into any atmosphere," she said, pointing to a knee-length black sheath with a muted rhinestone appliqué at the modest neckline.

Jasmine gave the dress a dismissive glance. "Sure you could, if Pluto had atmosphere. You don't want to look like you've just got out of a business meeting. You want to look like you enjoy life, and you're happy with your body."

"I do enjoy life," Maya insisted, hanging the dress back in the closet. "As for my body, well, I could wish for bigger breasts, but I'm not into silicone."

"You look just fine," Jasmine disagreed, going through the pile closest to her. "Trust me, if I thought you needed bigger breasts, I'd say so."

"How could I forget?" Maya asked wryly, remembering other times "Officer Jasmine" had accused her of committing crimes against fashion.

"The push-up bra you're wearing will do just fine, we just need the right top to accent it," Jasmine said. "Amora's Retreat is a dance and dinner place, very upscale and very romantic."

"Really?" Maya said, intrigued. "How do you know about it?"

"I went there for dinner before senior prom, remember?"

Jasmine's senior prom was three years ago. "My date took me to Benihana."

"That should tell you something."

It told her nothing and everything. Nick choosing an upscale *and* romantic place for their first date? The night was getting even more interesting. "I certainly don't want to wear black then. Wouldn't want to fade into the background."

"Exactly. See? You're not fashion hopeless after all."

"Gee, thanks a lot," Maya said, rolling her eyes in her sister's direction. "Stop criticizing me and tell me more about this place."

"It's close enough to downtown to be trendy but far enough away to be comfortable," Jasmine said, sorting through bottoms. "It's got a killer view of the skyline and the most delicious chateaubriand you've ever tasted."

"I don't think I've ever tasted chateaubriand," Maya said, feeling definitely outclassed by her younger sister. She knew what to wear for an interview, for a high-stress presentation, for a power lunch and after-work drinks with clients. She didn't know the first thing about what to wear for a romantic first date of dinner and dancing.

"You know, I've got a pair of wide-legged silk pants," Maya said, looking through the mound of fabric on her bed. "They're an ivory color, with a soft shiny look, and I think they have pearls along the hem." She pulled the pants out of the pile. "What about these?"

"Perfect," Jas said. "Do you still have those gold strappy sandals?"

"You mean the ones you always borrow?"

Her sister had the decency to look sheepish. "Yeah, those."

"I think so." Maya headed to the closet, found the high-heeled sandals, and rejoined her sister. "Do you see anything that would go with these?" she asked, sitting in the one empty spot on the bed so that she could slip into the pants.

"Hey, what about this blouse?" Jasmine asked, pulled out a scarlet off-the-shoulder sleeveless blouse made of a clingy fabric and boasting a deep neckline.

"Uhm, it probably would work," Maya said, eyeing the blouse her sister had given her last Christmas. It would definitely be daring, something she hadn't been in a long time. "You think it'll be appropriate for this place?"

"You've never even worn it!" Jas said, showing her the tag still attached.

"Look at the dip in the front," Maya argued. "Did you think I was going to wear that to work?"

Jas waved her hand in dismissal. "Throw a blazer over that and it would be no big deal."

"If I leaned forward, I'd be offering proof that it was no big deal," Maya retorted.

"The neckline's not that bad," Jasmine said, holding it against Maya.

"That's because there isn't a neckline," Maya shot back. "It's a belly-button line."

"Then that makes it perfect for tonight."

"No."

"Come on, Mai. There's a reason you called me, remember? Trust me on this. Relax and let yourself go.

You need to have a good time, no matter where this leads."

Maya sighed. She knew Jasmine was right. Thinking about consequences would only ruin what could be a wonderful evening. She'd spent too many dismal hours thinking about the what-ifs in her life. Now it was time to let go and have fun.

"You win," she finally said. "Hook me up."

———

By six-thirty, Jasmine pronounced her perfect, gave her two condoms, and left. Maya had quickly put them in her medicine cabinet, not wanting to think of her youngest sister having sex. Heck, she couldn't even imagine herself having sex, at least not tonight.

Not that she didn't want to. Nick was beyond attractive, with those sapphire blue eyes and mink brown hair that begged to be touched. Not to mention that smile that made him look boyish and mischievous and sexy as hell all at the same time.

She remembered how his body had felt when they'd kissed for the first time. Long and lean with evident strength, she'd enjoyed the way his body felt against hers. In her athletic shoes, she'd reached the center of his chest; with the heels she had on now she'd probably be able to rest her head on his shoulder. Perfect for dancing close, perfect for stealing kisses...

The doorbell rang, causing Maya's heart to leap. She glanced at her watch: precisely seven. Checking her appearance one final time in the hall mirror, she opened the door.

God help her.

She noticed his eyes first. The perfect blue of his eyes still amazed her, and the way his gaze widened in apparent appreciation made it even better. She noticed the blue of his shirt next, how it enhanced the color of his eyes. He'd paired it with loose-fitting yet tailored trousers of charcoal gray and a matching jacket. A subdued tie of blue and gray completed the ensemble, except for the single rose he held.

"Hi," she finally said when she found her voice.

He blinked. "Amazing," he managed to say. "You look amazing."

She gave him a huge grin. "I can clean up pretty well when the need arises," she said, grabbing a small purse and an ivory wrap off the hail table. "You're looking pretty good yourself."

"Thanks. This is for you," he said, extending the rose to her.

She accepted it with a murmur of thanks, holding it to her nose to inhale the subtle scent. She hadn't expected him to bring her flowers, but she liked it even better that he'd brought her a single rose instead of an entire bouquet. 'Course, she wouldn't dwell on what his intentions might or might not have been by giving her a single rose.

"Shall we go?"

Maya locked her door, then slipped her hand into his, letting him guide her to the car. Stars gleamed brightly overhead in the velvet of the night sky, and the cool air wrapped around them like a gentle caress. The scene was set for a beautiful night.

Nick's reaction to her appearance had given Maya that final boost of confidence she'd needed. It was one thing for Jasmine to declare her a success, but it couldn't compare to Nick's genuine admiration.

She'd meant it when she'd said that he looked good. Actually, good was too lame a word. The blue of his shirt made his eyes even more stunning. A lock of his hair fell over his forehead, just begging to be smoothed back into place, and his cologne sent a subtle scent of musk and spice her way. She breathed deeply. Lord, she was a sucker for a man who wore cologne.

"I have to tell you, I've been looking forward to this," she confessed, settling in as Nick pulled the car out of the driveway. The import purred to life as he shifted into drive, sending them cruising down the street.

"Really?"

"Oh yes." She thumbed the vent in front of her closed. "Getting dressed up, going out, and talking to someone who isn't a co-worker or related to me...this is almost like Christmas!"

Nick laughed. "I'm glad I could oblige you, ma'am," he drawled. "But you can't tell me that you're a homebody."

"Okay, maybe not a homebody, but I like being at home," she admitted. "I mean, I spend a lot of time out with my sisters or hanging out over at my parents' house, but home is heaven as far as I'm concerned. Besides, I'm addicted to home improvement shows. I tend to turn off the phone whenever there's a *Trading Rooms* marathon on."

"So what you're telling me is that I shouldn't leave you alone in my house for two days."

"Nope. The first thing I'd do is get rid of that 'country kitchen' style."

He tossed a look her way before getting on the highway. "What's wrong with country kitchens?"

"Nothing, if you live in the country," she retorted. "City people shouldn't have pale blue geese with cute red ribbons tied around their necks prancing on their walls. Or cow-covered appliances. It's just wrong, I'm telling you."

"And what if I happen to like country kitchen?" Nick asked with a smile.

"Then I'd get you some help. I've heard that Betty Ford can cure almost anyone."

"Okay, okay, I give up," Nick said, lifting one hand off the wheel. "I don't really like country kitchen. It came with the house. I tend to like clean and simple when it comes to decorating. You know, solid patterns, no bright colors."

"I know. I saw your bedroom," Maya blurted out. She immediately winced.

She could feel Nick's eyes on her "You did?"

Maya pulled her wrap about her shoulders. "The night you had to work late," she said softly, feeling her cheeks warm. "I went through the house, making sure everything was locked up, and well…" She took a deep breath. "I was curious, okay?"

"I got no problem with you being curious," Nick said.

Laughter was obvious in his voice. "Are you laughing at me?" she asked, trying to decide whether to be amused or ticked off.

"At a woman who said she doesn't leave witnesses?" He coughed. "God forbid. I was just thinking I'm glad I didn't leave underwear on the floor."

The image had her bursting with laughter. "God, I hope I wouldn't think less of you for that."

"I hope not either."

"Even if I did, you still have brownie points from the show you put on Sunday," she reminded him.

He slowed down for the traffic light. "You're not going to let me live that down, are you?"

"Sure I will," Maya grinned. "Sometime next year."

They settled into an easy silence for the remainder of the drive. Maya spent the time watching Nick's hands. He moved easily, shifting gears with an almost absent-minded gesture. She liked the way he gripped the steering wheel, liked the play of his fingers on the gearshift. With hands like that, he could have been a concert pianist, or perhaps even a maestro with the guitar. Instead, and most importantly, he used those hands to save lives.

She knew his fingers were warm, soft without being feminine. Strength and grace ruled his hands in a heady combination that made her throat dry. What would it be like, she wondered, to feel those hands sliding over her bare shoulders? How would she react to the tips of his fingers grazing her breasts?

Her breath caught in her throat, and she had to shift against the erotic image that suddenly filled her mind in glorious detail.

"Penny for your thoughts."

Startled, she turned to find Nick staring at her, his expression curious in the reddish glow of the traffic lights. Disconcerted at being busted, she leaned forward to turn on the stereo. "Just wondering what sort music you're into."

Pop music filled the air. "I do have a seven year-old, you know," he reminded her, pushing a button to change the station to some sort of soft flamenco-style music. "Personally, I like a little bit of everything. But I have a feeling that that's not what you were thinking about."

"Really?" she asked, trying not to feel nervous. He really couldn't tell what she had been thinking, could he? "And how would you know?"

"Your breathing deepened, as if you'd become excited or anxious," Nick explained, shifting the car into gear as the light changed. "Not exactly a reaction I'd have if I were thinking about music."

He had her there. Still, she decided to play it out for as long as she could. "You must think you're a doctor or something."

"Something." He flashed her a grin. "So, what were you thinking about?"

She decided to 'fess up. What harm would there be in that? "All right, I was admiring your hands."

"My hands?"

"Yes. Don't tell me you don't know how incredibly sexy your hands are?"

"No," he said slowly, as if thinking about it. "I just think of them as tools, important tools, that I need to get my job done."

He smiled again. "You know, I've heard of women who like eyes or go gaga over a man in a pair of tight jeans, but I never heard of a woman with a thing for hands."

She tilted her chin skyward. "Didn't you know? I'm not like most women."

"I'm finding that out. And what a pleasant discovery it is!"

He cleared his throat, keeping his eyes on the road. "You know, there's something we need to talk about."

Uh-oh. That sounded serious. "What do we need to talk about?"

"That kiss we shared a couple of weeks ago."

Maya adjusted her wrap with nervous fingers. Why so serious about that one kiss? Okay, technically it was two kisses, but it hadn't been a big deal, had it? Maybe he wanted to make sure it didn't happen again. But if he didn't want it to happen again, he wouldn't ask her out, right?

"I've got a better idea," she said, determined to keep the night on a light note. "Why don't we kick seriousness to the curb and swear that we'll let our hair down and have a good time?"

When he remained silent, she poked him in the arm. "Come on, doctor, surely you're allowed to have a little fun?"

"All right," he finally agreed. "Fun it is. Frankly, I'm looking forward to relaxing and having a good time."

He certainly was, Nick thought, as he slowed the car for a turn. His first glimpse of Maya had short-circuited his senses. He'd thought her beautiful before;

how she looked tonight he didn't even have adjectives for. Mysterious, exotic, sexy—they all fit but seemed woefully inadequate. He'd actually felt a jolt when he saw her, and he knew he'd never forget the seductive scent of her perfume.

Maybe he'd been single too long. He had no other way to explain his overwhelming reaction to Maya. What he'd thought was just a mild fascination in late March had grown into full-blown attraction. He wanted her. He'd been wanting her since their late-night kiss. Seeing her tonight, with the blood red blouse framing her throat and the hollow between her breasts, he wanted her even more.

Taylor also wanted Maya. His poor little girl had only his mother and their housekeeper as nurturing women in her life. He understood how she could latch onto a woman like Maya, a woman who possessed such a kind and generous spirit. Hell, he'd latched onto her himself.

Taylor didn't understand the complexities of relationships, and Nick didn't know how to explain them to her. He was far from an expert himself. It wasn't as simple as going up to Maya and asking her to be Taylor's mother. He had to like her as much as Taylor did. They had to have something in common, they had to be compatible. And Maya had to care for them, and want to be with them. She had to know his hang-ups and be all right with them. He needed to know hers. Hell, he needed to know a lot of things about Maya, and that wasn't the sort of stuff that could be covered in one date.

Sure, he had more than his own problems and urges to think of, but Maya was right. Tonight needed to be a relaxing, no-pressure sort of night. There would be time enough for taking stock of things tomorrow.

He pulled the car into the curved drive, feeling his excitement rise. A beautiful night with a beautiful woman. Things certainly couldn't get much better, he thought as the valet opened his door, allowing him to step out into the cool night. He accepted his claim ticket and pocketed his change, turning in time to see Maya exiting the car on the other side, looking very much like a ruby and pearl goddess. Her beauty hit him anew, infusing him with pure lust. Want rushed through him. He wanted her, wanted to pull her clothes off layer by layer, slowly revealing her secrets. He wanted to run his fingers over her skin, taking his time to discover every curve and dip.

And he wanted it soon.

He moved around the car to offer her his arm. "Ready to have fun?"

She gave him a brilliant smile as she fell into step beside him. "Absotively positlutely. But I thought we were going to a restaurant."

"We are."

"So why are we making a pit stop at this hotel?" she asked, gesturing to the lobby.

"A hotel? Really?" He led her past the lobby. "I didn't notice."

"Sure." She slowed her pace. "You know, most women liked to be wined and dined before they go to a hotel with a strange man."

Nick pushed the button at the elevator bank. "I'm not a strange man, and you said you aren't like most women."

"Point taken." She shot him a look. "But I do know *tae kwon do.*"

He grinned. He couldn't help it. "Duly noted. But Amora's Retreat takes up the top floor of the hotel." He guided her into the waiting car. "I heard that it's pretty spectacular."

NINE

Spectacular proved too tame a word in Maya's opinion. The elevator opened onto a lush tropical garden open to the sky. A double row of electric candles and a forest green canopy guided them to the restaurant's entrance. She stopped suddenly, causing Nick to bump into her. "What is it?"

"I think it's heaven," she replied, staring into the heart of the restaurant. Either the ceiling was made of glass or some artist had done a magnificent job of simulating sky. Stars seemed to twinkle in the velvet canopy of the night sky. Lush vegetation and burnished screens gave diners candlelit privacy. Beyond the dining area, she caught a glimpse of a dance floor.

"Welcome to Amora's Retreat," the hostess said, giving them a smile. "Do you have a reservation?"

"Yes, for Whitfield," Nick said.

"Ah, yes. If you'll come this way, I'll show you to your table."

The hostess led them along a muted burgundy and gold pattern carpet to a secluded table for two. Almost immediately, a waiter appeared to seat Maya. "Good evening, have you been to Amora's before?"

Maya looked at Nick, and they both shook their heads. "Then you are in for a treat here at the Retreat," their waiter said. "We take great pride in stimulating all the senses of our patrons. Our first and only rule is that you enjoy yourself, and to do that, you must take your time and set a leisurely pace."

Maya exchanged amused glances with Nick again. "I think we can do that," Nick said.

The waiter informed them of special dishes, took their wine order, then retreated. Maya looked at Nick in amazement. "This place is incredible."

"I agree. But not as incredible as you."

She blushed despite herself. "Flattery like that will get you everywhere."

He learned forward, giving her that sexy smile. "I certainly hope so."

The waiter returned with a bottle of merlot, and they placed their orders. When he retreated, Nick leaned forward again. "I think this is the part of the date where we tell each other about ourselves."

"We've never done that, have we?" she asked. "Okay then, what would you like to know?"

"Taylor told me that your father's black and your mother is Vietnamese."

Maya took a sip of her wine, taking her time with a reply. She decided on the direct approach. "That's true. Is it a problem?"

"Would we be here if it were?"

"I don't know," she said, instinctively defensive. No one got away with downing her family. "You tell me."

He smiled again. "What if I tell you that I find you extremely attractive?"

"I'd say that you were avoiding my question."

"It doesn't bother me because it's nothing to be bothered about," he said. "You are who you are, and I like who you are."

Relieved, she took another sip of her wine. "Then why bring it up?"

"Call it curiosity. I'm wondering what it was like for them, being an interracial couple back then. I mean, if it's not exactly mainstream now, I can't imagine what it was like in the seventies and eighties."

Maya settled back in her chair, feeling the warmth of the wine spreading through her limbs. "If Mom and Dad ever had any problems with people, we kids never felt it. They said after all they went through to be together, people's opinions weren't worth worrying about."

Their entrees arrived, lobster tails for her and steak for him. "So how did they meet?" Nick asked as he sliced into his meal.

"In Vietnam, at the beginning of the war. Dad was in the Army Corps of Engineers, building roads. My mother was a driver and translator for one of the French bigwigs in a private construction consortium."

Maya smiled. "Dad will tell you that it was love at first sight. Mom will tell you that she made him dangle for a while. Either way, they fell deeply in love, secretly married, and had Carson Junior and my older sister Nadine. They don't talk about it much, but supposedly Dad had some trouble getting them out of the country when his rotation was up. I think he had to bribe some pretty high up people."

"Wow." Nick gave her an impressed smile. "That sounds more like a novel than real life."

Maya laughed. "I know. One thing I can say for sure, that story really impressed us growing up. We were all extremely close, and still are. Back then, kids learned early on that it was easier to be our friends than our enemies."

"That must mean you've got big brothers."

"Well, we just liked everyone, and we had so much fun that everybody liked us, too," Maya explained, pausing to take another bite of her exquisite meal. "Ours was the house that all the neighborhood kids gravitated to, and my mom was always willing to help other mothers on our street. I think she was the first person to organize a neighborhood watch."

"It sounds like you had an almost idyllic childhood."

"We weren't the Cosby kids, but we were pretty decent," she answered. Her smiled waned as memories crept upon her. "We waited until we were adults to mess up our lives."

He reached across the table, taking her hand in a gentle yet comforting grip. "You're talking about your divorce?"

"Among other things," she murmured, remembering past pains in her family. She squeezed his hands once, then let go. "So what about your family? I'm not going to be the only one here giving my life story."

"My family's typical mainstream America," he answered. "Mom and Dad are still together and living the good life in Florida when they're not traveling in their RV. I have one sister named Caroline, younger than me and still a brat."

"What made you decide to go into medicine?"

"Believe it or not, it's always something I wanted to do," he answered. "Even as a kid, I was always running around, wrapping my sister up like a mummy, making a papier-mâché cast for my dog, making my mom and dad say 'ahh'." He smiled, and she wondered if she'd ever become immune to it. "So no divine calling, no tragedy in my past making me decide to be a doctor. I just wanted to help people.

Though sometimes, you get brutally reminded that you can't help everyone."

Maya heard the pain in his voice and wondered if he meant his wife or the patient he'd recently lost. It felt rude to want to ask about his wife and how she died, and she didn't want to make him relive that, especially since he hadn't pressed her on the details of her divorce. "What was the outcome of the review board?"

He blinked, focusing once again. "No negligence or wrongdoing on my part," he said, sounding distracted.

"You have mixed feelings about that?"

"Not really," he said, then paused to take a long swallow of his wine. "Okay, maybe a little. I mean, I'm glad that my peers realized that I did everything I could, but that doesn't bring my patient back."

This time she reached across the table to take his hand. "How do you deal with it?"

"Badly," he said with a grimace. "You just have to learn not to internalize it, and focus on the next patient and the next."

He lifted her hand to his lips. "You know, this night isn't supposed to be a downer. Dance with me."

It was a request Maya wasn't about to refuse. She didn't want the night to be about talking, especially talking about the past. She placed her hand in his and allowed him to lift her to her feet. Conscious of his hand at the small of her back, Maya let him guide her to the dance floor.

A ten-piece band serenaded them with a smooth groove. Several couples were already swaying to the music, gliding around a floor painted to simulate the ocean. Nick swept her into his arms, holding her close. She rested her head on his shoulder, swaying dreamily as the seductive beat washed over them. This is what the night is supposed to be about, she thought to herself. Giving over to the dance, the vertical expression of horizontal desire.

Horizontal desire. Oh yes, she thought, turning her lips toward his throat. The desire to be with this man threatened to do away with all her common sense. Even now she could feel her normal reserve eroding, and the wish to throw caution to the wind and let the night lead them grew ever stronger.

She nearly lost her breath when she felt Nick's hand slide down her back, resting just above the rise of her buttocks. His lips turned, grazing her cheek, and she had to close her eyes against the sensations that filled her. She pressed even closer, wrapping both arms around his neck, swaying against him with blatant suggestion. Two years without someone sharing her bed was two years too long. And judging from the telltale bulge she felt, Nick thought eight years was eight years too long.

"I could dance like this with you forever," he whispered against her cheek.

"Ditto," she murmured, pressing her lips against his pulse. It jumped beneath her mouth, and she had to smile, pleased with her effect on him.

"Do you know how incredibly sexy you are?" he wondered, his voice deep and husky as he dipped her head to taste her throat.

"No, I've never thought of myself as sexy," she admitted. "Most of the time, I tend to be just pretty. I like being described as sexy much better."

"Trust me, it definitely fits," he said softly. "I almost forgot my name when I saw you for the first time tonight."

"That's quite a compliment," Maya said, puffing away to smile up at him.

"You should take it as one," he replied, holding her close again as the music deepened, became even more sensual. "Thanks for coming out with me tonight."

"You're welcome," she said, the magic of the moment making her drop her guard. "Though you really didn't have to go to all this trouble."

He stilled. "Why do you think this was trouble?"

Maya heard the careful tone of his voice and could have kicked herself. Great, she'd put her foot in her mouth; might as well make a meal out of it. "I know you've been looking for ways to thank me for taking care of Taylor," she said lamely, keeping her face firmly pressed against his lapel. "This is just more than I thought."

They stood in charged silence for the space of a heartbeat. Then he spun her in a twirl, and the next thing she knew, they were on the balcony. A metal railing separated them from high glass wall that afforded them a stunning view of the Atlanta skyline. If she wasn't so busy chewing on her own foot, she'd have appreciated the panorama.

He took a step away from her, and she could tell by the set of his jaw that she'd angered him. Way to go, moron, she thought to herself. She opened her mouth to apologize. "Nick, I—"

He turned to face her. Without the smile to light his face, he looked hard, emotionless. But she knew he was angry. She could tell by the set of his shoulders. "Is that how you think I see you?" he asked, his voice stiff. "As a substitute caregiver for Taylor?"

She turned to the railing, not wanting to see his anger. "I don't know how you see me," she said honestly, staring out into the night. "The neighbor lady who came to your rescue to look after your daughter, the friend who occasionally invites you over to dinner…"

She trailed off, her voice threatening to betray her. "I don't know what you think of me."

"Then let me clear the air." He came up behind her and placed his hands on either side of hers on the rail, effectively caging her in. "Get this straight, Maya Hughes: you are the most attractive woman I've ever met. From day one, I was attracted to you, but since I didn't know what you think—and by the way, I still don't know—I decided to keep it to myself and hope that it would go away. After all, you were doing me a big favor by looking after Taylor for me after school. But I've decided that it's stupid to keep seeing you and talking to you and not find out one way or the other."

He wrapped his arms about her waist, pulling her back snug against his chest. "This is why I'm doing this, Maya," he whispered in her ear. "Not because Taylor likes you, but because I like you. I like the feel of your hair, the way you smell, the way your lips curl and your eyes crinkle when you smile. I especially like this moment, because now I know how your body feels when I hold you close."

Leaning against him, she closed her eyes and gave in. "I like this, too."

They returned to their table. Their dinner plates had been whisked away, their wine and water glasses refilled. A gilded dessert menu lay on the table. "If I haven't said it before, I really like this place," Maya said as Nick seated her.

"You have to admit, they're definitely good at what they do," he said, picking up the dessert menu. "Would you like to have dessert with me?"

Her stomach clenched in response to the innocent question. She wanted a lot more than dessert with him. She wanted to undress him and explore every part of his body. She wanted to know where he was ticklish and where he was particularly sensitive. She didn't know if it stemmed from sexual deprivation or what, but the attraction she felt couldn't be denied.

"I would love to have dessert with you."

His eyes brightened, and that long slow smile appeared. Luckily their waiter appeared, and they ordered the signature dessert. They decided to take another spin around the dance floor while waiting. Maya went eagerly into his arms, and couldn't resist stealing a kiss or two as they swayed together.

Nick held her comfortably close, his body swaying against hers with an innate grace. In her heels, her cheek reached his shoulder. Her arm dropped about his waist, and she closed her eyes as the music swelled around them. The music caused her imagination to transport them into a fantasy realm where she was a princess and Nick her prince.

How long they danced, she neither knew nor cared. A symphony performed in her head, and she nestled her cheek into his shoulder, breathing in the spice and musk that was Nick alone.

His hand tightened at the small of her back, his fingers brushing the rise of her derriere.

He pulled away slightly to stare down at her, the blue of his eyes darkened. "Am I crazy, Maya? Am I alone in this? Let me know now, before I get in too deep."

She raised their clasped hands, pressing her lips against his skin. "No, you're not alone. As for crazy, let's just say that you'll definitely have company if they come to take you away."

He smiled, and her stomach did a drunken somersault. "I'm glad," he said in a soft voice, then pulled her close again.

Dessert was purely decadent, definitely deserving of its name, "Chocolate Sin." Fudge rum cake served as the bottom layer, with a generous padding of dark chocolate icing between it and a mousse-like top layer. Atop it all was a hard shell of white chocolate drizzled with a Chambord-inspired raspberry sauce. Framing it were two humongous chocolate dipped strawberries.

"Oh my God," she breathed. That one generous slice probably contained more calories than both their meals combined.

"I don't think God had anything to do with this," Nick said, picking up a fork and slicing into the confection. "Let's see if it lives up to its name," he said, offering the first bite to her.

"I think the only sin will be finishing the thing." Keeping her eyes firmly glued to his, Maya leaned forward to accept the bite.

"Oh God." Her eyes rolled into the back of her head. "That is so good!" She shivered as rum, Chambord, and chocolate slid down her throat, gripping the edge of the table to hold on.

After she finished the bite, she opened her eyes to find Nick staring at her with a mixture of surprise and intrigue lighting his features. "Two questions: Will that be your reaction with every bite? Don't get me wrong, I'm enjoying the show. I don't know how the rest of the restaurant feels about it, though."

She picked up her water glass, needing to cool off from the near-orgasmic delight. "It's a damn good dessert," she said defensively. "Anyone who thinks otherwise is dead from the lips down."

"I guess I'll have to see for myself." He handed the fork to her. "Will you let me have some?"

From the heated way he looked at her, Maya could tell the question wasn't nearly as innocent as it seemed. "Of course you can have some," she all but purred. "But I have to warn you: too much of a good thing can be deadly."

"At least I'll die happy." His teeth clicked on the edge of the spoon.

TEN

Nick shifted the car into park and killed the engine. Except for that embarrassing moment when he thought he'd pass out from chocolate overload, he considered the night a success. For the first time he regretted having a manual transmission. It would have been good to have Maya curled up close to him on the drive home. Still, it felt pretty darn terrific to have her hand resting lightly on his thigh, the other teasing at the back of his neck. Getting out of the car with his arousal proved difficult.

Hand in hand, they walked up the drive to her front door. He really wanted to plant his hands on her butt and squeeze her Charmin all the way to the couch. It was all he could do not to flatten himself against her as she fumbled to unlock the door. Heat had been streaking through him all night, heat sparked by desire. He wanted to wrap himself in her softness and make them both really happy.

Once inside the front door, she turned to face him. "I had a wonderful night."

He stepped to within a breath of her. "So did I."

He gave in to his urge to touch her, pulling her close and capturing her lips with his. She responded by wrapping her arms around his neck and threading her fingers into his hair and kissing him back with equal fervor. His hands slid up her hips to her ribs, the tips of his thumbs brushing against the underside of her breasts. She pressed her hips against his with unspoken invitation, and his hands found their way beneath her blouse to her bare skin.

"Wait, wait." She pulled away from him, breathless.

"Why?"

"Because I'm sure the sitter saw you pull up," she said, still breathing hard. "She'll be waiting for you."

"You're right," he said, leaning his forehead against hers. "I know you're right. That doesn't mean that I want to leave."

"I don't want you to leave either," she whispered, cupping his face in her hands. She pressed several quick kisses against his mouth. "But I know you have to."

He sighed. Dammit. "I'm glad one of us is thinking."

She laughed, low and throaty. "Oh, you don't know what I'm thinking."

"Try me."

She leaned forward to nibble at his ear. The touch of her teeth on his earlobe made his arousal jump, and he damn near came in his pants. "I'm thinking how good it would have been to take that Chocolate Sin dessert, rub it all over your body, and take my time licking it off."

He almost jumped out of his skin at the erotic image that filled his mind. "What?"

She stepped back from him, eyes wide. "Tell me I didn't say that out loud."

"You most definitely did."

"Oh God." She covered her eyes with one hand. "I shouldn't even be thinking like that on a first date, and certainly not talking like that."

"I don't mind." His hands slipped down her back, pressing her hips closer. "You should keep talking like that."

He grinned. "Actually, that gives me an idea."

He felt her shiver as he nibbled at her ear. "What sort of idea?" she asked, her voice breathy.

"I'm going to call you, and we're going to talk to each other until we're both satisfied."

"Satisfied? You mean…oh." She shivered again. "H-have you done that before?"

"No, but tonight I'm inspired to give it a try."

"Ooh, I like it."

"You keep talking like that and it won't take me long at all."

She ran a finger along the edge of his ear. "Don't disappoint me now."

"One thing I will promise you," he said, dropping slow kisses along the curve of her neck. "When we come together, I swear you won't be disappointed."

"Promises, promises," she teased. "When will you call me?"

"Give me half an hour," he said, running his hands down her arms. "Then be ready."

Maya lay back against her pillows, nervous and expectant. Actually, she felt the same kind of excitement she'd felt on her wedding night. Entering into a new, uncharted area intrigued and excited her. She'd been excited already, by Nick's hands, his lips, his body, all working a magic that easily captured her.

How would they start? Would they just talk about what they want to do with each other, or would they build a fantasy?

Maya smiled to herself. She could do whatever she wanted to, she realized. In his instance, the power would be hers.

When the phone rang a few minutes later, she was ready. "Hello?" she purred into the phone, lowering her voice to a husky seductive tone.

"It's me," she heard Nick whisper.

"Are you ready to go on a little journey?" she asked.

"Oh yes."

"Then close your eyes and come with me."

She settled back against the pillows. "The room is completely dark, with only the glow of the moon coming through the open bay windows. You're lying on the bed, spread-eagled and naked, with the sheet just covering your middle. I can hear you breathing, hot and heavy with anticipation."

"Yes," he breathed. "And where are you?"

"I'm moving towards you, wearing a white negligee so sheer it leaves nothing to the imagination. I stop at the end of the bed, surveying your magnificent body, perfect, hard and ready for me. I have to touch you, feel the heat of your body. I trail my hand slowly up your leg, the lace of my cuff causing you to shiver. You lift your hips off the bed, wanting me to touch you."

"Touch me."

"I like it when you plead for my pleasure," she said, caught up in the magic of the moment. "I pull the sheet off you slowly, and you groan at the sensation of the cloth sliding over your skin. You want me to touch you, to give you that most intimate kiss. But I'm not ready to give you that final pleasure just yet. Instead, I lean over to kiss your belly button, slowly kissing my way up your ribcage to your nipples. I take the left one into my mouth, biting it just enough to make you moan. I swirl my tongue around it to take away the sting, then move to the right."

"Oh, yeah."

"I trail kisses down your ribcage. I know what you want, and now I'm ready to give it to you. I wrap my hands around you, enjoying the feel of you. I lower my head to place a slow, wet kiss on the tip."

"God, yes," he breathed.

"You taste so good," she continued. "So warm and ready in my hands. I taste you completely, taking you just the way you like it, slowly at first, then faster. I love the sounds you make, I love knowing that I have the power to pleasure you. But now I need to please myself."

"Maya…"

"I'm ready. I pull loose the ties on my robe and let it slip from my shoulders to the floor. Then I stand on the bed, straddling you. I can feel the heat of your gaze as I slowly lower myself, ready to be impaled on the hot heavy length of you. I'm wet with anticipation; I don't know how long I can ride you, but I know it's gonna be wild.

"Slowly I sink down until I'm straddling your thighs. I can feel your erection bumping against me. I wrap my hand around you, causing you to moan, and rub the head against me. You're ready, I'm ready, and there's no reason to wait any longer."

"No, don't wait," he whispered harshly. "I want to be inside you."

"And I want you inside me," Maya breathed, caught up in a swirl of sensation. "I push down as you move your hips upward, and I can feel every delicious inch moving deeper inside me. Oh, you feel so good. I lift up, then sink down again. You lift up to meet me, and we fall into a seductive rhythm."

"Ride me," he demanded.

"I lean forward to kiss you, our tongues matching the pace of our bodies. Your beautiful hands slide up my waist to my breasts, teasing my nipples, sending me closer and closer to the edge. We move faster and faster, and I'm so slick and so ready and need you so bad…"

"I'm almost there…"

"I'm riding you hard and fast like a magnificent stallion, feeling your power, feeling you thrust into me over and over and over again. I can feel it building inside me, feel it coming, coming…"

When it came it surprised her, causing her to drop the phone as waves of pleasure swept over her. She had to bite her lip to keep from crying out, riding out the rolling pulses of the orgasm. It took her a moment to come back down to earth, to remember that she had been on the phone with Nick.

She fumbled for the phone. "Are you there?" she asked as she tucked the receiver under her chin.

"Y-Yeah," he said. He took a deep breath. "Damn, you're good."

"I was inspired," she admitted. Now that it was over, a blush crept up her cheeks. "I've never come like that from flying solo."

"Me either," he admitted, his breath still fast. "You sure you've never done this before?"

"Never," she answered, her heartbeat taking its time returning to normal.

"Would you like to do it again?"

"Tonight?" She didn't think she'd have the strength.

"God no," he said. "There's no way I could go another round right now. But since you did all the imagining tonight, I feel it's only fair to return the favor. I'd enjoying sharing one of my fantasies with you."

Completely satisfied, Maya felt sleep tugging at her. "I'd like that. Good night, Nick."

"It certainly was. I'll see you tomorrow."

ELEVEN

Saturday morning dawned bright and cheerful. Maya awakened from a deep sleep with a smile on her face and a blush to her cheeks. After slipping out of bed, she pulled on her robe and padded downstairs to let her boys into the backyard. She opened the kitchen window to let the spring air in, then reached for the coffee canister.

"Hey, sis."

Maya shrieked, dropping the canister and sending ground coffee spilling across the beige tile. She whirled to find her brother Brandt standing in the doorway.

"God, Brandt, you scared the crap out of me!" she gasped, clutching at her chest. "How long have you been here?"

"Not too long," he answered, moving into the kitchen to grab the broom and dustpan from the pantry. "Those animals of yours are useless as watchdogs. And I see you didn't remember any of the defensive moves I taught you."

"Hamlet and Horatio aren't supposed to be guard animals, and why would they attack you when they love you more than they love me?" Maya picked up the canister. Since it still contained enough grounds, she continued her coffee preparations. "And I remember the karate you taught me. I just wasn't planning to use it in my own kitchen on a Saturday morning. And why didn't you let me know you were here?"

"You were sort of busy, so I didn't want to disturb you."

"I wasn't that busy," she said, feeling a blush creep up her cheeks as she remembered the knee-wobbling kisses and more that she'd shared with Nick last night. "You know I would've wanted to talk to you."

"It's all right." Brandt emptied the dustpan then returned it and the broom to the pantry. He was the spitting image of their father, broad-shouldered and strong, with dark wavy hair and gray eyes wide-set in his cinnamon face. "I just got tired of being at home. It was way too quiet."

Maya nodded in understanding, turning on the coffeepot while her brother settled his large frame at the breakfast table. Even though he'd sold the house and moved into a small apartment, she knew how awful the silence could be for him.

"I'm assuming you want breakfast?" Of all her brothers, Brandt was the one she was closest to. Growing up, he didn't seem to mind her following him around, asking him questions, getting in the way while he built things. Brandt was the one she'd cried on when she'd revealed the reason for her divorce. And she'd returned the favor last year, just after he'd lost his wife and son.

"I'll need my strength to work in your yard," he informed her. "You've got stuff for pancakes?"

"And bacon and eggs and anything else you want." She brought a cup of coffee over to him. "Did the nightmares start up again?"

He accepted the cup, quelling a sudden shaking in his fingers that Maya pretended she hadn't noticed. "I'm dealing with them," he said in a tone that warned her not to press him further.

Being the caring sister that she was, Maya ignored the warning. "Next time, don't wait until morning to talk to me."

Brandt gave one of his rare smiles. "Considering the view I got from the couch, it seemed to me like you didn't need to be disturbed."

She ignored the heat that rose to her cheeks, gathering the ingredients for pancakes instead. "How much did you see?"

"Enough to decide it'd be better to take myself up to the guest bedroom to sleep and talk to you this morning instead." He sipped at his coffee. "Nadine told me you had a new man."

Maya cracked an egg with harder force than necessary. "He's not my man."

"That's not what it looked like to me," her brother said, a sly, amused tone to his voice. "I'm surprised you two didn't set off the smoke alarm."

"Brandt."

"Hey, I'm just saying." Putting his mug down, he crossed to the cabinets, then started pulling out dishes to set the table. "Is he still here?"

"Of course not!" She beat the pancake batter as if she was Phil Collins doing a drum solo.

"Just want to make sure I'm not taking you away from anything important."

"You're not," she said forcefully. "Anyway, you're important, too."

"So who is he?"

Maya set the griddle on the stove, then turned on the heat. "His name is Nick Whitfield. He's my next-door neighbor."

"Convenient."

"You keep on, you're going to be wearing pancakes, not eating them," she retorted, mixing the batter again with vicious strokes. "Why am I even telling you this, anyway?"

"Because you know I won't run to Mom and Dad."

He had a point. It was one of the reasons why they were so close. Maya loved her parents dearly, but they had a tendency to ride to the rescue as if all the kids were still underage. Though there were some days when she needed her mother's fiery protectiveness and her father's bear hugs, she didn't want them running her life. And if they knew she was dating...

"I'm definitely not ready to expose Nick to the family just yet," Maya said, ladling batter onto the grill. "It's still new, so new that I still don't know what to make of it. Last night was the first time we went out."

"You're that hot and heavy after seeing him once?" Brandt asked, surprised.

"No. Yes. Look, I'm not telling this right, so let me start over." She put bacon strips on a microwave rack, then put them in the microwave before turning back to the griddle. "Nick and his daughter moved next door about seven months ago. I didn't really interact with them until the day their housekeeper broke her hip. After the ambulance took Mrs. Henderson to the hospital, Taylor stayed with me until her father got home. Since the housekeeper had to stay home on bed rest, I offered to look after Taylor after school. Sometimes we're here, sometimes we're there. Sometimes I cook dinner, sometimes we go out, and sometimes Nick will cook. All of us just hit it off, and we enjoy being together."

Brandt took the bacon out of the microwave. "So what are you to them? A new housekeeper?"

"That's not fair. I was the one who offered to look after Taylor. I like taking care of people, Brandt. You know that."

"I do know that." His dark eyes grew serious. "Taking care of people is as necessary to you as breathing. I just don't want to see you to get taken advantage of."

"No one's taking advantage of me." Maya took the stack of pancakes to the table. Brandt followed her with the bacon and syrup. "Nick lost his wife just after Taylor was born. He's been raising her alone for eight years. I just…they need me right now. And I like being needed."

Her brother filled a plate for her, then himself. "What are you going to do after the housekeeper comes back?"

"He's already got a temporary replacement. She started this past Monday."

"So where does that leave you?"

"I don't know. Nick wants to date me."

"Why? Does he want to take a walk on the wild side?"

"Do you really think that's a fair accusation to make?"

"Any white man dating someone of a different race needs to be asked that question," her brother said. "And any black woman who wants to date a white man needs to know the answer."

"But Mom and Dad didn't need to get answers?" she asked.

"That's different."

"Really." Sarcasm dripped from her voice. "I didn't realize there were different rules for black men."

"Come on, Mai," he said, gesturing with his cup. "Don't you want to know if he's just after you for an exotic after-dinner mint?"

"He's not like that," she insisted, not wanting to argue with her brother and definitely not wanting him to be right.

"I hope he's not," Brandt said. "But if he's serious about wanting to date you, he needs to know what to expect. I don't want you getting hurt because the guy proved to be too weak to handle an interracial relationship."

"You're not being fair to him, Brandt," Maya said, no heat in her voice. "Sure, he asked what it was like for Mom and Dad, but believe me, I'd know if this was nothing more than the 'fever'. I can tell you that it's not. He really does want to date me."

"Do you want to date him?" Brandt asked around a mouthful of bacon.

"Yeah." Maya stared down at her pancakes. "He's the first guy to even notice me in two years."

"That's no reason to jump into dating," Brandt argued. "Besides, maybe if you got out once in a while instead of wrapping yourself in work and the family, you'd get some play."

"First you're worried that Nick's just taking a walk on the wild side, and now you're saying I need to get some play?" Maya shook her head. Only she and Brandt could have this conversation without her getting embarrassed. God knows she couldn't talk to her other brothers about it.

"Honestly, I'm not jumping into anything. We're taking things slowly. He's a great guy, and he's gorgeous and he dotes on his daughter. But if it'll make you feel better, I'll have the talk with him."

"Are you going to tell him about the other?"

Maya fiddled with her coffee. She knew what her brother meant. "No. We've just had one date. I don't know if there'll be another, or even if this has the possibility of being long-term. I'm determined to take things one day at a time and see where it goes. If things get serious between us, then I'll tell him."

Brandt frowned. "If you get hurt—"

"I'm not going to get hurt," she interrupted. "If Nick starts making any plans about the future, I'll tell him that if he wants more children, he's betting on the wrong horse. And then I'll walk away."

She lifted her coffee to avoid saying anything else, feeling her heady mood dissipate. Things had seemed so right with the first light of day. But reality had a way of turning things gray. Still, she meant what she'd said. She'd enjoy every minute of her time with Nick and Taylor, but if he started to talk about the future, started to talk about children, it would be over. She'd tell him the truth and then she'd leave. Better than the other way around. Much better.

They concentrated on their breakfast, settling into the easy silence they'd shared since they were kids. Brandt was the true middle child; she'd come along a year later, with Jericho two years after that and Jasmine another two years later. With the next oldest sibling three years ahead of them, Brandt had appointed himself Maya's guardian, and he still continued to watch over her. Maya knew he wanted the best for her, wanted her to be happy. She appreciated the concern, but it didn't dim her concern for him.

"So," she said, picking up a last piece of bacon, "did you read that book I gave you?"

Brandt lifted his coffee. "What book?"

"The book I gave you last month—*The Phoenix Principle* by Willow Zane."

"Oh. That book." He set his coffee down and attacked his pancakes.

Maya lifted one eyebrow. "Well?"

"Well what?"

She sighed. "Did you read the book or not?"

"No."

"No? Why not?"

Brandt pointed his fork at her "I don't need no New Age fruitcake telling me how to run my life."

Maya lay her silverware down. "She's not a New Age fruitcake, she's a psychologist. You won't talk to Nadine, so I thought this might help some."

"Help? And just how is it supposed to help?"

"It helps you understand the reasons why bad things happen."

With a loud scrape, her brother shoved his chair back, then stood, his large hands bunching into fists. "Understand the reasons?" he repeated, his voice coarse. "How can I understand the reasons when there aren't any? What reason was there for Brady to die? What reason was there for Sarah to kill herself? To punish me because I wasn't a decent enough husband and father?"

Maya jumped to her feet, coming around the table to throw her arms around her brother's waist. His outburst was the most he'd spoken about losing his wife and son in more than a year. "It's not your fault, Brandt," she said for the thousandth time. She'd keep saying it until he believed it. "There was nothing you could have done."

"Yes there was," he said, his muscles wound tight. "I could have gone with them."

"I'm sorry," she whispered, miserable for having pushed him. "I just wanted to help."

Brandt's hands settled heavily on her shoulders. "I know, Mai, but you can't help everybody. Some of us are beyond help."

"Brandt." Maya closed her eyes, her throat too thick with tears to say anything more.

He patted her shoulder. "Hey, I'll make you a deal. Fix me a good lunch after I work in the yard, and I'll start the book tonight."

"Fix you lunch?" Maya forced a laugh as she stepped back. "You'll be lucky if I remember to order you a pizza."

"Pizza? I'm going to break my back fixing your broken-down backyard, and all I get is a pizza?"

Maya crossed to the sink. "No, that's not all you get." She tossed him a towel. "You also get to help me clean up."

TWELVE

"Daddy, can we go see Maya today?" Taylor asked as she grabbed her orange juice.

"Maybe later on," Nick said, sliding an omelet onto her plate. "We don't want to bother her first thing in the morning. She might need to sleep some more." And recover from the night before. Lord knows even his dreams had been active.

"No, she's awake," Taylor said, then added, "I saw a man on her porch. Now he's in the backyard, messing with the grass and stuff."

"Really?" Nick glanced at his watch. Ten o'clock. Not exactly early, but not exactly prime time for visitors either. "Have you seen this man before?"

"No, Daddy." Taylor stabbed her omelet with her fork.

Nick sat at the breakfast table across from his daughter, suddenly not interested in his favorite breakfast. Maya had a man over her house first thing in the morning, after a night he believed they both thought incredible. Maybe he was the landscaper. Maybe he was her brother. Maybe Nick was reading too much into the situation.

Then again, maybe he wasn't.

"I'll tell you what, pumpkin. We'll stop over on our way out and see if Maya needs anything."

Two hours later, they crossed the drive to Maya's front door. Standing there forcibly reminded Nick of the time he'd spent with Maya the previous night. He remembered then how she'd run hot and cold, how she'd brushed aside any talk of anything other than the moment. Was this man in her backyard the reason why?

He gave the doorbell an impatient push. He was not jealous, he told himself; he and Maya hadn't talked about dating exclusively. Heck, they hadn't talked about dating at all. He'd spent so much time convincing her that last night hadn't been a thank you night out that he didn't get the chance to ask her out again.

The door opened, and Nick found himself face to face with Maya's guest. Towering, muscled, and skin like polished mahogany, the man stared at them as if they were specimens to be dissected. "Yes?"

"I'm Nick Whitfield and this is my daughter, Taylor," Nick said. "We're here to see Maya."

Those gray eyes flicked over him again. "I know who you are," the man said, no emotion in his voice. "Come in. Maya's upstairs taking a shower."

Nick wanted to turn heel and leave, but Maya's pets came scrambling around the corner. Taylor pushed past the man. He stiffened as if he'd been stabbed, then turned to follow her Nick stepped forward. "You must be one of Maya's brothers," he said as he stepped over the threshold.

"Brandt. Might as well come in." With that glowing invitation, Maya's brother stepped back to let Nick in.

Taylor had already taken Hamlet and Horatio out the back door. He could hear her laughter and shrieks of delight filtering down the hall towards them. Brandt didn't look too enthused with the noise filtering from the backyard. Nick wondered how the man could be related to Maya and her warm disposition. He'd seen icebergs that exuded more warmth.

"You want coffee?"

"Sure." Nick followed the large man into the kitchen, determined to kill him with kindness. "I noticed that you're planning on doing work in Maya's backyard. Do you own a landscaping company?"

Brandt poured him a mug of coffee. "Something like that," he replied, thrusting the mug out. "What do you want with my sister?"

Nick took the mug, deciding to ignore the rude question. Almost. "Like to get right to the point, don't you?"

The other man remained silent, crossing his arms against his chest while balancing a matching cup of coffee. The beige porcelain resembled a child's teacup in his massive hand.

Nick took his time sipping his coffee before setting the cup on the kitchen table. "I really don't think what I want with Maya is any of your business."

"Oh, it's definitely my business," her brother said. "Nobody plays games with my little sister."

"Your little sister is a grown woman," Nick pointed out. "And I'm assuming she's been making her own decisions for a while."

Brandt placed his mug next to Nick's. "I'm her brother. I'm supposed to look out for her."

"I can understand that. So where were you when her ex-husband broke her heart?"

Brandt took a step forward. So did Nick, refusing to be intimidated and preparing for the worst.

"Something smells in here." Maya's voice sliced the tension. "Must be all the testosterone."

She entered the room, placing herself squarely between Nick and her brother. "I hope all the chest beating and defending of my virtue is over?"

"Just getting to know each other," Brandt said easily, reclaiming his coffee. He continued his emotionless staring at Nick. Not that Nick intended to let it bother him. Maybe the guy just didn't know how to be polite.

"Yeah, just talking about brothers and sisters, the usual stuff," he explained. He deliberately turned from

Brandt to capture her gaze. "How are you this morning?"

She dropped her head, probably to hide a blush. Nick thought it extremely cute. "I'm fine," she finally said. "How about you? Did you sleep well?"

"Best sleep I've had in a long time," he answered, unable to tone down his smile. Damn, she made him feel good, and he didn't care if her brother knew it.

Brandt grunted. "I need air."

Nick waited until the other man stepped outside before posing a question to Maya. "Is he always that friendly?"

A worried expression crossed her face, then quickly disappeared. "Don't worry about Brandt," she said lightly. "He's been my protector since I was in diapers. Not to be rude, but what are you doing here? I thought we were all getting together this evening."

"Taylor wanted to come over," he explained, his hands itching with the need to hold her.

"Uh-huh," she said, her disbelief clear.

"It's the truth," he insisted, even though it wasn't the whole truth. When she just stared at him, he added, "All right, after she told me about the strange man in your backyard, I decided to come on over."

She grinned. "Got a little jealous, huh?"

"Got a lot of jealous, if you must know," he answered, finally grabbing her wrists to pull her close. He gave her a proper hello kiss before releasing her.

"Of course, then I realized that I had no legitimate reason to be jealous because we've never set boundaries on our relationship. Actually, we should probably decide what our relationship is going to be first."

Her smile faded. "You're right. We do need to discuss this."

Uh-oh. The seriousness of her tone caused a warning bell to go off in his brain. "Is this something I want to sit down for? If so, let's go outside, so I can keep an eye on Taylor."

"All right." She pulled open the kitchen door, leading him out to the deck. It was a perfect day for yard work and generally being outside. Cotton-like clouds fluffed up a robin's-egg-blue sky, and the late spring heat of the sun was tempered by a gentle wind.

"I have one question first," he said as she sat on a weathered bench. "Does this have anything to do with your brother not liking me?"

"Brandt doesn't dislike you," she said as if surprised he'd think so.

"How do you know?"

"You're still standing."

Point taken. He sat beside her on the bench, noting Taylor tossing a bright yellow ball for Hamlet to chase. Damned if the cat didn't go chasing after it as well.

"Am I going to get the third degree from the rest of your brothers?" he asked. "It may take some time to order a flame-retardant suit."

She laughed. "They're not that bad, not really. Dad drilled into the four of them early on that they had to watch out for us girls."

"Did you have trouble growing up?" he asked, keeping his eyes on Taylor's progress.

"Not a lot," she said, settling back against the bench. "Because of the way we looked, girls thought we were stuck up and boys hoped we were easy targets. Like I said before, it only took a couple of busted heads to get the point across, and most kids became our friends."

"What about after high school?" Nick asked. "Did you have any problem then?"

She stayed silent for a moment, and Nick realized that Taylor had stopped playing catch to follow Brandt around the yard instead. "It took a while to get comfortable in my own skin. I mean, I know a lot of kids go through an identity crisis, but it's harder for mixed race kids. I didn't want to deny my mother to honor my father."

She looked down at her hands. "I'm a part of both worlds, but if I think about it, I don't belong to either. I have a couple of Vietnamese friends from college, but their brothers wouldn't even think about dating me. Their families are very traditional and although they talk with my mother and invite us to dinner occasionally, it wouldn't occur to them to push me or my sisters to their sons. We're just not Vietnamese enough. And other black people think I have it good because my skin is light and I can fit in better. Because I don't use a lot of slang, I can get accused of 'acting white.' And all the time I'm thinking that I'm just me."

She sighed. "But it's okay. I've got a strong, loving family who'll be there and support me no matter what. I'm okay with who I am."

Moved, he reached over to clasp her hand. "I'm okay with who you are, too."

She squeezed his hand. "Are you sure? Even in this millennium people who date interracially have problems."

"People who date have problems," he retorted, keeping hold of her hand. "No matter what color they are. I think as long as no one plays games with the other, most problems can be solved just by talking."

"Have you ever dated someone who wasn't white?"

He cast back in his memories, trying to remember who he'd dated before he married Jessica. "My first year of college, I had a six-week affair with a girl named My Ling."

"Really?' Her voice rose with curiosity. "Why only six weeks?"

"She got drunk during a keg party and confessed that she'd heard that white guys were freaky in bed and she'd decided to test the theory," he said, memories making his voice harden. "Then she told me that she'd picked me because I was the exact opposite of who her parents wanted her to date. Like I said, I'm not into playing games, no matter how good the sex is, so I left her at the party."

"Why did you go out with her in the first place?" Maya asked softly.

"I thought she was pretty," he answered. "I'd never met anyone like her before."

"So you wanted to date her because she was different."

Nick looked up. "Do you believe that's why I want to date you?" he asked, trying unsuccessfully to squash the sudden anger he felt. "Because you're different?"

To her credit, she didn't back down. "Isn't that one of the reasons?"

"I didn't make a list, Maya," he said, sighing with exasperation. "It just felt like a good idea at the time, because I'm attracted to you."

"Attracted to our differences, you mean."

"I have a feeling that there's no right answer to that question." He turned on the bench to face her. "So what do you want me to say, Maya? I'm probably as white bread as they come. My sister and mother both have blonde hair. The most exposure I got to black people before college was MTV or the nightly news. So yeah, I'm white. And no, I haven't had anything bad happen to me because of it. That doesn't mean that I can't be open-minded."

"I'm not saying that you're not open-minded," she said. "I'm just saying that something as simple as dating becomes less simple when you mix races."

"Who said dating was simple?" He threw up his hands in frustration. "All right, we're going to have problems. We haven't even had a second date, and we're already having problems."

She put a hand on his arm. "I just want you to understand."

"Then maybe you need to explain a little better," he said, feeling anger welling inside him again. "I want to date you. I thought you wanted to date me."

"I do."

"Sounds pretty simple to me."

"It is," she agreed. "And it isn't. How comfortable we are when we're just staying in for the evening is completely different from how it will be when we go out."

"We went out last night," he argued.

"In a dark restaurant where the most important color was dollar-bill green. It'll be different going out to a Denny's or something, especially if Taylor's with us."

He climbed to his feet, needing the space, needing to pace. "So are you saying that you don't want to date me? Or you do want to date me, but not be seen in public with me?"

"Nick." She reached out a hand to him, then pulled it back.

"Tell me something."

"Something like what?" Maya asked.

"Your ex-husband," he said, waving his hand between them, "was he black or white or something else?"

"Does that make a difference?"

"I'm not a psychologist," he said, his mouth in a taut line. "You tell me."

Her shoulders slumped. "He was black."

"And did he marry you because of your color? Because you're light-skinned? Was he 'taking a walk on the wild side' as you so eloquently put it?"

"His family thought we'd make beautiful babies," Maya said, her throat so tight she could barely speak.

"So the way you looked had something to do with him falling in love with you," Nick pressed.

"If you want to look at it that way, then yes."

"And are you thinking that I want to date you for the same reason?"

She sighed. "It probably doesn't matter now. I have a feeling that I've pissed you off enough that this whole discussion has become a moot point."

"Then you obviously don't know me very well," he said. "Just like I don't know you and the reason behind this conversation. Are you afraid that we're going to get too deep, and something will happen with some Cro-

Magnon idiot and I'm going to want to throw in the towel? I don't give up that easily, Maya. If I did, my daughter and I wouldn't be here."

He reclaimed his seat beside her. "I'm going to say this one last time. I want to date you, Maya Hughes. I want to get to know you. Because you opened up your home and your life to me and my little girl. Because you have a giving spirit and a warm heart, and I'd like to share some of it. Obviously there are reasons that you feel the way you do, but I'm not going to back away from something that hasn't even begun on the basis of what might happen while we're out. All that matters is what you think and what I think."

"What about what Taylor thinks?"

"I already know what Taylor thinks," he said. "I asked for her okay before I asked you out. She definitely gave the idea two thumbs up."

Maya finally smiled. "Cool."

He leaned closer to her. "So what do you say? Can we at least give this a shot?"

She looked up at him. "If you're sure, I'm sure."

"I'm sure." The discussion settled, he put his arm around her. "But there is one question I forgot to ask you."

"What question is that?"

"You know, I didn't ask you the most important question yesterday," he said, keeping his voice casual. "Are you seeing anyone?"

"No, I'm not," she answered. "How about you? Any hot nurses setting their sights on young Dr. Whitfield?"

"Probably," he admitted, "but I'm not interested."

"Really?"

He smiled at the obvious sarcasm. "Really. I'm not looking for someone with as crazy a schedule as mine. Actually, I wasn't looking at all. But they say that when you aren't looking, that's when you're sure to find something."

She didn't say anything to that, but he took her silence as acceptance if not outright agreement. He'd have plenty of time to convince her later.

"Hey, do you think we should rescue Brandt from Taylor, or vice versa?"

He knew his daughter had an overly inquisitive disposition, and had a tendency to try the patience of Job. If Brandt hurt her feelings, Nick would have to defend his daughter, and he wasn't up to either him or Brandt going to the emergency room today.

"Probably," she said, standing beside him. "It's about time for lunch, anyway."

"Why don't we all go together?" he suggested, giving her a grin. "I hear there's a Denny's just up the road."

THIRTEEN

Early spring grew into late spring as everything in Atlanta burst into a pollen explosion of green. Although they hadn't had the opportunity to have another date, Nick and Maya spent almost all of their free time together, getting to know each other and taking Taylor out and about.

"Maya."

Maya looked up from her laptop to see Taylor in front of her, hands clasped behind her back, sneakered toe digging into the carpet. "What is it, Taylor?"

"Are you going to your office the day after tomorrow?"

"As a matter of fact, I am. Why?"

"Because." Taylor looked down at her pink sneakers. "That's 'Take Your Child to Work Day'."

"Oh." Maya controlled the rush of pleasure she felt, deciding to be cautious. "You'd like to go to work with me?"

"I'll be really good and quiet," Taylor said eagerly, her blue eyes wide with pleading. "My friends are going to work with their mothers, and I thought I could go with you. I won't get into trouble, I promise. Please?"

Good Lord. Maya was beginning to realize that she had little in the way of willpower when it came to this precocious child. "I have to talk to my boss and to your father, but I'll give it my best shot, okay?"

"Okay." Taylor threw her arms around Maya's waist and squeezed. "Thank you so much!"

"You're welcome," she replied, dropping a hand to Taylor's braid. "But remember, we have to get your father's permission and let my boss know. All right?"

"'Kay." Taylor skipped off as if permission was a minor obstacle to overcome.

Maya sighed, then reached for the cordless to punch in her boss' mobile number. Roger Denton wasn't only her boss, he was her friend and mentor. He'd probably pitch a fit and get all up in her business before he'd give in. "Denton here."

"Roger, this is Maya. I just wanted to let you know that I'm bringing my neighbor's daughter in on Wednesday for 'Take Your Child To Work Day.' "

"You're kidding, right?" he asked over the sound of traffic.

"No, I most definitely am not kidding."

"Let me pull over. This is not a conversation I can have while navigating traffic." She heard honking and brakes for a few seconds, then the sound of him disconnecting the hands-free cord. "Okay. Now why can't your neighbor take her own kid to work Wednesday?"

"Because *he* has to perform major surgery on Wednesday, and she stays with me in the afternoons anyway."

Roger paused, and Maya could swear she heard the gears in his head turning. "Why are you doing this?"

"Because I think it will be a good experience for Taylor." Maya moved into the breakfast nook for more Privacy. She didn't want Taylor to hear if Roger shot the idea down. "I know we're scheduled to demonstrate the beta version of *Princess Power and the Petty Penny Pincher,* but what better than to have a member of our target audience there with us? Besides, the whole point of the day is to inspire young children about the workplace. Taylor's a bright and inquisitive seven-year-old. She won't be any trouble."

"That's not what I meant, Maya, and you know it."

She managed to stifle a sigh. Roger knew way too much about her private pain. But she'd worked for him since college, and she knew he and his wife considered her the daughter they never had. "Roger, please. Taylor's a wonderful child, and she doesn't have a mother. This will be a good experience for her, and me."

"All right," he relented. "Not that the presentation needs help, but Kingsland might look favorably on us inspiring tomorrow's business leaders."

Maya laughed. "You always have to find an angle, don't you?"

"Didn't you know? That's why they pay me the big bucks. Now, are there any last-minute issues with the demonstration?"

"Not a one. I'm going through it again right now. I've already burned it onto a disk and emailed a backup to my office computer."

"Good thinking. The presentation is scheduled for ten, so I'll see you in the office at nine?"

"At the latest. And thanks." Maya disconnected, expelling a breath. Getting Roger to agree had proven surprisingly easy. She just hoped Nick would be as amenable.

She broached the subject with Nick while he prepared spaghetti for dinner. "I'd like to take Taylor to work with me on Wednesday."

"You would?"

"Sure. Where do you keep the strainer?" She turned around in the large navy and white kitchen. "Do you actually like 'country kitchen' style?"

"No, it came with the house, and stop trying to distract me," Nick said, flipping open a lower cabinet with his foot. "Strainer's in there. Why do you want to take Taylor with you to work?"

Maya bent over to retrieve the strainer. "Because she asked me to. Are you looking at my butt?"

"You don't mind, do you?" Nick asked in a tone that said he didn't care if she minded or not. "It's a terrific view. But you're still trying to distract me."

"Okay, I'll tell you the truth. I want to use her as a test subject."

"I thought you were going to tell me the truth."

"All right." Maya straightened, strainer in hand. "Wednesday is 'Take Your Child to Work Day'."

Nick's expression softened. "But Maya…"

She held up a hand to stop him. "I know. She's not my daughter. That doesn't mean that she won't learn from the experience, and she can't exactly go with you into surgery, now can she?"

"No, but still…"

She put the strainer in the sink. "It's important to Taylor. I'm honored that she asked me. I'll take good care of her."

"That I don't doubt for a minute." He turned from the stove to pull her into his arms. "I just don't want you taking too much on yourself."

"I'm not, really. My boss already gave the okay, pending your agreement of course."

"Sounds like I've been outvoted." He tightened his arms about her waist. "Do I even get a consolation prize?"

"I think we can arrange something."

As she leaned up to kiss him, Taylor poked her head into the door. "Does this mean I can go, Daddy?"

Maya would have pulled away, embarrassed at being caught, but Nick hung on to her waist.

"Sure thing, pumpkin, but I expect you to be on your very best behavior and do whatever Maya tells you to."

"I will, Daddy, I promise." Taylor grinned from ear to ear.

"Good. Now, why don't you go wash up so you can help set the table."

"Kay." She retreated, then poked her head in again. "Are you going to kiss Maya now?"

Maya felt her ears start to burn. She opened her mouth, prepared to deny everything. Nick beat her to it. "Of course I am. You don't mind, do you?"

Taylor giggled. "No."

"Thanks, pumpkin. But I still want you to go wash up. Now."

Giggling anew, Taylor made a loud production of stomping away.

"Are you sure she's just seven?" Maya asked, wishing she could sink through the floor.

"I'm not sure of anything, especially where women are concerned," he said, nuzzling her cheek. "Can I kiss you now?"

"No." She pressed against his shoulders, but he wouldn't relax his hold. "Not when she knows we're kissing."

"She knew we were kissing a couple of weeks ago," he admitted, pulling her ever closer.

"What?" Horrified, Maya managed to wriggle out of his grasp. "You told her?"

"I didn't have to," he said, grinning as if he found the whole conversation amusing. "Remember when we were watching that movie with the talking animals in it, and we thought she'd fallen asleep?"

"Yeah, so?"

"Apparently she's not as deep a sleeper as we thought."

"Oh God." Maya covered her face, remembering the particular night. Taylor had been on the floor with Hamlet and Horatio, leaving the couch to Maya and Nick. He'd had his head in her lap, and they'd occasionally stolen a couple of kisses during some of the louder scenes. Guess those scenes weren't loud enough.

"Hey, it's no big deal, you know."

"Maybe not to you, but it is to me."

"Why?"

"Because…" Maya foundered for an explanation. "I just don't like the idea that your daughter knows I'm making out with her father."

"If it will make you feel better, she actually likes the idea of us liking each other," Nick said. He leaned against the counter, propping his chin on his hand. "Is that a bad thing?"

What a loaded question. Maya couldn't think of a graceful way to answer it. She wanted to be cautious when it came to Nick and his beautiful daughter; it would be far too easy to lose her heart to them both. She wasn't ready for that, wasn't ready for the loss sure to come. If she and Nick got more serious than they already were, she'd have to tell him the truth about her divorce. Once she did that, she was certain that her wish for this fairy tale to continue would come to a screeching halt.

Nick straightened. "You know, when you go all silent like that, it tends to make me nervous."

"You nervous?" Maya forced a laugh. "I find that hard to believe."

"Believe it." He lifted the pot of spaghetti off the stove, then poured it into the colander. "I can almost hear the gears grinding in your head every time I ask you something. As if you're pondering the ramifications of your response. Not every question needs a King Solomon answer, you know."

"You're right," she agreed, popping the top on a jar of spaghetti sauce. "Just call me jaded. I'm not as leap-before-looking as I used to be. Divorce has a way of dimming your enthusiasm, you know."

"I know," he said, understanding filling his voice. "I understand taking things as they come. I even understand slowing things down a bit when they seem to get out of hand. But we're talking about Taylor liking us liking each other, that's all."

Perhaps it was simple to him, but it wasn't simple to her. "All right." She poured the sauce into the pot, then began work on doctoring it. "I don't think it's a bad thing for Taylor to like us liking each other. I mean, with all the time the three of us have been spending together lately, I'm sure she'd have said something if she didn't like it." She darted a glance at him. "Wouldn't she?"

"She would. Trust me when I say she's been extremely positive about this whole thing."

"I just don't want her to get her hopes up," she said, stirring the sauce. "I mean, she's just a child. She doesn't understand that things aren't as simple for adults as they are for children."

"I know," Nick said as he sliced Roma tomatoes for the salad. "I've tried to explain that to her. We're just dating, not getting married."

She should have been reassured by his words, but they didn't sit well with her. Did he not consider her marriage material? She decided not to think about it. "Exactly. I mean, it's natural for her to have wishes and dreams. It's just up to us to keep them in check."

Sure, she could help him keep Taylor in check. But who would help her rein in her own wishes?

———

Nick dropped a sleepy-eyed Taylor off right at seven-thirty the next morning. "Are you sure about this?" he asked.

"Of course I am," she replied, gathering Taylor to her with one arm on the girl's shoulder. She smiled down at the yawning child. "We're going to have lots of fun today, aren't we?"

Taylor nodded, leaning against her with half-closed eyes.

Maya smiled at Nick. "I don't suppose she can completely follow in my footsteps and have a grande mocha latte?"

"And have her bouncing off the walls for the next five days?" He shuddered. "I don't think so."

"All right. I promise I'll return our precious cargo a little smarter, a little happier, and a little tired."

He gave her a brilliant smile, then leaned forward to whisper in her ear. "Did I ever tell you how turned on I am by a woman in a conservative gray suit?"

She laughed, tucking a stray curl back into place. "No, but it will have to wait until we get home," she said. She pressed a kiss to his cheek. "We'll see you when you get in tonight."

"Okay." He ruffled his daughter's hair, then pressed two fingers to the bit of lipstick Maya had left on his cheek. "Until tonight," he said, pressing his fingers to his lips.

Maya fought a ridiculous urge to smile as she locked her door and shepherded Taylor to the car.

The weeks that she'd been seeing Nick and Taylor were some of the best since her divorce. Every domestic scene she shared with them answered a silent wish in her heart, the need to be a part of a family. Whether they were shopping at the neighborhood superstore or taking Taylor and her nieces to a ballgame, Maya found herself looking forward to spending time with Nick and his daughter.

Even though it still proved difficult to find time to spend alone, they had established one ritual: their bedtime fantasy phone calls. Maya blushed at the memory of the previous night's installment. Nick's imagination and husky recitation had left her breathless and yearning for more. They had to find time to be alone, and soon. She stood a dangerous chance of spontaneously combusting.

"What are you going to do today?" Taylor asked, following Maya into the parking deck's elevator.

"Today, my boss and I are presenting a software program to his boss and an outside client," Maya said, punching the button for the lobby level. "You saw part of it. Remember the princess game?"

"Oh yeah." She looked up at Maya. "You made that game?"

"Sure did," Maya said, leading the child out of the elevator and into a carpeted hallway. "And you get to help me with the presentation."

Taylor's eyes grew round. "Really?"

"Really. I'll introduce you to my boss and then we'll get started."

<hr />

The presentation went over like a dream. Taylor pushed the proper buttons on Maya's laptop at the proper time, and generally charmed Maya's boss and her client with energetic and genuine responses to the game.

"What a wonderful little girl," Benson Anderson, the chairman of Whitehorse, said. "You must be very proud of her."

"I am," Maya replied. The fact that Taylor wasn't her daughter didn't make the statement less true. She was proud of her.

Mr. Anderson leaned closer to her. "I have a blended family myself," he said in a conspiratorial whisper. "Hope you're as happy with yours as I am with mine."

Taken aback, Maya could only manage a non-committal answer. She could feel her boss' eyes on her and knew that if he didn't grill her later, his wife sure would the next time they all had dinner together.

"Why don't I take you all to lunch?" Mr. Anderson suggested. Maya began to refuse. "Thanks, sir. I appreciate the offer. We—"

"Would be delighted," her boss finished for her "Shall we go?"

After a leisurely lunch discussing educational software in the guise of games and blended families, Maya and Taylor returned to the office for wrap-up meetings and then headed home. "What did you think of your day?" Maya asked the little girl as they pulled out of the parking deck.

"People sure talk a lot," she answered, referring to the myriad of meetings and discussions Maya had before leaving. "But I like playing the games, especially the Power Princess one."

"That one came from our princess parties," Maya said.

"It did?" Taylor sounded impressed. "Cool."

Cool indeed, Maya thought. Her success today, though a group effort, would cement her drive to continue working from home. "I've got a couple of starters at home; maybe you'd like to take a look at a couple of them?"

"Yeah!"

They kept up a steady conversation on the ride home, with Maya giving suggestions on the report Taylor would have to write of her experience. As they pulled into the driveway, Taylor said, "Thank you for taking me to work with you today."

"You're welcome," she said as they both exited the car. "I had fun. I hope you did too."

"I did." Taylor pushed her door shut.

Maya watched as the child joined her on the path to the front door. "Why do you sound so down?"

"I'm not," Taylor refuted, holding her backpack close.

"You sure?" Maya asked, unlocking the door.

Taylor waited until they were both inside before saying, "I just think that you'd be a cool mom."

"Oh." It took her a couple of tries to put the latch on the door as she blinked rapidly against sudden tears. "Thank you, Taylor. That-that means so much to me."

The little girl looked down at the floor. When she spoke, her voice was barely a whisper. "I wish you could be my mom."

"Oh, Taylor." Everything slipped from her hands so that she could hug the child.

"I can be good," Taylor said, holding on tight. "I can do whatever you tell me to, and I can take care of Ham and Harry, and whatever else you want."

"Sweetheart, it's not that simple," Maya tried to explain as she cupped the child's teary-eyed face in her hands. She was far from dry-eyed herself.

The porcelain features drooped with disappointment. "But don't you want to be my mommy?"

How could she answer that? "I would love to be your mother, but...but there are other things that have to be considered."

"Like what? All you have to do is marry my daddy."

Maya suppressed the urge to groan. Just how many more shocks would Taylor drop on her? "It's not that easy," she said unsteadily, desperate to find words to explain what she didn't know how to explain.

"I thought you liked my daddy," Taylor said, her face twisted in confusion. "He likes you."

Maya suddenly wished she were somewhere, anywhere else. Getting her legs waxed maybe. Or her teeth cleaned.

She sat back, trying to gather what remained of her wits. "Sweetheart, I do like your father, very much. But when you talk about marriage and family, you have to be careful. Those things are important, and there's a lot of stuff grown-ups have to think about."

"Like what?"

"Well, your dad and I have to like each other a whole lot, enough to want to spend the rest of our lives together. And your father would want to make sure that you and I get along as well."

"But we do," Taylor said, her mouth set into a stubborn line.

"I know we do now," Maya said patiently. "But your dad would want to make sure that he and I agree on how you should be taught, and how you should be punished if you do something bad."

"I'm not bad."

Would this pint-sized debater shoot down every one of her arguments? "I know you aren't. But there are other things to think about, too. I haven't met your daddy's family, and he hasn't met mine."

"There sure is a lot of stuff to think about," Taylor said.

"There sure is," Maya agreed, hoping that would put an end to the conversation.

"Does it take a long time to think about this stuff?"

"It can. Months, even years." That should do it.

Taylor thought about that for a moment. "Are you and my dad boyfriend and girlfriend?"

Where in the world were these questions coming from? "Not really," she answered. "We only went out on one date."

"But you kiss and stuff," Taylor pointed out.

Out of the mouth of babes…Maya wondered if the Spanish Inquisition had been this difficult. And she didn't even want to know what Taylor meant by the "and stuff." *God, if she'd overheard us on the phone…*

"Okay, maybe you can call us boyfriend and girlfriend," Maya said, "but we're just starting out."

"If you're boyfriend and girlfriend, you could move in with us."

"What?" Who was this child, and what on earth had she done with Taylor Whitfield?

"Amy Marshall's mom has a boyfriend and he lives with them," Taylor explained. "He sleeps in her mom's room and everything. So you can do that too, since you're daddy's girlfriend."

Maya sat on the floor, hard. That was the final straw. "Taylor, I know this can be confusing. But just because other people do it, doesn't mean we have to. If someone wanted to go play in a minefield, would you go with them?"

"Huh?"

"Never mind." God, she was starting to sound like her mother. "Why don't we see what time your father's coming home? Maybe we can go out to dinner tonight. And you can pick the place."

"Cool."

"And Taylor?"

"Yeah?"

"Let's just keep this conversation between you and me for right now, all right?"

"Why?"

"You remember what I said about adults doing things differently? This is one of those things."

"All right." Taylor lifted her backpack over her shoulder and headed for the stairs. "Grown-ups sure are weird."

Maya closed her eyes with a sigh. Grown-ups weren't the only ones.

FOURTEEN

Maya covered her mouth, trying unsuccessfully to smother her laughter. "What's so funny?" Nick demanded.

"That's not what you're going to wear, is it?"

He looked down at his khakis and white polo-style shirt. "What's wrong with what I'm wearing?"

"Nothing—if you're planning to sell insurance."

Taylor giggled along with her Nick tried not to frown. "I'm on call, Maya. I may have to leave at a moment's notice."

"So put those clothes in a gym bag or something. Don't you have anything casual?"

Nick folded his arms across his chest. "This is casual for me."

"This is the Memorial Day barbecue at my parents' house, not golfing with your fellow doctors," Maya informed him. "My dad won't let you in the house wearing that, and if he did, my brothers would probably beat you up and then throw you into the pool."

"The pool?"

She nodded. "Either that, or bruise you in a volleyball game. Or basketball, or football. Mom and Dad encouraged us to be artists and athletes. They wanted to have a Hughes compete in every event of the Summer Olympics."

"Did you?"

"No, but one of my brothers did run in the 400-meter relay with Carl Lewis."

Nick put his fingers to his temples to stave off a headache. "Okay, I'll go change. What should I wear? Or would you like to pick out my clothes for me?"

"I'm sure you can come up with something," she said, giving him a generous smile. She pirouetted before him. "Look at how I'm dressed. This is the Saturday of the three-day weekend. Today is all about relaxing and overeating. If you don't have a good time, you'll make my mother cry. And that will make my father and my brothers very unhappy."

"There's no way in the world I'd want to do that." He shuddered at the thought. "I'll be right back."

He headed back upstairs, taking the steps two at a time. Changing was probably a good thing—especially since he'd gotten an erection when Maya had spun around in front of him.

It was a reaction that occurred more and more with each passing day. It didn't matter if she wore the little hot pink shorts and white shirt tied above her navel that she had on today, or a business suit. He'd been wanting her for weeks, and doing his level best not to. But that damn smile, those eyes, and the sway of her hips when she walked stalked him in his dreams, haunted him when he was awake.

The phone fantasies they shared only served to make him need her more, not less. The need had grown and grown until he had to touch her whenever they were in the same room, whether for a few minutes or a few hours. Thanks to their careers, they hadn't had the chance to have another night on the town, and it pleased him that Maya never suggested he shuttle Taylor somewhere so that they could be alone. If anything, she enjoyed Taylor's presence as much as Taylor loved being with Maya, and he knew he couldn't hope for a better relationship between them.

Yet despite their late-night phone fantasies, Nick had the feeling Maya held back from him. He couldn't put it into words, and he didn't want to ask her about it, but it seemed that as much as she lavished attention on his daughter, Maya seemed to be reserved with him when they were together. Oh, she held his hand and initiated kisses, but he had the feeling that she was holding back, as if afraid to fully give herself.

That reservation didn't ease his need for her, however, he thought as he changed into a pair of shorts, sneakers, and a t-shirt. Speaking of need, he wished he had time to take care of his growing problem. 'Course, the way he felt now, it wouldn't take long. He looked at the clock on his nightstand. Five minutes and his imagination should do the trick.

He crossed the room to his bathroom and shut the door. Leaning against it, he dropped his shorts and gave his mind over to the fantasy that had haunted him for weeks. Maya, wrapped in nothing but moonlight, walking toward him. He imagined how her breasts would feel in his hands, how soft her sigh would be as he took one nipple into his mouth, suckling it to complete awareness. His hand would slip down the smooth curves of her body, making sure she was ready for him. She would be ready, hot and sweet, whispering in his ear what she wanted him to do, what she would do for him. He'd push into her slowly, enjoying that first moment of their first time. Then the heat would take over, and her legs would wrap around his waist as he drove into her again and again, harder and faster until she shuddered and convulsed around him, calling his name…

"Nick, are you coming?"

That did the trick. "Yeah, I'm coming!" he yelled, grabbing a towel as his orgasm hit. "I mean, I'll be right down!"

Hurriedly he cleaned up and left the bathroom, stuffed his other clothes into the bag, then headed back downstairs. Maya and Taylor and the pets were waiting by the front door. "Are you all right?" Maya asked. "You look a little flushed."

"I'm fine," he assured her, hoping that his ears weren't bright red. "All that running up and down stairs, you know. Are we ready?" He hustled everyone outside.

Maya's parents lived on a tree-lined street that seemed right out of a Norman Rockwell painting. Kids were actually playing outside, riding bikes, tossing a Frisbee, chasing pets. Hamlet and Horatio started bouncing up and down in eager anticipation. "They seem to know this is a big deal," Nick observed.

"It is," Maya agreed. "Mom and Dad tend to make summer holidays into block parties. Dad's even won a couple of contests with his barbecue recipe."

"That's pretty cool," Nick said, meaning it.

"Trust me, he had plenty of opportunity to perfect it," she said. "There were a few times when he'd be gone because of work, but when he came back home, there was always a celebration, with food and music and fun. After he took early retirement, he got into building things. Bought the house next door, renovated it, then moved my mother and the remaining siblings into it so he could improve the main house. Now my mother was not to be outdone, so she took interior decorating and upholstery classes. Now Dad has a renovation business and my mother does interior design."

She directed him to pull over behind a long line of cars. "Mom has a gift for knowing what needs to be done and what will make a situation better. Believe it or not, she would always have cookies or something ready for us after school, and anytime one of the neighborhood ladies needed something, Mom was there. I think she was PTA president the entire time I was in elementary school. Our house was always the one everybody hung out in, and I think a lot of that had more to do with Mom than us and our friends."

Nick stopped the car. He barely got the door open before Hamlet and Horatio scrambled out of the car and went careening into the nearest clump of kids. "Daddy, I see Leila and Tamera!" Taylor said excitedly. "Can I go play with them? Please?"

Over the hood of the car, Nick looked to Maya, who nodded. "All right, but stay out of trouble."

Taylor disappeared as fast as the animals did. "I guess that leaves you and me, kid," Nick said, trying to control the apprehension that had grown since he'd started the drive. "Should I be worried?"

"Yes." Maya shut her door as he came around the corner to her. When he stopped in his tracks, she went to him, putting her arm through his. "It won't hurt much. My mom's five-four on a good day, but she acts like she's an Amazon. She's demanding that I get back on the horse and get married again. Daddy worries about me being in my house alone with two useless pets. Most of my brothers don't have wives to distract them, so they tend to be very protective of us girls."

"How many of you are there again?" Nick asked, struggling to remember her family history.

"Officially there are three girls and four boys."

"And unofficially?"

"Unofficially, the entire neighborhood calls my parents Ma and Pa Hughes. You'll see what I mean when you meet them."

She led him around the assortment of kids playing basketball to the back of the house. Smoke plumed in the air, signaling that barbecuing was underway. The backyard stretched for another acre it seemed, and teemed with kids and adults. A fenced-in pool anchored the left corner of the yard just beyond the massive deck. The far portion of the yard held a number of picnic tables all decorated with red, white, and blue. Citronella candles sprouted around the tables like so many tiki torches, keeping the mosquitoes at bay. A volleyball net waited in the far right corner of the yard, and several women watched children play on a jungle gym across from it.

"Oh my God."

Maya grinned. "To hear my father tell it, God stops by for his barbecue, too."

She led him over to a grill that looked like an oil drum cut lengthwise in half. A huge medium-skinned black man stood in front of it, wearing a stars-'n-stripes chef's hat and an apron that read "We're #1!" above an eagle flexing its muscles. "Dad, I want you to meet Taylor's father, Nicolas Whitfield. Nick, this is my father, Carson Hughes, Senior."

Maya's father put down his spatula and held out a beefy hand. "Taylor's dad. Beautiful daughter you have there. You ever been in the service?"

"Yes. Thank you. No, sir, I haven't." Nick tried to keep his answers straight as Carson Hughes' hand engulfed his. The man had twenty years on him easily, but his grip could have taken down a bull.

"Too bad," Carson said, and Nick felt as if he'd disappointed the older man. "Good discipline, the service is. Should be required for every kid leaving high school."

"Are you a preacher or an engineer?" a woman asked sarcastically. Nick watched a small Asian woman, beautiful with her immaculate hair and pale green sundress, walk up to Maya's father and pinched him on the butt. "Forgive my husband," she said, smiling at Nick. "It's hard to let the sergeant in him go sometimes."

"Nick, this is my mother, Loan. Mom, this is Nick Whitfield."

"Pleased to meet you, ma'am," Nick said.

Loan laughed at him. "Not what you expected?"

"Not exactly," he admitted. "But when I met Nadine and Jasmine I thought they might be adopted or multiracial. I mean, no one's exactly any one thing anymore, are we?" He scratched his head. "I'm botching this, aren't I?"

"Honey, put the man out of his misery," Carson said to his wife.

"Why should I?" she asked, a devilish smile on her face. "I'm having great fun."

"So," Nick drawled, looking for some safe topic to start with, "Maya told me the amazing story of how you two met."

Loan Hughes laughed. "Maya, you didn't tell him that your father was trying to kill my little brother and I wouldn't let him, did you?"

"What?" He couldn't have heard her right. He looked to Maya for confirmation or, hopefully, denial. "She's kidding, isn't she?"

"Yes, she is," Carson Hughes said in his rumbling voice. "I met her in 'Nam, at a little outdoor place in Saigon. When was it? Around '64 or '65, I think. Prettiest little thing I'd ever seen." He looped an arm about his wife's shoulders. "She had a flat, I was off duty, and I tried to help her."

"He fell flat on his butt in the mud," Loan interjected.

"That wasn't the only falling I did," Carson said with a grin. "Little ole thing handling that big ole Truck. I just wanted to help her, but she ended up helping me. And she's been helping me ever since."

The diminutive woman smiled up at her husband. "Of course. You can't live without me."

"You got that right. It took me twenty years and half a world to find you. I don't intend to let you go."

"Isn't he wonderful?" Mrs. Hughes winked at Nick. "More than thirty years together, and he still makes my heart go vroom-vroom."

"Mom!"

"Come on, honey," Loan said. "Just because the nest is empty doesn't mean the chicken and the rooster stopped playing house."

Nick joined the laughter, falling head over heels for Maya's mother. Even Maya forgot her embarrassment and had to smile as she pulled him forward to meet the rest of her family.

"Nick, this is my sister in-law, Amanda, who has the tough assignment of keeping my brother Dwayne in line."

"Oh, come on," a thirty-ish man in a green t-shirt and loose blue shorts said. "I'm not that bad."

Every woman in the family just looked at him.

"Okay, okay," he said, throwing up his hands. "I know when to keep my mouth shut." He stuck out his hand to Nick. "I'm Dwayne, by the way."

"I kinda figured that out," he said with a smile.

"These are my other brothers."

Nick assessed the men before him as much as they assessed him. They all took after their father in height, though their features were a blend of their parents'. Carson Junior had his father's height and a runner's build, and the thin glasses he wore only added to his quiet, studious aura. Nadine was the second oldest, followed by Dwayne, the troublemaker of the family.

Brandt came next in line, then Maya, followed by Jericho, and finally Jasmine. Nick took an instant liking to Jericho, especially when he revealed that he was also a single father, of a little boy named Jaremy.

"You guys could have at least worn t-shirts with your names on the back," Nick complained, holding his head with the effort to tie faces with names.

"What, and miss the opportunity to poke fun at you?" Jericho said with a grin.

"Poke fun all you want; maybe it will help me get y'all straightened out in my head."

"Don't worry if you don't," Maya's father said with a laugh. "It took me while to get everyone straight. I thought about calling them by numbers for a while."

"Hey, doc," Dwayne said, "you up for a game of volleyball?"

"Sure," Nick said, glad to be invited to play.

Maya glared at her brothers. "Be nice."

"We're always nice," Jericho said, eyes innocently wide. "I'm sure your doctor can handle playing 'dirty ball.' "

"What's dirty ball?" Nick asked Maya.

"Combine rugby with volleyball, you get dirty ball," she explained. "Brandt, I expect you to make sure Nick doesn't get hurt. He's on call today."

Brandt nodded. "I won't let him get hurt, sis," he promised. "Much."

FIFTEEN

"Dirty ball" was an understatement, Nick thought. "Lowdown-and-dirty-ball" would be more appropriate. He felt like setting up a clinic on the spot to handle the bruises and scrapes and cuts everyone had gotten. The only reason no one had gotten seriously injured was because Carson Senior declared it was time for the kids to eat and Loan threatened to turn the hose on her sons.

With her father and Carson Junior serving up the last of the barbecue, Maya helped her mother and a couple of the neighbors arrange food on a couple of folding tables. Every available space in the backyard held spread blankets, folding chairs, and patio furniture from nearby houses. When the Hughes family had a cookout, everyone on the block contributed.

It took half an hour to get the kids washed up and through the self-serve line, but soon every child had a burger and hot dog on their plate. Then the adults went through, and soon everyone settled down to the serious business of eating.

Conversation, sparse as it was, bounced through a variety of topics: politics, the economy, and movies.

Maya watched Nick weigh in with his opinions and fought the urge to smile. Growing at ease with her large and boisterous family took a hefty combination of confidence and friendliness; they could overwhelm by sheer volume.

Her mother leaned towards Dwayne's wife, Amanda. "Now that's what I like to see, a good appetite. Dwayne, refill her plate."

"I guess I'd better," Dwayne said with a grin. "Especially since she's eating for two now."

Loan spread a hand against her chest. "Are you saying what I think you're saying?"

"Yep, in another seven months I get to be a daddy." Dwayne looped an arm around his wife's shoulders.

Amanda smiled up at him, then turned to Loan. "We were going to wait until after dinner to tell everyone the news."

Maya felt her heart seize in her chest. A baby. Dwayne and Mandy were going to have a baby.

Everyone gathered to congratulate the pair. Maya remained glued to her seat, heartache weighing her down. A baby. A precious little baby…

Nick's voice cut through her emotions. "Are you all right?"

"I'm fine," she said, taking a deep breath before summoning a smile. She noticed that Brandt also hung back, and that motivated her to leave her seat. Her brother stood as silent and immoveable as a statue. She touched his shoulder, causing him to stare down at her. The emptiness in his eyes caused her heart to contract painfully; he hurt as badly as she did, but for different reasons.

Maya squeezed her brother's arm before moving to Dwayne and Amanda. "I'm so happy for you," she told the couple, giving both huge hugs.

"You okay?" Dwayne whispered in her ear. "This isn't the way we wanted to spring this on you."

"What better time than when we're all gathered together?" she whispered back before kissing him on the cheek, then stepping away.

Brandt seemed to shake himself from his mood. "Way to go, bro," he said, clapping Dwayne on the back. "Mandy, what are you going to do with two children running around?"

"Hey!" Dwayne cut in. "I resemble that remark!"

Everyone laughed, and those who felt the tension relaxed. "I'm gonna grab some more beers," Brandt announced. "Anybody want anything while I'm in the house?"

"I think we're out, son," Carson Senior said. "Would you mind going for more? And see if they have any of that sparkling cider."

"All right." He dug his keys out of his pocket.

"Want me to come with you?" Maya asked, concerned. Sure, her brothers could drink enough beer to fill Lake Lanier, but Maya knew Brandt used the beer run as an excuse to get away for a while.

"Nah, I'll be fine." He gave her a slight smile, then turned and headed for the driveway.

Amanda's face fell. "I'm sorry," she whispered. "I didn't want to make a big announcement. I just—"

"It's all right," Loan said, wiping tears from her cheeks before giving her daughter-in-law a hug. "You know we're all happy for you, especially Brandt."

"I think I'll go check on the ice cream," Maya announced. "I'll be back." She retreated into the house, conscious of Nick's gaze at her back. Facing him right now would be impossible.

She headed for one of the upstairs bathrooms in search of privacy. Gripping the edges of the sink in both hands, she hung her head and took deep breaths in an effort to keep her emotions at bay. She was thrilled for Dwayne and Mandy, she really was. Just as she'd congratulated Nadine and her husband on both their daughters, and Jaremy when he became a father. She was happy for all her siblings, yet she burned with jealousy and anger. Why was she the only one who couldn't have children? Why had such a fundamental female right been denied her?

"Maya?"

She wiped at her face as Nick entered the room. "Hey. What's going on?"

"I though I'd ask you the same question." His blue eyes darkened with concern as he tilted her chin up. "It's your sister-in-law, isn't it?"

"It's stupid, I know," she said, wiping at her eyes again. "I'm happy for them, I really am. Sometimes it just gets to me though, seeing everyone else with their children. And Brandt, it's got to be horrible for him, too."

"What happened with Brandt?"

"He lost his wife and son last year," she said, her voice trembling with emotion. "Their son drowned in the backyard pool. Brandt's wife killed herself later. He's still taking it very hard."

Nick pulled her close. "I'm so sorry, Maya."

She stepped away from him, wiping at her eyes with shaking fingers. "I'm worried more about Brandt than myself. I mean, it's not like I just learned that I'm broken."

"Broken? What do you mean, *broken?*"

She pulled herself together long enough to stare up at him. "I can't have children, Nick. That's why Russell divorced me, because I'm broken inside."

"Maya." He gathered her into his arms again. "You're not broken. Did you see a doctor?"

"I tried everything," she said, her voice low and hollow. "Shots, hormones, standing on my head. I did everything right, I swear I did. But it didn't work. I didn't work."

"I'm so sorry," he whispered against her ear. "What about your ex-husband? Did he get tested?"

"Russell?" She laughed, a broken sound with no humor. "Russell was so mad. He thought I'd deceived him, but I didn't know. How could I know? And when I suggested that he get tested, he dropped the bombshell that he didn't have to because he already had a child by a woman he'd known before he met me."

Nick held her close, running his hand up and down her back in slow comforting motions. "I wish there was something I could say or do to make you feel better."

"Just hold me for a moment," she whispered, settling her cheek to his shoulder.

He did, running his hand up and down her spine and pressing tiny kisses to her forehead. She could feel the emotion running through him, tightening his muscles. Whether it was anger or something else, she didn't know.

"Two years after the divorce, you'd think I'd be used to it. I've accepted it, but that doesn't make it any easier. Especially when I see these teenagers running around pregnant and leaving their babies to die in dumpsters," she swallowed down her anger. "I'm thinking about adoption now. There are a lot of children out there who need homes. If I can't go through the state, I'll try private adoption."

His hand slipped to the back of her neck. "The doctor in me wants to do everything I can to help you," he said, his voice rumbling low in his chest. "The man in me thinks your ex is a putz and didn't deserve you. I don't suppose you know where Russell is now?"

She pulled away to see his face. "He moved out of state a month after the divorce was finalized. Why?"

"Because I'd really like to hurt him for hurting you like that."

"Nick!" Surprise shocked her out of her misery. "You can't do that—you're a doctor!"

"I didn't say that I'd leave him hurt. I would patch him up afterwards. I'm just saying that as wonderful and giving as you are, you should never see a day of pain."

"Nick." She found it hard to look at him, she was blushing so hard. She finally decided to stare at the center of his chest.

"Is this the reason you've been throwing up barriers in our relationship?"

"Yes," she admitted. "I thought that if you found out, it would change things between us." She peeked up at his face. "So, uhm, this doesn't change anything between us, does it?"

His hands dropped from her shoulders. "Do you think it should?"

Her eyes burned as she dropped her gaze back to his chest. "I can understand if it does," she finally said, her voice low and tight. "I mean, I know our relationship isn't far along or anything, but if you decide you want a wife and a mother for Taylor, you should choose someone who can give you more children, if that's what you want. I plan to enjoy whatever time I have with you and Taylor, and when it's over, it's done, no regrets."

He stepped away from her, leaning back against the sink, and a shiver crawled over her that had nothing to do with the air conditioning. "So you're saying that you want to be with us, have a good time with us, but if I start to think about marriage and family, I have to look for someone else?"

It sounded callous explained that way, but it didn't make it less true. "Yes."

His ears went scarlet as he loosed his anger. "What kind of man do you think I am?"

"A man that loves his child," she shot back. "A man who loves family, a man who will want a son to carry on his name. I can't give you that, Nick. Don't you understand? I can't give you children."

"Have I asked for any?" he demanded. "Have we even gotten that far?"

"No," she said softly, knowing that they probably never would. "But you need to know now, before we get too deep."

He crossed his arms across his chest, but she could see the anger draining from his face. "So breaking up with you because you're infertile," he said slowly, "that would be the logical thing to do, wouldn't it?"

She couldn't bring herself to look at him, afraid tears would start leaking from her eyes. "Yes."

"Logically speaking, if I were looking for a wife and a mother for Taylor, I wouldn't choose a woman of mixed heritage. I mean, that would just be asking for trouble, wouldn't it?"

The damned tears started leaking anyway. "Yes."

"And surely, logically speaking, if I wanted to have more children, especially, say, a son of my own blood, I would certainly want him to be close to the genetic makeup of my current child, and not a mix of three different races. But that's incidental since the woman in question can't have children anyway. I mean, there's a boatload of logical reasons not to keep going with this, right?"

Not today. Nails dug into the palms of her hands. Dammit, this wasn't supposed to happen today. She was supposed to do the walking, not the other way around. She tried for a tough, I-don't-give-a-damn attitude. "Yeah, that's what I'm trying to tell you. Logically, you should run. Now."

"Bullshit."

Surprise jerked her head up. "What?"

He held her gaze, sapphire eyes sparking with anger and something she could only describe as hunger. "Listen to me good, because I might not say this right again. When I think of you, logic flies out the window. All I can think about is how you've been there for Taylor and me, helping us, making both of us happy in so many ways."

He pushed off the sink, taking a step towards her. "When I see you, rational thought leaves, and I get all tongue-tied. I'm struck senseless by your smile, your warmth, and your scent, and it's enough to just be in the same room with you."

He stopped in front of her, so close she could see the variegated shades of blue in his eyes. "And when I touch you, well, it's definitely not this head I'm using." He tapped his forehead.

She didn't know what to say. He'd completely and eloquently thrown her for a loop. Unable to form a coherent sentence, she let herself be pulled into his arms.

"Maya, I have no idea what tomorrow holds. You could decide you never want to see me again or Taylor could suddenly become allergic to cats. But for now, all I can tell you is that for me, your not being able to have children doesn't make you anything less. I wanted you before you told me, and I still want you after. In fact, I want you right now."

"You do?"

"You have no idea what you do to me, do you? Spinning in front of me in that skimpy outfit, making me hungry for you." His hands framed her face, his gaze burrowing into hers as he used his thumbs to gently wipe the last of her tears away. "I want to make love to you, Maya. I want to know what it feels like to be inside you. I want to hear you sigh and moan and scream with pleasure. I want you to tell me what makes you feel good so I can give it to you over and over."

"Nick…" She couldn't think as her senses went into overload. She entwined her arms around his neck, pressing closer to him. The last of her fears melted away. It was a simple thing to lift her face for his kiss, to open herself to him. The moment their lips met, however, a wild rush of desire swept through her, more powerful than anything she had ever known. Nick's lips slanted across hers and she opened her mouth to receive him, to taste him as he tasted her. He backed her into the counter and she didn't care, didn't want anything except the heat of his skin against her own. Her fingers clutched his buttocks, pulling him closer as his mouth swept down to her throat, suckling her frantic pulse.

"Ahem."

They sprang apart, guilty at being caught. Maya fought to cool her heated cheeks as she glared at

Dwayne, who grinned from ear to ear. "Couldn't you have knocked or something?"

"Hey, be glad I wasn't Dad. He'd be hauling you to a justice of the peace right about now." He wiped at his forehead, then grinned again. "Is it hot in here, or is it just me?"

"It's just you," Maya retorted, pushing her rock of a brother out the door. "What do you want, anyway?"

"I just came to check on you, make sure you're all right." He looked from her to Nick. "I guess you are, huh?"

"I'm fine," Maya said through gritted teeth. "Now will you please leave?"

"I'm going, I'm going." He let her push him a couple of steps then stopped. "By the way," he said to Nick, the smile dropping from his face. "Maya's a big girl, and makes her own choices. But if you hurt her, I'll break you in half. Got it?"

"Got it." Nick quirked a smile. "And if you don't give us some privacy, I'll break you in half."

Maya shut the door on Dwayne's surprised expression, then laughed. "That was a ballsy move."

"Well, I'm feeling kinda ballsy right now." He looked down. "Okay, more than kinda. How about you? Are you feeling better?"

Better? She felt as if she were about to explode. "I know a way that I could feel a whole lot better," she said.

Light gleamed in Nick's eyes as he caught her meaning. "Tonight?"

"Yes."

He pulled her close again, and she could feel the hard length of his erection pressing between them. "Are you sure?"

She smiled up at him. "Very sure." She gave him a light kiss before turning back to the door.

"Maya." He moved up behind her, pressing her between him and the door. She could feel the heat of him against her buttocks, feel his breath warm on her Neck. Instinctively she pushed back against him, wanting to be filled as she'd never wanted before. He pushed his hand past the waistband of her shorts, beneath the lacy edge of her panties to the smoldering spot between her thighs. "Maya, it'll be good, I swear."

She pressed forward against his questing fingers, forgetting everything but the man with her. Turning her head and arching back, she pressed her lips to his cheek, his lips, his throat. The spicy taste of him burned her tongue, sending a delicious shiver down her spine.

His fingers moved faster, his thumb circling the center of her excitement while his fingers plundered Her. Without warning she exploded, gasping as pleasure swept through her. The motion of his hand sent aftershocks through her, unhinging her knees.

Only the press of his body and his arm around her waist kept her upright.

When he released her, she turned to face him, burying her face against his chest. "Nick." She couldn't find words to say and didn't know if she could say them anyway.

"I know," he whispered, his voice husky with a hunger that had nothing to do with food. "I know. Right now, though, I need you to leave."

"Leave? Why?"

His eyes bored into hers, darkened with desire. "Because all I can think about is how easy it would be to turn you around, lean you over the sink, and make us both really happy."

"Nick!" Heat blossomed in her cheeks as the erotic image ifiled her mind.

"I know, I wouldn't actually do that in your parents' house. Your mother would draw and quarter me. But if I try to go out right now, everyone else will know what Dwayne already does—that we were in here making out. And I really don't want to be beaten up by your brothers. I'm going to need a few minutes to cool off."

"Oh. Okay." She turned to the door, then turned back. "I could, uhm, take care of it for you."

"God, no." His eyes rolled up in the back of his head.

"Why not?" she asked, confused. "Most men in their right minds wouldn't turn down an offer like that."

He opened his eyes, and Maya would swear she actually felt his gaze on her "I'm not in my right. mind," he said, his voice hoarse. "You've driven me right out of it. I don't think I can keep quiet when I'm with you."

"Ah-oh." Heat spread to her ears again. "Uhm, in that case, I think I'll just, give you some privacy."

Just before she opened the door, his pager went off. She turned around to find him glaring at the readout. "Is it the hospital?"

"Yeah," he answered. "I'll call them, but more than likely I'm going to need to go in."

"Do you think you'll be able to make it back?" she asked.

"I hope so," he answered, opening the door for her. "I don't like missing any time with you, even if it means I have to get the third degree from your family."

"They're not that bad," she protested, leading him down the hall. When he didn't say anything she turned around. "Okay, maybe they are that bad, but they have good intentions."

"I know they do, and I don't blame them. Actually, I'm kinda jealous of your family. I mean, mine isn't bad, but what you guys have here..." He smiled. "Every family should be so lucky."

SIXTEEN

"Where's Nick?" Loan asked.

"Getting changed."

"Did he have an accident?" Dwayne asked with an innocent expression.

"No, he got a page," Maya said, glaring at her oldest brother. "He has to go to the hospital."

"It's not anything serious, is it?" their mother asked.

"I'm not sure. But they wouldn't page him unless it was an emergency."

Nick exited the house, the gym bag in his hand. "There was a deck collapse. A couple of people are going to need major surgery."

"Oh, those poor people," Loan murmured.

"Have you seen Taylor?" he asked.

"She's around front playing four-square with the other girls," Nadine supplied.

"Thanks." Nick crossed to Maya's father. "Thanks, sir, for a wonderful afternoon. You have a terrific family, and I appreciate you letting me and my daughter be a part of it today."

"If you make my daughter an honest woman, you could be a part of it every day," Loan informed him as Carson shook his hand.

"Mom," Maya complained, her cheeks reddening.

"What?" her mother asked in Vietnamese. "If you won't work it, someone has to."

"What did she say?" Nick asked, seeing Maya's mortified expression.

"I said, you need to give me a hug. The women in this family don't shake hands." The petite woman held out her arms, and Nick obligingly gave her a hug with a kiss on the cheek for good measure.

Loan slanted a glance at Maya. "Nice muscles," she said in her native language. "I think this one's a keeper."

Maya felt heat creep up her ears. Thank God her mother was speaking Vietnamese. "We haven't been dating that long, Mom," she said.

"You mean you haven't gone to bed with him yet?"

The family members within earshot burst into laughter. "Oh my God," Maya said in English, putting her head in her hands to keep it from exploding. "I can't believe you said that!"

"What did she say?" Nick asked, which caused everyone to laugh again. "It was about me, wasn't it?"

"Nothing. Why don't I walk you around to the front of the house?"

Nick waved goodbye to everyone else, then followed Maya to the driveway. "Your mother didn't say anything about my butt, did she?"

Maya tripped on a piece of gravel. "What makes you say that?"

"Because she felt me up when I hugged her. I don't know if I should be flattered or scared that she wants to roast me on the grill."

Heat crept up her neck, slow-roasting her in embarrassment. "I'm sorry, Nick."

He stopped her with a touch on her arm. "Have I told you how beautiful you are when you blush?" he teased.

Her mortification disappeared with a laugh. "You're just as bad as the rest of them. You're gonna fit in just fine."

"Cool."

She elbowed him in the ribs. "I didn't mean it as a compliment."

"Too bad. I'm gonna take it as one."

"You know, I can still have one of my brothers beat you up."

"You wouldn't do that," he said with confidence.

"Oh yeah? What makes you think so?"

He put his arm around her waist, pulling her close. "Because you want me, you really want me."

Laughing, she half pushed him towards the front yard. Jasmine and Jericho were cheering the neighborhood kids on in a massive game of dodgeball. "Hey," Nick called, "can I borrow my daughter for a moment?"

Jasmine called time out, and Taylor ran over to them. "Hey, Dad, why did you change clothes?"

Nick bent to Taylor's level. "I have to go to the hospital."

"Are you gonna come back?"

"I'm going to try, but it sounds very serious."

She looked at Maya. "Are you going, too?"

"Nope, I'm going to stay here."

"I can still spend the night with Leila and Tamera, right? Auntie Dina and Uncle Kevin are taking us all to Six Flags tomorrow."

"Of course you can. I just wanted to tell you bye and to have a good time tomorrow. Daddy-kiss!"

Maya watched as Taylor threw her arms around Nick's shoulders as they made air-kisses against each cheek before rubbing noses. It was a ritual she'd seem them perform many times, but repetition made it no less poignant.

"Bye, Daddy." Taylor gave him a final wave before hurrying off to rejoin her friends.

Nick looked up at Maya. "Auntie Dina and Uncle Kevin?"

Maya shrugged, not sure when Taylor had started calling her sister and brother-in-law by those titles. "I have no idea when that started, but I know Nadine and Kevin don't mind. A lot of kids call them that. They're following in my parents' footsteps."

He stopped at the car. "What time is this shindig usually over?"

"When the last neighbor drags himself home," she answered. "But I don't plan to stay that long. I've got a special night ahead of me."

"Indeed you do," he said in a low voice, causing her insides to contract. "How will you get home?"

"I'll get Brandt to take me," she said. "I want to talk to him anyway, make sure he's all right."

"And what about you? Are you all right?"

"I haven't felt this all right in two years," she admitted. "Thank you for that."

"My pleasure," he said, giving her a sensual smile. "Will you do me a favor?"

"What sort of favor?"

He dug into his pocket, producing a set of keys. "When I come home tonight, I want to find you stretched out on my bed, in some cute little sexy number, or maybe even completely naked. I want to think about you waiting for me, just like that, while I'm at work."

"While you're at work, you need to keep your mind on other things," she reminded him, although she couldn't deny the heat that swept through her at his words.

"The voice of reason strikes again," he said, opening the car door and tossing his bag inside. "Can I at least have a kiss to sustain me?"

"Of course you can." She wrapped her arms around his neck and laid one on him. Catcalls and whistles rose in the air. They broke apart and turned to see the dodge ball kids pointing at them and laughing. "You know, having an audience is not one of my fantasies."

"Mine either." He kissed her again, then got into the car. "I'll see you when I get home."

"I'll be waiting."

"I hope so," he said, starting the car. He gave her a wink and a wave before shifting the car into gear and driving off.

Her stomach performed cartwheels as she watched him drive away. She held the keys tightly. He'd just turned the corner and she already missed him. Soon, though, they'd get to be together, get to spend the night in each other's arms, get to act out the fantasies that had sustained them for so long.

After making sure the kids were okay, she returned to the deck. Her parents sat in matching deck chairs, holding hands as they surveyed the activity in their sprawling back yard.

"Did Nick get off okay?" her father asked.

"What?"

"Get your mind out of the gutter," her mother chastised. "Will he be able to come back?"

Maya took the chair opposite theirs. "I don't think so, but he said he'd try." She leaned forward. "So what do you guys think?"

"Does it matter what we think?" her father asked.

"Of course it does," she said. "I want you guys to like him."

"I know it's been a couple of years since Russell," her mother said, "so I'm glad you're coming out of your shell and dating again. But are you sure about this, a man and his daughter?"

"I wasn't, not for a long time," she confessed. "I mean, it seems a little too perfect, doesn't it? No wife, no mother, and they're right next door to me. But it really feels right, now."

"Did you tell him why that bastard Russell walked out on you?" her father asked.

"That's what we were talking about when we went into the house," Maya explained. "I was afraid to open up to him. I mean, Russell left me afraid to even try to have a serious relationship. But Nick…he's got this wonderful heart. When I'm with him, I feel comfortable with who I am and where I am. And when I'm with him and Taylor, I feel like we've always been together."

She sat back, gathering her feelings close. "I was afraid that I'd have to break up with him once I told him about my problem," she admitted. "I knew I'd have to consider that, so I didn't want to commit too much of myself. But he told me it doesn't make me anything less."

"Of course it doesn't!" her mother exclaimed.

Maya smiled. "You're my mother; you're supposed to say that. But hearing it from Nick, I believed it. I really believe he means it. And that means so much to me."

Her father reached over and took her hand. "I'm glad you found a decent guy," he said. "I can tell that he cares about you, that he loves his daughter, and that work is important to him. I like that."

"And he's not intimidated by your brothers," her mother added. "That's good. They never got along with he-who-shall-not-be-named."

Both of her parents made faces, and Maya had to laugh. The laughter felt good, making her feel lighter than she had in a long time.

Her mother rose to her feet, crossing the deck to give her a hug. "Daughter, you know we support you, no matter what you do. I've seen the way Nick looks at you, and I see how he loves his little girl. He's got a good heart, that one. And nice buns."

"Mom!"

Two hours later, cleanup was complete, and she'd sent Taylor off with Nadine. Brandt offered to give her a lift home, just as she knew he would.

"How you doing?" he asked.

"Better than I thought," she said. "What about you? Are you doing okay?"

"I'll be fine," he said. "You know me. I'm a survivor."

"I know, but that doesn't mean that I'm not going to worry about you."

"Don't I know it," he said. He tapped his fingers against the steering wheel. "I want to let you know that I started reading that book."

"What do you think?"

"I still think the woman's a quack, but there are a couple of parts that make sense," he admitted. "I'm not saying that I swallow all of it and it sure as hell doesn't explain what happened, but some of it's okay."

"I'm glad," she whispered, her heart full. There was hope yet that Brandt would find the peace and forgiveness he so desperately needed. She so wanted that for her brother, wanted that more than anything.

He pulled to a stop before her house. "I like your man."

Surprised, she turned to face him in the car. "You do?"

"Yeah. He cares about you. That's good."

"I care about him, too," she said, her voice soft.

Brandy gripped the steering wheel in both hands. "I remember a night, a couple of years ago, when you thought your world had ended. When you thought that you'd be alone for the rest of your life because no one would want you." He looked at her. "I think you're wrong."

Touched, Maya reached across to give her brother a hug. "Thank you," she said, her throat tight. "Thank you so much."

"You're welcome." He pushed her back with a gentle shove. "Now get out of my car and go wait for your man."

"Fine." Laughing, Maya got out of the car with her pets and almost skipped up the drive to her front door. After unlocking it, she waved Brandt off and stepped inside. Hamlet and Horatio made it as far as the living room before collapsing.

"You guys had a big day, didn't you?" she asked, tossing her keys and purse on the couch. "Don't get too comfortable yet. We're going to be spending the night at Nick's house."

Saying the words aloud stopped her cold. Tonight, she'd be spending the night at Nick's house, in Nick's bed. In Nick's arms.

Butterflies began to do cartwheels in her stomach as anticipation filled her. So many nights of so many fantasies were about to be fulfilled, she thought as she went upstairs to her bedroom. Remembering how Nick had touched her, how he'd looked at her filled her with yearning. Lord knew she needed this night, needed to show Nick in the most primitive and intimate way how much he meant to her.

She took a small duffel bag out of her closet, then begin filling it with the essentials for an overnight stay. She hesitated at her lingerie drawer, wondering what to take with her. Finally she pulled out a gossamer black robe, made of fabric so thin it almost couldn't qualify as clothing. She'd bought it a couple of weeks ago because it reminded her of the first fantasy she and Nick had shared by phone. What an appropriate choice for their first night together.

After gathering a few more things, she headed back downstairs. "Come on, boys," she called to her pets. "We're going next door to wait for Nick to get home."

Her exhausted pets dragged themselves to their feet and dutifully followed her from one house to the other. She fished into her pocket for Nick's house key, then inserted it into the lock. The significance of the gesture wasn't lost her on. Tonight, she'd be opening the door on a new chapter of her life, one that promised to be worth all the pain she'd endured up to this point.

Taking a deep breath, she entered the silent house, then headed to the kitchen to make sure there was water and food for Hamlet and Horatio. There was. It was one of those little things that demonstrated how deeply she'd become woven into the fabric of the Whitfields' lives.

She glanced at her watch. Nine-thirty. She hadn't really expected Nick to be home yet, but she hoped he'd arrive soon. Nerves threatened to get the best of her and she knew that if she let them, they'd give way to doubts. She didn't want doubts. She wanted Nick.

"Okay guys, you've got plenty of food and water," she told her tired pets. "Now you be good and stay down here while Mommy goes upstairs, okay?"

After making sure her boys were settled for the night, she took her bag and made her way upstairs to Nick's room. It was just as she'd remembered it, strong and masculine. The bed dominated her vision, calling to her like a siren's song. She'd be there soon enough, but first she wanted to take a shower.

Crossing the bedroom to the master bath, she paused at the door, fumbling for the switch. The room gleamed teal, chrome, and white. A large shower stood in the far right corner opposite a vanity area that led to the walk-in closet. Midway on the right was a door that she supposed led to the toilet, and the main double white marbled sinks were backed by a huge mirror that stretched to the ceiling. She could see the garden-style tub reflected behind her in the mirror, and turned around. It looked large enough for three people with its huge oval shape and whirlpool jets. "Wow."

As delicious as the tub looked, she opted for a shower, washing away the exertions of the day with her favorite jasmine-scented soap. She completed her bedtime ritual, brushing her hair, smoothing lotion into her skin, realizing for the first time how sensual the experience was.

Pure unadulterated lust cramped her stomach. God, she needed Nick. Please let this go right, she murmured to herself. Let reality match fantasy.

While slipping into the lightweight robe, she looked at herself in the mirror, then burst out laughing. Was she actually praying for good sex? Lord, what would her mother think?

'Course, knowing Loan Hughes, she'd already lighted a candle on Maya's behalf.

Still chuckling to herself, she turned down the bed, then crept between the sheets. Almost immediately, the day began to take its toll, pulling her towards sleep. It wouldn't hurt to take a cat nap, she thought. She had a feeling she'd need her rest once Nick came home.

And she was right.

SEVENTEEN

"Maya."

She was awakened by a whisper of touch, gentle and worshipful. "Nick? What time is it?"

"Shh." His admonition to silence and stillness skittered over her skin even as the languorous stroking continued.

Stroke. "I love the feel of your skin." Stroke. "It's smooth, like hot caramel sliding down a sundae." Stroke. "Beautiful."

Low, and filled with a huskiness Maya had never heard before, his voice mesmerized her in the darkness, his touch stirring the flame in her core. Heightened by the lack of vision, her other senses, including her somnolent sexual sense, hummed to life.

The incessant stroking of her cheek shifted. His fingertips now grazed her throat, her wildly pounding pulse.

"I've been watching you sleep for the last ten minutes." Stroke. "Watching the curve of your hips, the way your arm falls over your waist." Stroke. "The way your breasts rise and fall with each breath."

Breathe, a voice inside her head frantically whispered, and she realized that she had forgotten how to perform that basic involuntary function. Nick knelt beside her on the floor, his eyes glinting in the faint light from the window. Again the rhythmic stroking shifted to the small expanse of skin between her throat and the rise of her breasts.

"I watched your face, too." Stroke. "You looked so innocent and relaxed while you slept, and you were smiling." Stroke. "I hope it was a good dream." Stroke. "I hope it was about me."

Not only had he robbed her of breath, he'd robbed her of speech and thought. All extraneous senses burned away, leaving only two: hearing his voice and feeling his touch.

And one more, the blaze of desire, on its way to becoming an inferno.

Her hypnotic languor deepened as his voice and hands continued. "What did you dream, Maya? Did you dream about me coming to you, holding you, touching you?" Stroke. "Did you dream about me kissing you, tasting you? Did you hope it would become real?"

"Yes," she managed to answer. "Oh yes."

His hands slipped lower still, parting her robe, exposing her breasts to the night and his gaze. "How beautiful you are, lying there like the goddess you were named for." Stroke. "I wonder how sweet you are, your lips and your breasts." Stroke. "I'm not going to wonder anymore." He lowered his head.

Her vocal cords awakened with the searing heat of his mouth coaxing her nipple to perfect awareness. She gasped his name as her body hummed with desire, wanting his touch further, to be branded by his hands and lips.

He lifted away from her. "I need to see all of you," he whispered, his voice husky. "Can I do that, Maya? Can I see all of you?"

"Please," she breathed.

His hands gently tugged at the gossamer peignoir, parting it completely. She sat up so that he could slip it off her shoulders. The flimsy fabric slid down her skin like a whisper until her chest was completely bared to him.

"Beautiful," Nick whispered, his voice reverent. She could feel his stare, hot and heavy on her skin. His hands reached for the small scrap of black lace that passed for panties and she lifted her hips, helping him free her from the suddenly confining garment.

Finally she lay bare to his gaze. Her nipples tightened as he surveyed her from head to toe in a leisurely perusal. His fingers reversed his gaze, skimming up her calves to her thighs, brushing lightly over her most intimate place. Her hips lifted involuntarily, wanting more of his caress, but he continued his slow meandering up her body, trailing his fingers over the soft curve of her belly upward to the slopes of her breasts. Both hands cupped her, warm like massage oil, the pads of his thumbs at once rough and gentle on the aroused peaks of her nipples.

"Just like my fantasy, so very beautiful," he breathed. The way he stared down at her, Maya believed him.

His hands slid down her belly again to the juncture of her thighs. "I don't know whether to just keep looking at you, keep touching you, or make love to you. I want you badly, Maya, so badly I don't know how I'm gonna last with you. I want to see every emotion wash over your face as I touch you, taste you, and take you."

His voice served to drive her out of her mind. "Nick." She writhed on the mattress with need, her fingers digging into the sheets.

He pressed his thumb against the center of her arousal, moving in slow lazy circles. She gasped at the heady sensation, lifting her hips off the bed in a silent quest for more of his touch. He obliged her by slipping a finger inside her moist heat, making her moan in appreciation.

"You're gorgeous when you're aroused," he whispered, his eyes glazed as he stared down at her. "I can see the need gathering in your eyes like a storm. Rain for me, sweetness. Let me feel the thunder inside you."

She shuddered, close, so very close to unleashing the storm he wanted. She gasped for breath as sensations built within her, boiling like a tempest. So when he withdrew his fingers, she cried out in protest.

"I want to take this slow," he said shakily, unbuttoning his shirt. He pulled it off quickly, then reached for his belt. "I want to enjoy each and every moment, every second, every heartbeat."

"Yes," she sighed, watching him undress. They had all night; they could take as much time as they wanted. "I want to feel your skin on mine."

Finally he stood beside her, gorgeously naked. She sat up, the better to run her hands over the long, flat planes of his chest, the dark whorls of hair tickling her hands. She threaded her fingers through his hair, pulling him down for a kiss, pulling him down beside her on the bed.

Given unprecedented access, she let her hands roam his body, running them lightly and slowly down his cheeks to his throat, then across his shoulders and down his arms. She lifted his hand, separating the fingers, sucking each one into her mouth one after the other. Nick moaned, dragging her close to capture her breasts. She took slow nibbles down his arm, tracing back the way she had come, enjoying the sounds he made and the movements of his body as he tensed, then relaxed.

Measured bites took her down his throat to the expanse of chest. Working in his yard had given the expanse of his chest a warm, peachy glow shadowed by whorls of dark hair. Moving with tiny nips, she reached his left nipple. She closed her teeth gently over his skin, softening the bite with a sweep of her tongue. He hissed, then groaned with pleasure, his hands stroking whatever parts of her skin he could reach.

She turned on the bed, shifting so that she could continue the sensual feast of his skin. Nibbling down his chest, she made her way to his navel, swirling her tongue along the outer edge before following the slight line of hair further down. His erection rose hard and proud from a nest of dark hair, waiting for her touch.

Not planning to keep him in suspense, she lightly ran her fingers from base to tip before wrapping her hand around him. He moaned in response, causing a wave of pure lust to hit her She wanted to drink him down, to take every bit of him, to take and take until he could no longer give.

She felt his hand on her hips, pressing her legs apart. Heady with sensation, she automatically complied. His fingers moved over her, soft yet sure, making her moan around him. When his lips replaced his fingers, giving her an intimate kiss, she had to cry out at the pleasure. She increased her pressure and rhythm, determined to shake him as he'd shaken her.

Nick's groans told her more than words how much he appreciated her attention. His whole body went rigid. "Not like this," he whispered harshly. "Not for the first time."

She drew away from him, but had to reach out, needing the contact with his skin. He stretched out atop her, causing her insides to sizzle with desire. Burning with need, she leaned up to kiss him, tasting him, tasting herself, telling him wordlessly exactly what she wanted.

He rose above her, the muscles in his arms prominent beneath his skin. "Are you ready?"

She'd been ready from the moment he'd touched Her. "Yes," she breathed. "I need you inside me."

His hips flexed beneath her hands, and she could feel the tip of his arousal pressed against her entrance. He moved slowly, bathing the head in her natural moisture with a sensuous movement. She moaned with urgency. "Please," she whispered. "Please."

Nick ignored her entreaty to rush, pushing oh-so-slowly into her. Every inch of his entry made its presence known by causing tiny shocks along her nerve endings, making it difficult to catch her breath. As if they played a game, he advanced, then waited, driving her to the brink with the blind basic desire to be filled.

She wrapped her legs high around his waist in encouragement, opening for him. His hips thrust forward. One moment she was empty and the next filled, so completely filled that she lost her breath.

"Did I hurt you?" Nick asked, his voice harsh and low.

"No," she breathed, sighing as her body welcomed him. He withdrew again and then slowly advanced. "It feels…so good."

Her body hadn't been filled like this in more than two years, but it remembered and hummed with pleasure. She lifted her hips to meet him, wanting to feel him moving inside her, needing the lust and the power and the sex.

Nick had other ideas, pumping into her slowly then quickly, then pausing altogether. "You feel so damn good," he breathed. "I want to make this last all night."

"I can't last that long!" she exclaimed, then emphasized her point by latching onto the curve of his neck with her teeth, then wrapping her body around his as tightly and completely as she could. She rocked against him, determined to shake his resolve, determined to make him lose control and take them both over the edge.

He made a strangled noise, her name choking out of him. His hips drove against hers as his pace slowly increased, filling her over and over. She clutched at his shoulders, rising to meet him, desire raging through her like a massive storm. He shifted against her, and she went ballistic. Gasps ripped from her throat as her body convulsed in wave after wave of pleasure so powerful, so pure, she thought she would explode.

He shifted against her again, and this time she did explode, emitting a sharp cry as her senses scattered in fragments of white-hot orgasm. The world tilted as her body reduced itself to her innermost core, her inner walls holding on for dear sweet life to the erection that continued to throb inside her. She felt him jerk in response, then suddenly push deep into her, his body stiffening as he came.

She came to her senses slowly, helped by the way that Nick had all but collapsed on her. She didn't mind, enjoying the magical sensations that continued to pulse inside her, but his stillness made her worry. "Nick?"

"I'm here," he muttered. "I think."

He raised up on his elbows, and she drew in a cool breath of air. "I thought I felt the earth move," he said. "Now I know why."

It took her a moment or two to realize that somehow they had made the mattress slide off the box spring, and it now hung half on, half off the bed frame. "I gotta tell ya, you definitely rocked my world," she said, bursting into giggles.

He laughed with her, causing deep aftershocks to rocket through her and steal her breath again. "Would you believe me if I said that that was the most amazing experience of my life?"

"I'd have to agree with you," she replied, lifting her head to kiss him. "But I guess we'd better straighten the bed up so you can get some sleep."

"Who said anything about sleep?" he wondered, shifting inside her. "I thought we'd try to move the mattress the rest of the way."

She sighed as he moved against her. "I think that's a most excellent idea, doctor."

EIGHTEEN

The next morning, Maya awakened to bright sun and singing birds. It suited her mood perfectly. She felt like Audrey Hepburn in *My Fair Lady*, except it was a different kind of dancing she could have done all night.

Nick's arm lay heavily yet comfortably about her waist, holding her snug against his chest. She could feel his morning arousal pressing against the cleft of her buttocks, the stubble on his chin resting in the curve of her shoulder. It felt like paradise.

Scratching at the bedroom door interrupted her reverie. Hamlet and Horatio would have urgent need to go outside, she realized. She didn't want to leave the comfort of the bed—and Nick's arm—but she didn't want to start the day by cleaning up after her pets either.

As soon as she tried to lift his arm, Nick's grip tightened. "Where do you think you're going?" he rumbled in her ear.

The sleep-roughened tone of his voice sent a delicious shiver down her back. "To let the boys out," she said, turning to face him. Tousled dark hair streaked across his forehead, hanging almost into those brilliant blue eyes. The lips that had given her so much pleasure the previous night stretched into a smile as he reached up to cup her cheek.

"I'll let them out. You just lie there looking gorgeous." Before she could argue, he planted a kiss on her, slipped out of bed, and padded over to the door. "Come on, guys," he said as he opened the door. "I'm the only male getting Maya's attention today."

Flabbergasted, Maya watched Nick's beautiful buns disappear into the hallway, then got up to visit the master bathroom. After using the toilet, she caught sight of herself in the mirror over the vanity and groaned. With her hair sticking out at strange angles and her eyes full of sleep, she was hardly cover model material. Maybe all the lovemaking had made Nick blind.

She slid back into bed just before Nick returned. He leaned against the door, staring at her with a satisfied smile. "I like way you look in my bed," he said, his voice husky with possessiveness.

Heat crept up her cheeks at the compliment. "I can't believe you went downstairs like that."

"I didn't want to take the time to dress," he answered, moving towards the bed. "Especially since I'd just be taking everything off again as soon as I came back."

He slid into bed beside her, folding her into his arms again. "We've got about twelve hours before we have to pick up Taylor," he said between nuzzles to the curve of her neck. "What would you like to do today?"

She ran her fingers through the light scattering of hair on his chest, enjoying the feel of his muscles flexing beneath her touch. Then she leaned forward, planting a kiss on one flat nipple. "Would it upset you if I said I just want to spend the day here, with you, with no outside distractions?"

"No." He sighed. "That doesn't upset me at all."

"Good." She kissed the skin over his heart, then sat up. "But I would like to take a shower. I can still smell my—uhm, enthusiasm—from last night."

Nick sat up on the opposite side of the bed. "I'm smelling a little enthusiastic myself. Let's take a bath."

She perked up at the thought of lounging in the large whirlpool tub. "Really?"

"Really. I've got this huge whirlpool tub, and I've never been in it. Taylor uses it as a swimming pool sometimes, and I'm pretty sure she's got some kiddie bubble bath around here somewhere. It's certainly big enough for two adults."

Fifteen minutes later, they were up to their necks in bubble bath. Maya leaned against the comforting planes of Nick's chest, letting her mind and the steam carry her away.

"I can feel you smiling," he said, his hands making lazy circles down her arms. "What's got you smiling like that this morning?"

She turned slightly sideways to get a better look at him. He still had that gorgeous tousled look that most men have when they just wake up, very handsome with those brilliant blue eyes contrasting with his dark hair and beard stubble. She found it difficult to believe that she was here with him like this.

"You've got me smiling," she said, turning in the water so that her breasts pressed against his chest. "I feel like I'm on a fantasy vacation."

"Good," he said, pulling her closer so he could drop a kiss to her forehead. "My ego feels much better now."

"Your ego doesn't need the reassurance, and neither does the rest of you. I seem to recall that you rose to the occasion several times last night."

"I had the best kind of inspiration." His fingers crept down her back to massage her buttocks. "You're like natural Viagra."

"You make me feel," she stopped, unsure of how to put the sudden surge of emotion into words.

"Like what?" Nick asked, the question rumbling beneath her ear.

"Like I'm this beautiful, sexy woman," she finally answered.

Nick laughed as he turned her around until she straddled his lean, muscled body. "You are a beautiful, sexy woman," he told her. "Don't ever think you're less than that."

The sincerity in his tone overrode the sentimentality of his words. She floated into his arms, kissing him with all the emotion and need she possessed. A particular body part poked her in the ribs at the same time that Nick's stomach rumbled.

She broke away with a laugh. "I guess we should get out and think about something to eat," she said with a grin. "You're gonna need your strength for the rest of the day."

"Aww." Nick gave her a boyish pout completely at odds with the heat of his gaze. "I was hoping we'd get to play a game before breakfast."

"What sort of game?"

"How about 'hide the submarine'?"

Maya burst out with laughter. "Man those torpedoes, captain, and prepare to dive!"

Sometime later, they sat at the kitchen table, feasting on western-style omelets and steaming cups of coffee. Nick's only concession to getting dressed was to pull on a pair of boxer shorts, though he had to admit that Maya looked damned good in his pajama top unbuttoned to her navel.

Nick raised his fork in salute. "Who knew that paradise could be as simple as good food, a good cup of coffee, and the company of a gorgeous woman?"

"I agree," Maya said, "though not necessarily with the order."

He grinned, feeling ridiculously happy. "I am a man," he reminded her. "Food and coffee are important to me."

"You remember you said that the next time Mr. Happy wakes up," she said, pointing to his lap.

He pushed back his chair to stare at his crotch. "You would pick now to be quiet," he said. "Look at the trouble you got me into. Now the stomach's going to ruin everything you worked so hard for. What do you have to say for yourself?"

He pretended to listen to his anatomy as Maya erupted into giggles. "Come on, man, speak up! What do you have to say for yourself?" He looked at Maya, whose face was red with laughter. "He told me to tell you that there is nothing more important in heaven or earth than a beautiful woman, especially when that woman is you."

She grinned at him. "Such flattery, Mr. Whitfield. One would think you're a poet instead of a doctor."

"It's not flattery, Maya," he said. "I mean it. You're amazing. I keep using that word, but it fits. Being with you has been amazing from day one, and it just keeps getting better."

"Nick." She dipped her head in embarrassment.

"It's true. When I woke up this morning and saw you beside me, I just…if it was a dream, I didn't want to wake up."

She reached over then, lightly pinching the back of his hand. "No dream. I'm still here, feeling incredibly lucky to have you."

He turned his hand over, capturing hers. "You know I won't be content with just one night. I want more than one day with you, Maya. More than one stolen weekend."

"Have you been talking to your daughter?"

The question threw him. "What, about you and me?" He shook his head. "That's not a conversation to have with a seven-year-old."

"Huh. You should have heard the conversation she had with me." He straightened, giving her his full attention. "What conversation?"

She glanced away. "The day I took her to work with me, on the drive home. She said—okay, it doesn't matter what she said, but your daughter has some definite ideas on our relationship."

Oh no. Nick suppressed a groan, remembering the talk he'd had with his daughter back before he and Maya started dating. "How definite?"

"About as bull's-eye as you can get," Maya answered. "She told me that if I married you, I could be her mother, and she really wants me to be her mother."

Yep, that definitely was definite. "What did you say?"

"What could I say?" she replied, spreading her hands. "I told her that things weren't that simple with adults. Then she asked me if we were boyfriend and girlfriend."

Taylor the Tenacious. He didn't know whether he should spank her or be proud of her for knowing what she wanted and going after it. "How did you answer her?"

Maya shrugged. "I hemmed and hawed and then said that we were. Then your seven going on seventeen-year-old announced that since we were boyfriend and girlfriend, we could move in together because that's what her friend's mom did and now her friend has a daddy."

"God." He put his head in his hands.

"That was pretty much my reaction, too," she said softly. "I didn't know what to say, so I just said that adults take their time with things like this, and it could take a long time. Then I changed the subject."

He sighed. "Taylor, what am I going to do with you?"

"You're not going to talk to her about it," Maya said. "I'm extremely touched that she thinks I'm mother material. That meant a lot to me."

Nick thought Maya great mother material himself, among other things. He kept his opinion to himself, though. Being intimate with Maya had taken their relationship to a whole new level, and he knew they both needed time to sort out what that meant.

Still, "I want to make this work, for all of us and on every level. I'm going to do my best to make it work, because I'm nowhere near ready to give you up, Maya. I hope you know that."

"I want to make this work, too, Nick, I really do. But I have to tell you, I would feel strange making love with you while Taylor's sleeping down the hall. You don't even want to explain the birds and the bees to her. How would you explain my presence every night and first thing in the morning?"

"I don't know." He sighed again. Their relationship was nobody's business but their own, so he didn't give a toss what his neighbors thought. Taylor, however, was a different story. She was only seven. Maybe she knew more than he thought she did, especially if Maya's conversation with her was any indication, but he wanted to live in blissful denial for a couple of years longer, if he could. It didn't matter that it was a new century. He didn't want his seven-year-old to see him shacking up with anyone, even if that anyone was someone she adored.

"We'll think of something," he said with more confidence than he felt. He had to think of something soon, because he knew one weekend with Maya would never be enough.

NINETEEN

As luck would have it, Maya's family seemed to sense their need to spend more time together. Nadine offered up several weekends at her house with Maya's nieces. Her parents wanted to have all the grandkids and Taylor stay with them during the week so that they could take advantage of an educational day camp. Then there was overnight camp for two weeks, and Leila and Tamera had convinced Nick to let Taylor join them.

"Does your whole family know we're doing it?" Nick complained as yet another of Maya's siblings offered to take all of the kids on another outing.

"They either know we're doing it, or know we're wanting to do it," she replied, grinning at him. "And honestly, we've been doing this for Dina and Kevin and even Jericho for a couple of years. I guess it's finally my turn."

"Far be it from me to refuse help," he declared, dragging her close. "Especially if it helps me get into your pants."

She slapped at his hands. "If you want to go there, you better go over Taylor's camp list with her while I finish up the food for our picnic. We have to put her on the bus tomorrow morning, remember?"

He remembered, and tried not to feel guilty about having some quiet time with Maya. But Taylor seemed just as eager to get away, chattering excitedly about going to overnight camp with her bestest friends and fellow princesses.

To celebrate, Maya had decided on a picnic, and invited Nadine and Kevin to come along, too. It was the perfect day for a picnic. Fluffy clouds that looked like cotton balls pulled apart dotted an azure sky. A breeze teased through the trees, dampening the edge of the day's heat.

The park they chose was an older one filled with huge shade trees. Nick and Kevin set up their spot while the girls, Maya and her sister brought out the food and games. Soon the women were racing between the trees, shrieking with laughter as they played tag.

"Want a beer?" Kevin asked, lifting the lid on a cooler.

"Sure, thanks."

Nick accepted the cold can, popped the top, then took a satisfactory swig. "That's what I'm talking about."

"Yep, I know exactly what you mean." He lifted his can in salute. "These women are amazing, aren't they?"

"That's the word I keep using," Nick said, turning to Kevin. "So it runs in the family?"

"Without a doubt." Kevin took another swig of his beet "They get it from their mother, whatever 'it' is. I fell for Dina the first day I met her. I'm guessing you did the same with Maya."

"I don't know about that," Nick hedged, not wanting to explore his relationship with Maya with anyone else. He'd barely begun to explore it with himself. He certainly wasn't ready to talk about his feelings.

Kevin laughed, deep and loud. "You know," he said sagely. "You just don't know you know."

Kevin's words stayed with him the rest of the day. Sometimes he just had to stop and look at Maya, amazed that such a beautiful woman wanted him and adored his daughter. After Jessica, he hadn't thought he'd ever have anything like this, this sense of bone-deep satisfaction. Maybe it was time, he thought, to forget about the past and start looking towards the future. Maybe Maya was the one to help him do that.

<hr />

"Come on, Dina, give me a Hail Mary pass!" Maya yelled. "We can't let the guys beat us."

She broke into a run as her sister launched the Frisbee. Running in a side pattern, she tracked the bright-orange disk as it began to glide down. She heard yelling, loud and insistent as she reached for the Frisbee. Her fingers brushed against the plastic edge just as the toe of her sneaker caught against a tree root. Momentum carried her forward, gravity pulled her down. An ominous crack split the air as her left foot slipped out from under her, sending her crashing against the tree. The last thing she remembered was slipping to the ground.

"Maya? Come on, Maya, answer me."

It took a couple of tries to get her eyes open. "Nick?"

His face, pale with worry, loomed over her. "Thank God you're all right."

"I hurt."

"You should. You crashed head-on into that tree. Your ankle looks like it's broken. I've iced it, but the paramedics will stabilize it when they get here."

"Paramedics?" she asked, confused. "Why paramedics?"

"Sweetheart, you've been unconscious for the last two minutes."

"Oh, that's bad, isn't it?"

He tried to smile and failed. "Yeah. That's pretty bad."

She took a deep breath. Pain knifed through her, making her nauseous. "I think I'm going to throw up."

"Move your head if you have to, not your body," he ordered, putting a hand lightly on her chest. "I don't know how badly you're injured, and I don't want to make your condition worse."

She closed her eyes, her smile more a grimace. "Trust me, I'm not going anywhere."

"Good." His hands cupped her cheeks. "Open your eyes for me. Do you feel any dizziness?"

"Nah…yes," she admitted. "Maybe that's why I want to up-chuck."

His hands moved over her from head to toe, gentle yet sure. When he reached her right ankle, she hissed. "I think we have a winner," he announced.

She groaned. "Funny, I don't feel like a winner. Is it all right if I pass out now?"

"No, you are not to pass out, do you understand?" Nick's face loomed over her again. "Stay with me, dammit!"

"You don't have to yell," she complained. "My ears ain't broken."

"Daddy, is Maya gonna die?" Taylor asked.

Taylor's worried voice snapped Maya's eyes open, and she answered before Nick could. "Of course not." Her vision swam. "I'm just…going to rest here a moment."

"She'll be just fine, pumpkin, soon as we get to the hospital," he decided.

Maya opened her eyes to see a sizeable crowd hovering over them. "I don't think that's necessary, Nick. Surely it's just a sprain."

"Hey, which one of us is the doctor here?" He looked up and past her. "Will you guys be able to get everything together? Taylor and I are going to follow the ambulance."

"Kevin's doing that now," Dina said, leaning over Maya. "Are you all right?"

"I'm fine," she lied. "Don't you dare call Mama."

"Nick?" Dina appealed for help.

Nick turned back to Maya. "It looks like your ankle's broken," he told her, his voice remote and professional. "In a few minutes, it'll be the size of a Christmas ham. And you may have a slight concussion. I can't say for sure, but one thing I do know is that you're going to the hospital."

"Yes, doctor." She closed her eyes.

"Maya, stay awake." Nick's voice cut through the fog that shrouded her brain.

She opened her eyes and focused on him again. "My leg hurts so bad it's going numb."

"That's because I put ice on it, to try to keep the swelling down."

The paramedics arrived. Maya kept quiet as she suffered the necessary embarrassment of being strapped into a neck brace and placed on a board as

Nick recited complex medical terms she couldn't pronounce, not to mention understand.

As they lifted her onto a stretcher, she caught a glimpse of Taylor and her nieces, all three crying hysterically. "Let me talk to them," she pleaded. "I have to show them that I'm all right."

At Nick's nod they stopped and she motioned the girls forward. "Don't try to touch her," Nick cautioned.

The girls crowded close. "I'm all right, fellow princesses," she told them. "It will take more than a mean old tree to get the best of me, all right?"

The girls nodded, wiping at their eyes. "I'm going to the hospital now, but if the doctors say it's okay, you can come see me. If not, I'll definitely call you. Right now, I need you to mind Dina, okay?"

They nodded again, and Nick gestured for the paramedics to load her She was proud of herself. She waited until the doors dosed before she gave in to tears.

<center>~~~</center>

"Gary, how bad is it?"

"Not too bad." Markowitz put an X-ray up on the screen. Nick winced. "She's got a good break, we should be able to patch it with no problem. Since she's got a small contusion on her forehead, we'll probably want to keep her for a couple of hours, maybe even overnight."

"I can observe her at home."

"Really?" Gary eyes brightened with curiosity.

"Really. She's not going to want to stay here, and believe me, you're not going to want her entire clan descending on you questioning your medical credentials."

Gary smiled. "Maybe you just don't want me putting the moves on your lady friend."

Nick smiled. Gary was very married, very short, and very devoted to his wife. "Exactly. I'll sit up with her, make sure she's okay."

"All right. As soon as she gets casted, I'll check her over. If I like what I see, I'll release her into your care."

"Fine. And you'd better like what you see."

TWENTY

By the time Nick rolled her wheelchair out to the car several hours later, Maya was more than ready to leave the hospital. Nadine and Kevin had done such an excellent job of informing her family that she'd had to field phone call after phone call, assuring every sibling, cousin, parent and friend that she wasn't seriously injured. It was just a broken ankle, not major surgery, and she wasn't staying in the hospital, so no one needed to worry. Besides, she had a very special doctor right next door.

Grateful to be home at last, Maya tried to get out of the car, but her new fashion accessory—a bright blue cast and matching crutches—made it impossible. Nick came around to the passenger side as she opened the door, then scooped her up into his arms.

"Nick, this really isn't necessary," she said, feeling heat creep up her cheeks.

He carried her toward his house. "I know you're an independent woman, but humor me, okay? I want to know you'll be okay for my own peace of mind."

Taylor hurried ahead, unlocking the door and holding it open for them. Nick carried Maya to the couch, gently depositing her among the cushions. "I'm going to freshen up the guest bedroom," he told her. "Use that notepad there and make a list of things you need from your house, and I'll go get them."

"You're kidding, right?" Maya asked when she could find her voice. "You want me to stay here?"

"Yep." Nick pushed an ottoman towards her, then lifted her leg into place. "There's no way I can sit over here without worrying about you trying to navigate your stairs with crutches."

"Nick, you don't have to do this for me. I'll be fine by myself."

"You want the truth? I'm not doing it for you. I'm doing it for me, and my own peace of mind."

"But—"

"Maya. You've taken care of me and Taylor for the last few months. Let us return the favor, okay?"

How could she argue with that? "Okay."

He smiled at her as he thrust the pad and pen towards her. "Now will you please make a list of things you think you'll need for the next couple of days?"

Well, maybe she could argue. "Couple of days?"

"Doctor's orders. I have to keep you up for a while to make sure you don't have a concussion, and I want to make sure there are no other ill effects from your spill today." He gave her a stern glare, and she wondered if his patients felt the way she felt then. "Or you could return to the hospital and let them keep you overnight for observation."

"No, thanks." She'd had enough of hospitals and doctors and tests to last a lifetime. If she had to choose, she'd choose Nick every time. She quickly scribbled a list of things she thought she'd need, adding her laptop and mobile phone charger as an afterthought. She'd call her boss in the morning and give him the news. It wasn't a catastrophe since she did the bulk of her work via modem, but she had a feeling she'd be little in the way of good until she could manage the pain and the medicine.

"I think that's everything I need," she said, returning the pad to him. "There's a carry-on suitcase in the closet in the guest bedroom. Oh, and will you bring some food for Hamlet and Horatio?"

"Will do." Nick added to her list, then turned to Taylor. "Pumpkin, why don't you stay here with Maya until I get back?"

"'Kay, Daddy."

Taylor turned a serious face to Maya after Nick left. "Do you want some water or Kool-Aid?"

"No, I don't need anything right now. Why don't you come sit by me?"

Taylor hopped onto the couch beside her. Maya looped her arm around the little girl's shoulders. She grew concerned as the child began to shake. "Taylor, are you all right?"

A sniffle answered her. "Taylor honey, talk to me. What's wrong?"

"I-I thought you were gonna die," the young girl said, her voice wavering. "I saw you hit the tree and I thought you were gonna die."

"Oh, Taylor." With an awkward motion, Maya pulled the girl into her arms. "I'm so sorry you had to see that. But I'm all right now, and in a few weeks I'll be even better."

"I don't want you to go away," Taylor said against her neck.

"I'm not going anywhere," Maya whispered, her voice thick. "As long as I can, I'll be here for you."

She sat the child back, brushing the tears from her cheeks. "We're friends and fellow princesses, remember? I'm going to try to always be around for you."

"I don't want you to be my friend!" Taylor exclaimed, fresh tears streaking her face. "I want you to be my mommy!"

Maya froze, not sure she'd actually heard Taylor correctly. The little girl shivered against her and spoke again. "I want you to stay here and live with me and my Daddy and love us and be a family."

"Taylor." Maya pulled the child close, her throat choked with tears. "I do love you."

"Then why won't you be my mommy?"

She didn't really have an answer for that. She couldn't say, "Because your daddy hasn't asked me." This was the new century; she could do the asking if she wanted to. Did she want to?

"I'll tell you what," she said, stroking the girl's hair. "I don't know how to be a mommy, so we'll have to practice, okay? But it will have to be our secret. Don't let your father know."

She rocked the little girl, unmindful of the throbbing in her leg. She wanted to give Taylor her wish, wanted it with all her heart. But what did Nick want?

By the time Nick returned, Taylor had cried herself to sleep. "Sorry about that," he said, coming to scoop her up.

"Don't worry about it," she said quietly, stroking the child's hair. "She just needed a little reassurance."

"Reassurance about what?" he asked, finding room on the couch to sit beside her.

"She was afraid I was going to die."

The look on Nick's face made her regret the casualness of her words. "She wasn't the only one," he finally said. "Everything slowed down. I saw you heading for the tree, and I tried to yell at you to watch out. I remember breaking into a run, thinking I would get to you in time, but I didn't."

He drew in a shaky breath. "I saw you hit the tree a split second before I heard it. You fell down, and you were lying so still…"

"I'm sorry, Nick," she whispered, her heart aching with what she'd put them through.

He lifted her hand, pressing a kiss into her palm. "Just don't ever do that to me again," he admonished. "I don't think the old ticker can take another jolt like that."

"Don't worry," she said, looking down at her cast. "I think my Frisbee days are over."

He stood, then reached for Taylor. "Let me put her to bed, then I'll come back for you."

"Okay."

———

Nick lay in bed a long while later, unable to sleep. His thoughts kept returning to Maya, sleeping a floor below him. So close, and yet so far.

They should be together. He knew that. Taylor adored her, Maya adored Taylor. He was on the verge of falling for Maya himself. If the past few weeks were any indication, they had the potential of being a terrific family. Taylor wanted a mother, Maya wanted a child. He wanted a woman who could love Taylor as if his daughter were her own, and who could love him in return.

He sighed. Love was probably too much to ask for. After what he'd gone through with Jessie, he didn't think he had the ability to love again. He certainly didn't know if he could hear those promises from someone else, give his heart to someone else, only to lose them.

But Maya…Maya was different. He knew that. Something about her spoke to him, soothed his soul, warmed his heart. When he looked at her, he felt like a patient who'd heard the doctor tell him that everything would be all right.

Hope. That's what was different. Maya Hughes gave him hope that someday, somehow, all the wishes he and his daughter had could come true.

He glanced at the clock. It had been two hours since he'd seen Maya to bed, an hour since he'd come upstairs to try to sleep himself. He needed to check on her, to see for himself that she was all right. A simple day at the park had ended with a broken ankle. It could have been worse, much worse. She could have broken her neck, broken a rib and punctured her lung, had a major concussion, internal bleeding—He threw the covers back and got out of bed. He'd just sleep in the chair beside her bed tonight. Just for tonight, to make sure she got through it without problems. It had nothing to do with the sudden loneliness that roared through him, the need to see her. Nothing at all.

Outside her door he paused, pondering the wisdom of his actions. Maya needed her rest, not some overprotective lovesick doctor camped out at her bedside. His hand froze on the knob. Lovesick? No. He was gone, but he wasn't that far gone.

He'd turned away, heading for the relative compromise of sleeping on the couch when a soft whimper of noise stopped him. He turned back, opening the door. "Maya?"

Another whimper of sound reached him. He crossed the room to the bed, pausing before turning on the bedside lamp. "You're supposed to be resting."

"I'm trying," she said, a tremble audible in her voice. "But my ankle's bothering me."

He glanced at the clock on the nightstand. "It's time to take another close of medicine." He opened the drawer and took out a bottle of pills.

"I'm not going to get addicted to that stuff, am I?" she asked. "I mean, I can stand a little pain if I have to."

"I know you can. But I promised to take care of you, and that includes making the pain go away and seeing that you don't develop any dependencies. Trust me, all right?"

"I do trust you, Nick."

The soft, simple words tore through him. She trusted him, and he'd let her get hurt. She trusted him, and yet he hadn't told her the full story about his marriage. Was there any way that he could feel worse?

He had to clear his throat before he could speak. "Let me get you some water. Do you want anything else?"

She shook her head. He headed for the door, conscious of her gaze on his back. He was suddenly feeling as awkward as a teenager on his first date. He had no idea why he was suddenly feeling so edgy around Maya. They'd made love every chance they'd gotten since the Memorial Day weekend, and while his hunger for her hadn't abated, he knew every nuance of her body intimately. So why was he jittery now, with her in his house, staying the night in the guest bedroom?

He filled a glass of water and returned to the guest bedroom. She'd managed to raise herself into a sitting position, but she seemed exhausted by the effort. "I can't believe how this has knocked me for a loop. I feel so helpless."

"You're far from helpless," he informed her. "You're an amazingly strong woman."

"Not right now," she said in a thin voice. "I feel incredibly shaky for some reason."

"Take your medicine, it'll make you feel better."

"Yes, doctor." She dutifully accepted the glass of water and the pills, making a couple of attempts before she was able to swallow the capsules.

He took the empty glass from her, placing it on the nightstand. "May I?" he asked, gesturing to her leg.

When she nodded, he pulled the bedcovers down. Her nightgown was a deep rose color that made her skin look like peaches in the soft light. He remembered that her dresser drawer had been filled with delicate, lacy things. Jessie had never worn anything dressier than a t-shirt to bed. Seeing Maya in her gown, even one as demure as this, made him appreciate the business that lingerie stores did each year.

Telling himself he was checking for signs of infection, Nick ran his hands down the softness of her leg. She shivered. "Did that hurt?" he asked softly, lifting his hands slightly.

"No," she whispered back. "I guess my nerves are a little oversensitive right now."

"Really?" Nick picked up her prescription to read the label again. "This is supposed to ease your pain, not sensitize you. I'll talk to your doctor in the morning, see if he can prescribe something else for you."

He put the bottle back on the nightstand. "Other than a little sensitivity, are you feeling okay?"

"I think so," she said softly. He could feel her eyes on him as he propped up her foot and covered her with the bedclothes again. "Thank you."

He started down into her face, wanting to say so many things, but not sure what the words were. "Then I'll let you get back to sleep." He turned and headed for the door.

"Nick?"

"Hhm?"

"Will you stay here with me, for a little while?"

He turned back to face her. Her face, scrubbed free of makeup, looked incredibly young and unsure in the soft lamplight. He didn't want to leave her, couldn't if he'd tried. "Of course."

He climbed atop the covers, then lay beside her, making sure a respectable distance remained between them. "Are you comfortable enough?"

She half-rolled to face him. "I think so," she whispered. "The pillows help."

Nick reached for the blanket at the foot of the bed. As tempting as it was, he couldn't get beneath the covers with Maya. If he did, he wouldn't be able to keep his hands to himself. As it was, he covered himself with the blanket and took her hand in his. "I'm so sorry you got hurt, Maya."

"It's not your fault. You weren't the one treating the Frisbee like a 'Hail Mary' pass in a bowl game." She smiled softly. "You have to admit, it was a beautiful catch."

Nick laughed. "All right, you win. It was a terrific catch."

Maya shifted closer to him. "There's that smile I love."

The admission surprised and pleased him. "You like my smile?"

"I love your smile," she corrected. "It lights up your whole face, and makes you beautiful. When you first smiled at me, I was like, 'whoa.' I was stunned."

Nick twined his fingers in hers. He knew the strength of the pain medicine Maya had, and told himself not to put too much into her words. Still, that didn't mean that he couldn't enjoy the conversation. "I don't think I've ever been called beautiful before."

"Don't go getting offended on me. I meant it as a compliment."

"I'm taking it as one. I don't get a lot of them."

She closed her eyes, and Nick spent a few moments just staring at her. Dark brows and lashes stood out in the creamy tan of her face. Her cheek curved soft and full, making his fingers itch with the desire to stroke it.

He gave in to the urge, lifting his free hand to rest his fingertips lightly against her skin, not wanting to disturb her as she drifted off to sleep. He could touch her like this, stare at her like this, every night for the rest of his life and consider himself the luckiest man alive.

"Nick?"

"Yes, Maya?"

"I think you should kiss me now."

He didn't need to be told twice. He leaned forward to capture her lips, puffing as much comfort and tenderness into the touch as he could. Maya sighed against his mouth, a soft, pleased sound. She pulled away slightly and opened her eyes. The look she gave him stole his breath and sent his heart rate into the stratosphere.

"I'm falling in love with you," she whispered. "It's kinda scary, but it's also kinda cool."

His brain short-circuited. He couldn't think of a single word to say. Only one word came to mind. "Maya..."

"Shut up," she said, putting a finger against his lips. "Don't ruin the moment."

He didn't. Instead, he cupped her fingers in his, pressing kisses to the back of her hand, knowing that he'd been given a precious gift and feeling extremely grateful for that.

"Nick?"

"Hhm?"

"I'm glad I'm here, and you're here with me."

———

Taylor crept down the stairs, careful not to make any noise. Sometimes she woke up in the middle of the night because Daddy fell asleep on the sofa sometimes. She'd turn off the TV, cover him with a blanket, then go back upstairs to her room. It made her feel good to think that she could sometimes do things for her dad the way he did things for her.

The TV in the living room sat silent, the couch empty. Taylor knew he wasn't upstairs in bed. Not finding him in the kitchen either, she decided to go to Maya's room. Outside the open door, she paused. One of her friends had told her about catching her parents kissing and pressing against each other. Was that what Daddy and Maya were doing? Only moms and dads did that, right?

Taylor hugged herself. She really wanted Maya to be her new mother. Maya made her feel all warm inside, and she didn't seem to mind when Taylor asked her all sorts of questions. She crossed every body part she could, including her eyes. "Please, please, please," she whispered, then peeked around the door.

Hamlet and Horatio raised their heads from the floor. She could see her dad on his side in the bed. Maya faced him, her cast balanced carefully. They were asleep, holding hands. Taylor grinned, and had to cover her mouth to hold in a whoop of excitement. They were going to be a family, really, really soon.

Shushing the pets, she carefully crawled onto the bed between Maya and her Daddy. She curled against Maya, facing her dad. He looked happy. She liked that.

"Thank you, God," she whispered, then linked her hand gently through theirs and settled into sleep.

TWENTY-ONE

Maya awakened to a paw in the middle of her back and a cold nose between her shoulder blades. She blinked her eyes open blearily, feeling her limbs as unresponsive as if they were encased in lead. In the early morning light she saw Taylor's dark head tucked up against her, with Nick on the other side. She remembered Nick coming in, making sure she was okay, but she didn't remember Taylor coming in. She didn't mind, though. She didn't mind at all.

"Wake up, sleepyheads," she called softly.

Nick stirred first, blinking and yawning into wakefulness. He gave her a sleepy-eyed smile, a smile that became an "O" of surprise as he caught sight of his daughter nestled between them.

"When did she get down here?" he whispered.

"No idea," she whispered back. "But it's okay. Can you let Hamlet and Horatio out for me? I'll wake her up."

He agreed, slipping carefully out of bed, calling for her pets to follow him. "Come on, Sleeping Beauty, it's Camp Day."

Taylor stretched, then sat up, blinking her eyes slowly. "I don't want to go. I want to stay here with you."

"Of course you want to go," Maya said, trying to reassure the little girl. "Leila and Tamera are still going."

Taylor pouted. "But—"

"You know if we're going to practice this mommy thing, that means you have to do what I say," Maya pointed out. "I want you to go on your camping trip and have butt-loads of fun."

Taylor broke into a giggle. "You said butt-loads."

"No, I didn't."

"Yes, you did."

"No, I didn't."

"Yes, you did."

Maya reached out to tickle the child. "No, I didn't."

"Children." Nick's voice had them freezing in their tracks. Maya and Taylor turned to see Nick standing in the doorway, holding a glass of water with his arms folded across his chest, an inscrutable expression in his eyes.

"Uh-oh, that's his doctor voice," Taylor said to Maya. "That means you have to do what he says."

"That's right. That means you get to go upstairs and get ready for camp. And you," he added, turning to Maya, "are supposed to be taking it easy."

"I am taking it easy," she argued, though the little tickling bout had tired her out. She lay back down. "See? This is me, taking it easy."

"Good." He crossed the room to her, handing her the glass of water. "Time for meds."

"Can't I get my meds in the form of a cup of coffee?" she asked.

"Nope. It's punishment for overexerting yourself with all that tickling."

She dutifully took her medicine, looking up at him through half-lowered lashes. "And what do I get for good behavior?" she wondered.

He broke into a smile. "You're impossible, you know that?"

"I know." She leaned back against the covers. "You love me anyway."

She didn't mean to let the words slip, and regretted them as soon as she saw him stiffen. Before she could apologize, he dropped a kiss on her forehead. "Let me go check on Taylor."

She sighed after he left, closing her eyes as she settled down. She didn't want to push him. She certainly didn't want him to make any promises or claims if he didn't want to. Still, it smarted that he hadn't reciprocated her declaration of love. Okay, it more than smarted. It stung like crazy.

Maybe she'd scared him with her accident yesterday. Maybe she'd reminded him of Jessica, and how powerless he'd been to save her. But she wasn't his late wife. He needed to realize that.

Father and daughter returned, fully dressed and bearing coffee and a muffin for her. "Thought you might like something to eat before we left," Nick said, putting the steaming mug on the nightstand.

"Oh yeah," she said, accepting the mug from Taylor. "Give us a hug before you go?"

Taylor carefully slipped her arms around Maya's waist. "Promise me that you'll have fun and write lots of letters and make me something nice for me while you're at camp, okay?"

"I promise," Taylor said as she straightened.

Maya touched the tip of her forefinger to the child's nose. "I'll be right here when you get back."

She glanced up expectantly as Nick approached her. He lifted her broken ankle and resettled it on the plump pillow at the end of the bed. "Call me if you need me."

She let him get as far as the door before she called his name. When he turned to face her, she asked, "Am I your patient?"

"No."

"Then why are you treating me like one?"

He frowned. "I don't know what you're talking about."

"I don't expect you to kiss your patients goodbye, but I do expect, as your girlfriend, to be kissed goodbye properly."

A fire sparked deep in his eyes, though his face remained set in stern lines. Maya heard Taylor smother a giggle as Nick walked towards her. He leaned over her, tilting her chin up. Maya closed her eyes, wanting the kiss that always made her knees weak.

She was disappointed. The kiss she received was nearly chaste, barely any emotion in it at all. She didn't even try to make the kiss something more. "Thanks," she said dryly. "I feel much better already."

He quickly straightened, so quickly Maya would swear she thought she heard his back crack. "Drive carefully," she said before he could say anything. "And both of you, have a great day."

She kept a smile on her face until they left, then sank back against the pillows. She never should have told him how she felt. Maybe if she were lucky, he'd accept an apology and explanation that her ill-timed declaration was the product of drugs, nothing more. If she were lucky, she'd come to believe it herself.

***

"Maya, wake up."

She blinked, rubbing at her eyes. "Nick, what are you doing here?"

"You didn't eat your breakfast," he said, pointing to the untouched coffee and muffin.

"I wasn't hungry," she said, attempting to sit up.

He helped her, piling pillows behind her back. "Would you like something else? You have to eat something."

The overly solicitous nature was beginning to work her last nerve. "I thought you were going to work after dropping Taylor off."

"I called in, said I had a family emergency and that I'd be late," Nick said, sitting beside her. "I want to make sure you have everything you need. Mrs. Henderson will be here about noon, and I know your mother plans on dropping by, but I don't want to leave you alone that long."

"I can take care of myself, you know," she said without censure. Honestly, she appreciated the attention he gave her, but she didn't want him to feel any sort of obligation to her. "I have a broken ankle. I'm not helpless."

"I know. But I thought there might be a few things I could set up for you in the living room so that you won't overexert yourself."

"I've gotten plenty of rest," she pointed out, fighting the feeling of being trapped. "I'm ready for a little exertion."

"There's a good girl," he teased. "Now, would you like to take a shower?"

"Can I?" she asked, eagerness pulling her upright. She thought she'd have to face sponge baths for the next eight weeks.

"Of course," Nick said. He gestured to a mound of plastic she hadn't noticed before. "We just need to make sure you don't get your cast wet."

"I won't," she promised, sliding her feet to the floor. Nick knelt before her, lifting her mangled ankle carefully to slip a plastic bag over it. He secured the bag with a large rubber band, then wrapped plastic wrap around it before slipping another heavy-duty plastic bag and rubber band over it all.

"Nothing's getting through that," Maya joked, lifting her leg to view his handiwork.

"That's the idea," Nick said, straightening. He reached for the crutches leaning against the wall beside the nightstand.

She took the crutches he offered her, then slowly levered herself to an upright position. She felt a little wobbly but grateful to be out of bed.

"It's probably going to be best if you shower upstairs in my bathroom," Nick explained as they headed for the stairs. "The shower's big enough for you to maneuver in."

"Sounds good," she said, "but I don't think I'm getting up the stairs on these things." It had tired her out just navigating the short distance from the guest room to the stairs.

"If you don't mind me getting all Tarzan on you…" He scooped her into his arms, then made his way up the stairs. Maya held his shoulders and her breath, trying to make herself as light as possible and not think about tumbling down the flight and landing at the bottom with worse than a shattered ankle.

"You can breathe now," Nick said, setting her down on her good foot.

"How do you know I wasn't?" she asked, hobbling beside him down the hall.

"You tensed up as soon as I picked you up," he explained. "My male ego has been bruised."

"Are you kidding me? You made it up the stairs and you're not even breathing hard."

"That's because your cast weighs more than you do." He led her into the bathroom and to the shower stall, opening the frosted glass door. "I put in more of those non-skid stick-on things, and a stool for you to sit down on. The main showerhead detaches from the wall. Just give a yell if you need anything."

"Uhm," she hummed, clutching the crutch she'd managed to hang onto during the trek up the stairs.

"I hate to say this, but I don't think I'm going to be able to do this by myself."

"It's all right. I'll help you, and I swear I'll be a perfect gentleman."

"I don't need you to be a perfect gentleman. I need you to get me into the shower stall without looking like an idiot."

Nick quirked a smile at her. "Would it help if I said you'd be the most beautiful idiot I've ever seen?"

"No."

"Can I think it?"

She smiled. "No."

Handing him the crutch, she balanced herself by placing a hand on his shoulder. She'd shrugged out of one pale blue strap before he'd placed the crutch in the corner. He held her steady with one hand to her waist while he slipped the other strap from her left arm. A shiver of pure female excitement bubbled up her spine as the silken gown puddled at her feet. How could someone feel sexy with a couple of pounds of plaster on their foot? Maya didn't know, but the way Nick stared at her made her feel aware that she had a power to use to her advantage.

He helped her step out of the gown, then lifted her in his arms again. "You're getting pretty good at this," she whispered.

"One thing for sure, I don't mind the practice," he whispered back, easing her into the tiled stall.

He held her steady, balancing her as she sat on the stool. "I feel like I'm ninety years old," she complained.

"You'll feel a lot better in a few minutes," he assured her, turning on the faucets.

Warm water, just a hair below hot, cascaded over Her. She closed her eyes, tilting her head back with a sigh. "This feels wonderful."

"Good. I'll give you some privacy now."

Maya sighed as the door closed, then lifted the showerhead to let the water sluice over her head. She told herself not to be bothered by Nick's diffident attitude, but she was. She realized now that she'd made a mistake by telling him her feelings and expecting him to have feelings in return. She had to tell him that she had no expectations from him, and he shouldn't feel pressured. Maybe then he'd warm up to her again.

"I'm sorry, Nick."

"Sorry for what?"

She jumped, not expecting him to still be in the bathroom with her. "I, uhm…" She took a deep breath. "I'm sorry for what I said to last night, and this morning. I didn't mean to put you on the spot like that. Just blame it on the medicine knocking me for a loop and forget it ever happened, okay?"

He remained silent. She hung her head, wondering if she'd blundered yet again.

The shower door opened. Nick stood there, wondrously naked. "I thought I'd offer to scrub your back for you."

"I'd like that, very much."

She watched as Nick's hands squeezed bath gel onto a plastic green puff, rubbing it to lather between his fingers. Her mouth went dry despite the steaminess of the shower as he helped her to her feet. The hand holding the puff moved over her body in gentle yet sure strokes, leaving her skin tingling and her senses reeling. He kept her balanced with his free hand at her waist even as she held onto his shoulders for dear life.

"Can I wash your hair for you?" he asked quietly.

Unable to speak, she nodded once, then carefully turned around. He lifted the shower head, sending warm rivulets of water through her hair. Sliding her eyes shut, Maya gave in to the sensual experience of having her hair shampooed.

His fingers worked lather through her hair, his fingertips massaging her scalp. The gentle ministrations soothed her, made her forget her pain and her helplessness and the outside world. She could feel the heat of his body as he stepped close to rinse her hair. She rested a hand lightly in the curve of his neck, balancing herself as he ran water and his free hand through her hair.

She felt him shift, and the water changed to the multidirectional spouts. He wrapped his arms about her, holding her close. There was nothing sexual or distant in his hold; instead she felt as if he were seeking comfort.

She turned in his arms, pressing her face against his chest, wrapping her arms tightly about his waist. She didn't want to ruin the moment with words, hoping that her body would tell him everything that he needed to know.

Finally he turned the water off, then helped her out of the stall. Silently he pulled a large navy towel from the rack beside them, squeezing water from her hair before wrapping it around her The expression he wore shone with such tenderness and something she couldn't name, she lost her breath. "Nick," she managed to say.

"I know," he whispered. "I know."

He lifted her in his arms once more, carrying her into his bedroom to deposit her on the bed. His fingers smoothed the towel over her skin, and it was all she could do not to moan. His slow, steady attention dried her skin but drenched her insides, causing steamy erotic thoughts to fill her mind.

With slow strokes, he ran the towel up her good leg, drying her skin but leaving her warm. Then he switched to her other leg, taking care to dry the plastic that still encased her cast. Next, he peeled away the plastic layers to free her cast. He pushed the towel up her thighs, and her legs fell open under his touch.

Her breath caught as he smoothed the towel over the sensitive skin of her inner thigh, the dark nest of curls. Desire had her pushing her hips forward in silent invitation. She raised her eyes to his, realizing from his expression that desire had as strong a hold on him. This time his fingers, not the towel, provided the intimate touch, and she let her head drop back with a sigh of satisfaction.

His thumb brushed over the crest of her arousal, once, twice, three times. Then she felt the delicious pressure of his fingers entering her, slowly advancing and retreating. Her limbs went weak, causing her to fall back against the covers. Still his fingers continued the erotic massage, loosening and winding tight her body and her senses.

She felt him shift and pull his fingers away. She whimpered in disappointment until she felt his lips brushing against her inner thigh. "Yes," she whispered, urging him on. "Oh yes."

Lifting her hips with his arms, he swept her crest with his tongue, and she moaned again. Again and again he delved into her, taking her to the brink before easing back. All she could do was call his name, begging, praying, demanding, needing. Her climax struck her with lighting force, causing her to cry out as her entire body began to shake until she feared she'd fall apart.

Nick drew her to the edge of the bed, then entered her while she still shook. She came again, her body going into overload as he made love to her.

And he was making love to her, she knew, being mindful of her leg as he surged into her with powerful, sure strokes. She dragged open her eyes to find him staring at her. The intensity of his stare and the effectiveness of his lovemaking sent her careening over the edge of ecstasy, shattering emotionally and physically. When she gasped her pleasure again he joined her, pouring into her the joy of his release.

He moved just enough to take his weight off her. She stared up into his beautiful face, moist from the shower and lovemaking, and…tears?

She reached up to cup his cheek. He captured her hand and planted a kiss in her palm. "You've sent me on an emotional roller-coaster ride the last couple of days," he told her, his voice unsteady. "I watched you get hurt. I watched you comfort my daughter and joke your way through your pain. And then you told me that you loved me."

He swallowed. "You gave me a gift, and I couldn't believe it. In just a couple of months you've made the last eight years of pain fade to the past. You've brought me and my daughter sunshine, and I love you for it."

He smiled down at her "I've been freefalling in love with you, Maya Hughes. Now I'm there, and it makes me feel damn good."

"Nick," she breathed, her voice too thick to say anything more.

"Ssh," he said, giving her a soft smile. "Don't spoil the moment."

TWENTY-TWO

"Daddy!" Taylor yelled down the stairs, "Gamma wants to talk to you!"

"Okay, honey!" Nick found the cordless and punched the talk button. "Hey, Mom, where are you guys calling from this week?"

"We're in Dollywood right now."

Since retirement, his parents had bought an RV and spent their summers tooling around the country before stopping by for a visit and taking Taylor to spend time with them in Orlando. "When are you guys coming through?"

"Next week, but that's not why I wanted to talk to you." Uh-oh. When his mother took that tone, Nick knew the conversation threatened to take a turn for the worse. "What is it?"

"This woman that you're seeing," Victoria Whitfield began. "Taylor's been telling me about her for weeks. I haven't asked you about it, because I didn't think you had the time to get serious. I've heard from your daughter, however, that this woman has spent the night in your house, and that my grand-daughter was there."

"Her name is Maya, and yes, she did spend the night here," Nick said, growing defensive and not liking it one bit. "Three weeks ago, as a matter of fact, when she broke her ankle, and a couple of times since then. I wanted to make sure she'd be okay."

"But Taylor—"

"What about Taylor?"

"She's an impressionable child, Nicolas," his mother said. "You should be careful what you expose her to."

"Expose?" Blood pounded in Nick's ears as he cradled his head in his hand. "You're making it sound like Maya's a disease, and I don't appreciate it."

"I'm sure she's a sweet girl. I'm also sure that there are plenty of women in Atlanta who would be more compatible than a black Vietnamese woman."

Somehow he resisted the urge to groan. "For the record, Maya and I are compatible, more than you know," he said with exaggerated patience. "Compatibility isn't based on color. It's based on personality and experience and emotion. We get along great together, and she and Taylor adore each other. I couldn't ask for more."

Victoria Whitfield switched to another tactic. "How do you think your father is going to react to this? You know he lost a brother in Vietnam."

Nick rolled his eyes. "Good grief, Mom. Neither Maya nor her mother pulled the trigger! I would expect Dad—and you—to be happy that I've found someone who loves me and my child."

"How serious are you about this woman?"

"Very serious," he replied.

"Nicolas, think about this," his mother urged. "Think about your position at the hospital. Think about your future. Think about how Taylor will feel with brothers and sisters who don't look like her."

He remained silent for a moment, fighting the urge to yell at his mother. "Mom, listen to me. My future is with Maya. My work and my personal life have nothing to do with each other, and frankly, I don't give a damn what people at the hospital think about who I'm with. Taylor adores Maya and her family and wants Maya to be her mother."

His mother drew in a sharp breath. "She said that?"

"Yes, she did, several weeks ago. Look, Mom, I love you, but I can't accept you making snap judgments about someone you haven't even met. Why don't you hold your opinion until you get here and meet her? Then you'll see for yourself why Taylor and I love Maya."

"And if I don't see it?"

"Then I'll tell you to get over it," he answered, his voice harsh. "Maya's in our lives to stay, and you'll just have to deal with that or not. It's up to you."

"You'd choose this woman over your own parents?" she asked, outraged.

"If you recall, Mom, I chose a girl you adored. Look at how that turned out."

Silence answered him, but Nick knew he'd made his point. "I don't expect you to be holding hands and singing Disney songs," he said gently. "But I do expect you to treat Maya with courtesy and respect. Can you do that for me? For Taylor?"

His mother sighed. "All right. You're a grown man. You don't need my blessing anymore."

"You're right, I don't," he said, keeping his voice soft. "But I do want your acceptance."

After getting a date and time of arrival from his mother, Nick disconnected, then dropped the phone onto the couch beside him. His mother's reaction surprised and hurt him. He'd always thought of his parents as warm, accepting people, and it was hard to reconcile his memories with his mother's conversation.

Why should Maya's color matter? Why shouldn't the most important thing be that she loved him and his daughter? Maybe once his parents met her and spent time with her, they would understand why Maya was such a necessary part of his life.

And if they couldn't understand it…Well, he'd deal with that when and if it happened.

On the way home from the movies that night, Nick decided to break the news. "My parents will be coming down next week."

"Really."

That one word said nothing and everything. "Yeah, they come up every year to stay for a couple of days before taking Taylor on vacation with them."

"And?"

The one word replies were beginning to make his teeth hurt. He darted a quick glance at her. She wore a pleasant enough expression, but her hands gripped her purse a little too tightly.

"And I want you to have dinner with us. With them."

"You want me to meet your parents?" Maya asked.

"I'd like it very much," he admitted.

"You'll like Gamma and Pa-Pa," Taylor piped up from the backseat. "They're very nice, and we have a lot of fun."

"I'll bet you do."

"Yep," his little girl said. "I told Gamma all about you. She really wants to meet you."

He could almost feel Maya glance back at him. "Is that so?"

"Sure is," Taylor said. "You'll like her, you'll see."

"All right, your father and I will talk about it later."

Nick knew from the tone of her voice that it wouldn't be an easy discussion.

Half an hour later, they sat at the dining room table drinking coffee. "Your parents really want to meet me?"

"Yeah. They're curious about you."

She ran a finger around the rim of her mug. "I guess that's to be expected."

"So I was thinking that we'd all have dinner together, then maybe take in a ballgame over the weekend."

"A sedate, structured dinner and the rowdiness of a day at the ballpark," she murmured. "Why don't you drop us off on a deserted island and see who survives?"

"Maya."

"I'm sorry, Nick," she said quickly, reaching over to clasp his hand. "I'm nervous about meeting your parents. And I can tell by your expression that it's not going to be all hugs and kisses."

He sighed, giving her hand a squeeze. "Probably not," he admitted, wishing things could be different, easier.

"So who do I have to worry about most?" she asked. "Your mother or your father?"

He wanted to play it off. "Who says you have to worry about either of them?"

She gave him a look that said he was out of his mind. "You know, I want to wish that your family will have no problem with us being together. I wish that everything would go perfect."

She raised their entwined hands between them. "But we have to accept the possibility that things won't go the way we want them to. That your parents will not accept their only son dating someone outside of his race."

"Are you saying that my parents are racist?" he demanded, torn between the need to defend his parents and protect her.

"I don't know them, so I can't judge them," she answered. She lifted her face, searching his. "But you know them. What do you think? Will there be a problem?"

He looked down at their clasped hands, wanting to lie to her, wanting to shelter her, wanting to prove her fears unfounded. Instead he told the truth. "There might be. My mother's not thrilled, and my father lets my mother do the talking. But I've told them how I feel about you, and that's not going to change. No matter what."

⟶⟵

It could have been worse. She could have been tarred and feathered.

"Mom, Dad, this is Maya Hughes. Maya, I'd like you to meet my mother, Victoria, and my father, Hanson."

Victoria Whitfield looked as regal as her name: tall, silvery blonde, clear blue eyes. She looked as if she'd never perspired a day in her life.

Maya mentally reprimanded herself and pasted on a smile. It wouldn't do to think negatively of someone she wanted to be on friendly terms with. Still, knowing that Nick's mother already disapproved of her put her on her guard.

Hanson Whitfield stood as tall as his wife, with still-dark hair and the same sparkling blue eyes. Contrasting with his wife's Nordic look, Hanson looked as if he'd spent his life toiling in the fields instead of wielding a scalpel. The hand that captured hers was strong, smooth, and warm. "It's a pleasure to finally meet you, Ms. Hughes," he said.

"It's a pleasure to meet you too, sir," she said, relieved to not receive the cold shoulder from Nick's father. "And please, call me Maya."

"I heard that you broke your ankle," Hanson Whitfield said, staring down at her cast peeking from beneath her crinkle skirt. "How're you doing?"

"Getting the hang of it, actually," she replied, pleased that he'd asked about it. "But the not scratching restriction is starting to drive me crazy."

"You only have a few more weeks of it," Nick assured her. "Then you're free to scratch to your heart's content."

"Why did you pick a colored cast?" Victoria asked.

Maya felt a blush creep up her cheeks. "Uhm, the blue reminded me of Nick's and Taylor's eyes," she admitted.

"Really?" daughter and father asked simultaneously.

"Seemed like a good idea at the time," Maya said.

"Cool," was Taylor's assessment.

They went into the living room to have a bit of wine before dinner. Taylor became Maya's public relations representative, telling her grandparents all the wonderful things Maya had done, how cool her family was, how her best friends were Maya's nieces.

"Taylor told me that your mother's from Vietnam," Victoria said, taking a seat beside Maya on the couch.

"Yes, she is," Maya said evenly. "She and my father met there."

"Really? Was she a spy or something?"

The question was so outrageous that Maya had to laugh. "Not likely. She was a driver and translator. My father was in the Army Corps of Engineers."

"You know, Hanson lost a brother in Vietnam," Nick's mother said.

"Tori," Hanson said, "there's no need to bring that up."

Maya agreed, but she decided not to vocalize her opinion. "I'm sorry to hear that. My father lost several friends over there, too."

"And he still married a Vietnamese woman?" Surprise shone dearly on Victoria's face. She leaned closer to Maya. "They did marry, didn't they?"

"And are still very happy together," Maya said proudly, determined not to allow Victoria Whitfield to get under her skin. "Dad said he wasn't looking for love, but he's sure glad it found him."

Nick sat beside her on the arm of the couch. "I can understand that," he said, smiling down at her. "I know I'm glad it found me."

He stood, offering her his hand. "I heard the timer go off. Why don't we move into the dining room?"

Maya allowed him to pull her to her feet, then reached for her crutch. "Let me help you carry the meal in."

"Nope. You helped make it, so it's rest time for you now." He guided her to a side chair. "Mom, would you mind helping me carry things in?"

"Of course not, dear," Victoria said. "You shouldn't have worked Maya so hard, preparing our meal."

Maybe she was being over-sensitive, but Maya didn't like the reference that she worked for Nick. "Oh, I love cooking."

"Good, because I love to eat," Hanson said, taking the chair opposite hers.

"It will depend on what it is, Hanson," Victoria said. "Remember your special diet."

Victoria followed Nick into the kitchen. "Special diet," Hanson muttered. He gave Maya and Taylor a conspiratorial wink. "Think she's forgotten who's the doctor in his marriage."

Taylor and Hanson kept up a lively conversation recounting the highlights of Taylor's time at day camp while Nick and Victoria brought dinner in. Maya gladly took a backseat in the gathering, needing the chance to gather her emotions.

She hadn't expected Nick's parents to welcome her with open arms, but Victoria Whitfield's politely framed put-downs were beginning to erode her pleasantness. Maya understood that Nick was their only son, and that they wanted the best for him, happiness for him. Maya wanted Nick to be happy, too, and she intended to be the creator of that happiness.

Nick, seated beside her at the head of the table, reached over to give her knee a reassuring squeeze. She smiled at him, instantly feeling better. He loved her, and a day hadn't gone by that he hadn't told her so. No matter what the future held, she felt confident that she and Nick would face it together.

～～～

Nick watched Maya interact with his parents, his heart swelling with pride. Things were going to work out, he thought to himself. His parents would see in

Maya what he already did: a warm, caring woman who lit up his life.

His father appeared to be taken with her already, judging by his smile and nod of approval over dinner. Mom, on the other hand, didn't seem won over. His mother acted distant and stiffly polite, as if Maya were someone just to be tolerated.

Nick frowned. His mother's attitude continued to bother him, more than he wanted to admit. His parents had raised him to be hard working, honest, and open-minded. Why his mother would dislike Maya because of her skin color made little sense to him.

It didn't matter, he told himself. He intended to ask his mother point-blank why she disliked Maya. No matter what those reasons were, he'd make his mother understand in no uncertain terms that Maya was in his life to stay.

"Maya, can we take Hamlet and Horatio for a walk?" Taylor asked after dinner.

"Sure. You know where their leashes are."

"You put a leash on a cat?" Hanson asked.

"On this particular cat, yes," Maya said with a smile. "You'll see what I mean in a moment." She hop-stepped to the living room doorway. "Ham, Harry, it's walking time."

Maya's pets lumbered into view. His father gave a low whistle. "That's a damn big cat."

Horatio growled. "Dad, you can't say the c-a-t word," Nick said. "He gets offended."

"Are you kidding me?"

"Nope."

His father laughed. "Well, you know I have to test this," he said. "I think I'll join you two ladies on your walk."

"Good," Nick said. "Maybe Maya will take your advice when you suggest that she slow down."

"I'll take my time, I promise," Maya said, settling both crutches beneath her arms. He stepped to her, giving her a light kiss. She gave him that smile that turned his insides to mush, then followed Taylor and his father out.

His mother had already taken dishes into the kitchen. He picked up a bowl and headed after her, mentally arming himself for battle. He found her vigorously wiping the counter. "Do you kiss like that in front of my granddaughter, or was that just for my benefit?"

"It was just a kiss, Mom," he said, wanting nothing more than to get the argument over with.

"I can't believe you're doing this," his mother snapped, throwing down the dishtowel.

"Can't believe I'm doing what?"

"You know what I'm talking about," she said. "You're going to ask her to marry you, aren't you?"

Her tone instantly put him on the defensive. "So what if I do?"

"So?" she repeated. "So? So it's wrong and you know it!"

"What wrong about it?"

"You know damn well what's wrong." She inched closet "You haven't told her about Jessie, have you?"

Nick stepped back from his mother's vicious anger. "I've told her."

"All of it?"

"Look, I know how you feel about Jessie, but that's eight years in the past. Taylor adores Maya, and I know Maya loves her, too. The three of us are going to be a family. You'd better start getting used to it."

"This is wrong," his mother insisted. "If you would just—"

"No," he cut in. "The past is over and done. There's no going back, and I don't want to. Maya is my future."

Victoria tightened her lips, as if reining in the urge to speak further. As far as Nick was concerned, there was nothing further she could say. Still, he wanted her to understand.

"Mom, I don't want to argue with you, not about this. I'm a different person than I was when Taylor was born. I'm in a completely different place. Maya is the best thing that could have happened to me and my little girl. Taylor's blossomed since she's known Maya. Isn't that the important thing?"

"It's not like you've given your daughter much of a choice, Nicolas," his mother said, "but I'm not going to argue further with you. You know what my thoughts are on this."

"Unfortunately, I do," Nick sighed. "The only thing I can do is hope that you'll come around, and that you'll be civil at the very least where Maya's concerned."

Victoria Whitfield drew herself up to her full height. "Don't tell me how to conduct myself, not when I'm the one that raised you." She headed for the kitchen door. "I have a headache, so I'm going to turn in early. Extend my apologies to your neighbor."

With that, his mother swept out of the kitchen. Nick slumped against the counter, feeling as if he'd retreated back in time, to the moment he'd first given his mother the news about Jessica. As supportive as she'd been then, Nick couldn't help wondering now if his mother somehow blamed him. Heaven knew he'd blamed himself often enough over the years.

He'd meant it when he'd said the past was past. He had a future now, he and his daughter. That future included Maya.

As if his thoughts had summoned her, Maya entered the kitchen. "There you are," she said with a smile. "I take it that mother-son talk didn't go well?"

"What mother-son talk?"

She leaned into him. "The one you had as soon as your father, Taylor and I took the boys on their walk," she said. "Or are my ears burning for no reason?"

"You probably over-exerted yourself," he said, not wanting to dissect the conversation with his mother just yet. He pulled her closer. "Where's Dad and Taylor?"

She laughed softly, then kissed his cheek. "Don't even try changing the subject," she told him. "I'm a big girl, and I'm not blind. I'm not high on your mother's Christmas card list, am I?"

Nick sighed, then decided to tell the truth; at least, part of it. "Mom still holds on to the best times with Jessie."

"Oh." She pulled away to look at him, her eyes dark with concern. "You must have loved her very much."

Pain struck him low in the gut as memories swept over him. "Yes, I did. It wasn't enough."

Silence fell between them, and he wondered if he'd offended her Then she squeezed his hand and said, "Sometimes it never is."

"This time it will be," he announced, cupping her face. "We can make this last forever, Maya Hughes."

"Are you sure about that?" she asked. "Forever is a long time."

"That's probably what it's going to feel like until my parents leave."

She laughed abruptly, her hand covering her mouth. "I can't believe you just said that!"

"Trust me, I know how trying and trifling my mother can be sometimes," he said, kissing the hand against her mouth. "What did you think about my dad?"

She moved her hand. "I think he's wonderful. He knows something about everything. And I mean that in a good way."

"My dad's the best," Nick said proudly. "He's as easy-going as they come. I know he likes you, so it's just a matter of time before my mother comes around. So don't let her attitude bother you."

"If it doesn't bother you, it doesn't bother me."

"Terrific. Now how 'bout we break open another bottle of wine and let ourselves stay blitzed until we put them back on the Winnebago they came in on?"

"That's two more days, you know."

"I know," he said. "That's why I bought extra."

Maya grinned. "I'll get the glasses."

TWENTY-THREE

Try as he might, Nick's mood only darkened. By the time the last two days passed and his parents drove off with Taylor, all he wanted to do was have a beer, watch a game, and try not to think about his mother or Jessica.

Jessica. Somehow, everything in his life seemed to come back to Jessica. They'd started out with such promise. He'd been a couple of years ahead of her in college, and wouldn't have crossed paths with her if he hadn't stopped to help a friend change a flat tire. He'd seen Jessica crossing the quad with a group of friends and he'd been mesmerized, thinking she was the most beautiful woman he'd ever seen. They'd married just after her graduation. He'd gone on to med school, then his residency. When she'd become pregnant, that was the beginning of the end.

Maya let her crutch fall to the floor as she threw herself down next to him. "Okay, out with it."

"Out with what?"

She chucked him on the chin. "With whatever's made you so talkative."

Or not so talkative. Nick realized he'd hardly said two words since they'd adjourned to her house after seeing his parents and Taylor off. "I guess I'm just bummed out not having Taylor around."

"Sure?"

He looked into her beautiful soft brown eyes and almost gave in. Almost told her every sordid detail of his past. But he didn't. Couldn't. Not yet. "You know, there are some days when I feel like I don't deserve you," he said, wrapping an arm around her shoulders. "This is one of those days."

"Now I know you're depressed," she said, poking him in the ribs. "Maybe we should fly down tomorrow and bring Taylor home."

Her unguarded words only made him feel worse. "See, that's what I mean." He leaned his head against the back of the couch. "Maybe you are too good for me."

"Are you saying this because of your parents' visit?"

"Yeah, partly." Even that white lie caused him to wince. He didn't want to deceive Maya, didn't want to start their life together with lies and half-truths. But Taylor deserved the truth first, and then he'd tell Maya. He just hoped that the women he loved more than life wouldn't come to hate him.

Maya stood. "When I'm feeling down, there's always one thing that's guaranteed to perk me back up."

"Really? And what would that be?"

She gave him a seductive smile. "Dancing."

"Dancing?" he echoed. "How do you plan to dance with a broken ankle?"

"I'll show you." She picked up her crutch and leveraged herself to her feet, then crossed to the entertainment center. She chose a CD and placed it into the player. A bohemian-sounding instrumental tune filled the air. She dimmed the overhead lights, then moved towards him, her hips rolling with the rhythm.

Smiling down at him, she pulled her shirt out of her cutoffs one-handed, then undid each button with seductive slowness. He watched the pale blue material part, revealing the swell of her breasts trapped behind leopard-print lace. His breath caught as she spun around on her good ankle, slipping the shirt down her arms. Letting go of the crutch, she slipped the shirt completely off, then tossed it over her shoulder. He caught it, bringing it to his nose so that he could inhale her perfume.

But the doctor in him wasn't ready to give up just yet. "Markowitz would have my hide if he knew you were dancing."

"Then don't tell him," she said over her shoulder. "But if it will make you feel better, I took ballet when I was a kid, so I can do all sorts of things on one foot. Besides, I've been practicing this next door all afternoon. Let me show you."

"All right." He swallowed audibly. That smile was going to kill him. It certainly killed the doctor in him, leaving nothing but the man appreciating a damn fine view.

"Dancing is good for you," she informed him as she pranced away. She lifted her arms as the seductive beat continued, her hips swishing hypnotically to and fro, as she lightly rested the tip of the cast on the floor. "Dancing gets your blood moving, makes your heart beat in time to the rhythm."

He watched as she unzipped her shorts. "Dancing is the vertical expression of horizontal desire," she said, her voice soft and sensuous. "Dancing is fire, passion, sex. It reduces us to our primitive nature. Don't you feel primitive?"

Her shorts slowly slid to the floor, revealing panties that had just enough fabric to them so that he could tell they matched the bra. "I'm definitely feeling something," he said when he found his voice again.

"Good." She undulated towards him like a graceful fire goddess, exuding sensuality and the promise of passion fulfilled. With a practiced move, she reached behind her, unclasped her bra, and let it slide down her arms. His erection strained against his shorts, making him feel confined. He reached for her, wanting to pull her into his lap, but she skipped back a step, dropping the bra to the floor. "Dance with me," she said, holding out a hand.

It was an offer he couldn't refuse. He took her hand, rising to his feet to follow her to the center of the room. She danced around him, running her hands over his shoulders, chest, back, stoking the fire that burned in him. Standing behind him, she pulled his polo over his head, tossing it to the floor. Wrapping her arms about his waist, she made him sway to the music. "Do you feel that?" she asked.

"Uh-hhm." He could feel Maya's body pressed against his back. He could feel the heat of her arms burning into his skin. And he could feel need building in him, stronger and stronger until he thought he would go blind.

Then he felt her lips, placing kisses along his spine as her hands undid his shorts. They dropped to the floor, along with his briefs. He felt her breasts pressing into his back, felt her hands reach around to hold him. He almost came then, and had to grit his teeth against the overpowering desire she'd aroused in him.

"Dancing is desire," she whispered, stroking him in time to the heady music. "Dancing is invitation, appreciation, consummation. Dancing is reflection and perfection."

She danced around him again, brushing her flesh against his. She turned her back to him once more, swaying as she pushed her panties down her hips. "Dancing is about male and female," she said, her breathing faster. "It's about male attracting female, female tempting male."

She pressed against him. "Are you tempted yet?"

Something in his brain snapped. Grabbing her around the waist, the turned her to the sofa, pushed her against the plush arm, then entered her without preamble. Her sigh of acceptance made him groan with pleasure. Need drove him, making him dive inside her again and again, urged on by her soft murmurs of satisfaction and encouragement. His right hand slipped around the curve of her hip, seeking the hard nub of her passion. She gasped when he touched her, demanding that he go faster, slamming against him as he slammed into her.

He increased his frenetic pace, driving them to the edge of ecstasy. Nothing mattered except reaching that point, finding relief from the white-hot passion that boiled through him.

"Nick." He felt her begin to tremble, felt her slick inner walls gripping him. She cried out, slamming back against him as her orgasm swept through her. Gripping her hips with both hands, he surged into her hard, once, twice, three times. With a hoarse shout, he pushed into her one final time, pumping his release deep inside her.

Next thing he knew, he was flat on his back on the floor, Maya straddling him and pressing light kisses across his face. "Woman, you are amazing," he breathed, struggling to catch his breath. "You are freaking amazing."

"So are you." She gave him a final kiss before sitting upright. "I think I saw stars that time."

His hands roamed up her thighs to her belly, and he realized that they hadn't used protection since she'd broken her ankle. For just a moment he kept his hands on the flat plane of her stomach. A fleeting wish swept through him, sharp and poignant, before it faded.

Maya's hands covered his own. The look in her eyes broke his heart, and he damned himself for causing her pain. "Maya…"

She blinked, settling her features into a smile, then lifted his hands from her belly. "The floor's got to be pretty hard by now," she said, her voice tight with forced pleasantness. "Maybe we should get up and think about getting something to eat."

He helped her rise, searching for ways to apologize for a half-wish he hadn't mentioned and she wanted to forget. "Do you want to go out, or order something in? I can even go pull some steaks out of my freezer if you want."

"Let's just order something," she said, gathering her clothes.

He grabbed his shorts and stepped into them. "What do you want?"

The look in her eyes held a wealth of meaning. "It doesn't matter," she said softly. "You decide."

She went to take a shower, and he let her have her space, wondering if he could ever make this up to her. He decided to order her favorite Thai dish for dinner, hoping that it would help.

It didn't. She came back downstairs as the food arrived, dressed in a pair of worn jeans and a t-shirt that had seen better days. Her face looked scrubbed clean of makeup, but he could see redness around her eyes, and knew that she'd cried in the shower.

Neither of them showed much interest in their dinner, and he finally gave up all pretense of trying to eat.

"Maya."

She stiffened in her chair, her hand a fist around her fork. "I wish I could do that for you, Nick," she whispered, keeping her eyes lowered. "I wish I could give you another child, but I can't. Not for you, not for anyone."

He reached out, wrapping his hand around her fist. "You know it doesn't matter to me."

"It doesn't matter now," she said hollowly, refusing to look at him. "But it will one day. You know it will."

"No it won't," he countered. "You matter to me. You mean more to me than your ability to have a child or not."

The hand beneath his trembled. "You say that now. You said it before, and I wanted to believe it. For a long time, I believed it. And then you placed your hands on my stomach." She swallowed. "I saw the look, the longing in your eyes, and I knew that it did matter."

He wanted to deny that the thought had come to him, but it would be a lie. He'd done enough of that already. "Maya, I would love to have a child with you. But more than that, more than anything else, I want you."

"Russell put me through hell before our divorce was finalized. He made me feel like half a woman, like I had some disease. He said that no man would want to be with a woman who was messed up inside, and that I deserved to die unloved and alone for betraying him the way I did."

"Don't tell me you believed him?"

"I didn't have to believe him. I'd already thought that myself."

Angry tears glittered on her lashes. "I told myself that I would never let another man treat me like that. I told myself that I would walk away if things got too serious between us, if you wanted another child," she said with a shaky breath. "I told myself that if I ever saw that look in your eyes, I'd have to leave."

His heart slammed into his chest. "No."

She looked at him, tears spilling down her cheeks. "I saw that look, and it hurt me. It hurt me, Nick. But I don't want to go. I still want to be with you."

He crushed her in his arms. "Then be with me," he said against her hair. "Be with me, no matter what anyone else says or does."

"I'm scared, Nick," she managed through her tears. "I'm so scared that I've given my heart to a man and child that I can't call mine. I'm scared that this is all wishful thinking, that it's just a dream and I'll wake up tomorrow and everything will be gone."

"It's not a dream, sweetheart. I'll still be here tomorrow, and the day after and the day after that."

She lifted her face to stare up at him, and he knew the weekend had worn on her more than she'd let on. "But what about later? What if you change your mind? What if you meet someone who looks more like Taylor's mother, and who can give you children?"

He cupped her cheeks in his hands. "I already have the woman I want. That's you, Maya. I can't think of what life without you will be like. I'm scared, too. Scared that you'll finally see all my warts and realize that you could do better."

"I won't, I promise I won't."

"I love you, Maya, love you so much I think my heart's gonna explode right out of my chest. I don't want anyone else but you. Do you believe me?"

She sniffed back tears, her reddened eyes still filled with hurt and pain. "I could go through all the tests again, if you want. They've probably made some advances since the last time I saw a doctor about it."

Knowing what those tests and procedures entailed, Nick knew how much the offer cost her. He would never put her through that kind of pain, not for anything, not even to have a son.

"No. No more doctors, and no more tests. If it happens, we'll consider ourselves blessed. And if it doesn't happen, we'll still be happy. All right?"

She nodded.

He stared into her beautiful dark eyes and knew, just *knew*, that this was the woman he wanted to spend the rest of his life with. He buried his face into her hair. "I love you, Maya Hughes," he whispered. "Never, ever doubt that."

"I don't doubt it, Nick. I know how lucky I am."

He was the lucky one, he thought as they went to bed. He'd met the one woman who fulfilled his and his daughter's wishes. He wanted her to share their lives and hold their hearts. But he couldn't do that until he told her the full story.

He had to tell her that Jessica was still very much alive.

TWENTY-FOUR

Maya hobbled through the packed department store, frantically peering at her list. Why in the world had she offered to take Taylor back-to-school shopping? Even though she now used a cane and could actually walk on the ankle, it was still tough going. The rainy weather and crowds did nothing to improve her mood.

Taylor wasn't exactly a ray of sunshine either. The little girl had been sullen since her return from her grandparents'. Maya could understand Taylor missing them, but she'd noticed that Taylor's mood soured only when she was alone with Maya. Her attempts to talk to the little girl had been met with resolute silence. Maya couldn't think of anything that she had or hadn't done, which led her to believe that Nick's mother must have said something to Taylor during her visit. With no proof, there was nothing Maya could do, and she'd finally decided to keep it to herself.

"Can we go now?" Taylor asked, sounding as cranky and tired as Maya felt.

"We're almost done," she promised, pushing past a large woman with a tiny dog sticking out of her duffel bag of a purse. Did everyone in Fulton County have to pick this particular time to visit this particular store?

"I wanna go home," Taylor sighed in that dramatic way that kids can. A woman looked at Maya strangely before hurrying on. Normally, Maya didn't let looks rankle her; after all, she'd gotten plenty growing up. But the more exasperated she grew, the less polite she tended to be.

Balancing the shopping basket and her cane, Maya reached down and took Taylor by the upper arm. "Taylor, honey, we'll be done soon. Stop acting up and behave."

The little girl tried to wrench her arm free. "No! You're not my mommy—I don't have to do what you say!"

Shocked by the outburst, Maya let Taylor go. The girl turned to run, only to smash into a security guard. "Is there a problem here, ma'am?"

"No, there's no problem," she retorted. "I just have a tired little girl and a crowded store working my last nerve!"

"Why don't you come along with me," the guard said, his hand wrapped around Taylor's upper arm. The little girl's face was pale and she seemed on the brink of tears. "Maya?"

"Come with you for what?"

"There's been some concern," the man said. "Why don't we go to the manager's office and we can sort this all out?"

"I don't know what sort of concern you're talking about, and there's nothing to sort out," Maya said, reaching for Taylor. The child reached for her, only to be pulled back by the security guard. Taylor burst into tears. "Let her go this instant!"

Another security guard came up behind her. "Ma'am, I suggest you do what we say. There's no need to cause a scene."

"Cause a scene? You're the one terrifying Taylor," she shot back, her frustration rising to the boiling point. "Let her go. Now."

"After we sort this out," the second guard said. "Come to the office with us. Please."

"Fine. If only so I can talk to your manager." Sandwiched between the two burly guards, Maya allowed herself and Taylor to be led to the office. But if she thought things would be over quickly and easily, she was mistaken.

The store manager on duty called in a female cashier to sit with Taylor in the outer room of the cramped office. When she saw that Maya would not be staying with her, Taylor burst into hysterics, screaming Maya's name repeatedly. Maya's heart

pounded with the need to comfort the child and lash
out at those making her upset.

She chose what, at the moment, was the better
course. "It's all right, sweetheart," she said to the
child. "I'll just be a few minutes straightening this
out. Then we'll be on our way home, okay?"

The two security guards took her into another
office, this one windowless and cramped. Both guards
stood in front of her, blocking her view—and route—
to the door.

"We need to check your purse," the first guard
said.

"The hell you will," Maya retorted.

The guard took a step towards her. She lifted a
finger in warning. "You lay the tip of one finger on
me, and I will have your job and any money you
could hope to make for the rest of your natural life."

"Now ma'am, there's no reason to get upset—"

"Upset?" Maya repeated, her voice rising. "You
think this is upset? I haven't even begun to get upset.
I've just spent the better part of an hour struggling
around your store with a bad ankle and a tired child
on my arm. Believe me, I can get a whole lot more
upset than this. And I promise you, you don't want to
see it. Now get your manager down here. Now."

"You're hardly in a position to make demands," the
security guard said.

Maya got to her feet, "Is this position better?" she asked, her anger barely in check. Her father had taught her and her siblings to try to use diplomacy but, if it came down to a fight, to fight to win.

The second security guard rose with the first. "Please take your seat, ma'am," he said. Only the politeness in his tone made Maya return to the chair, taking a deep breath to settle her temper. Getting angry wouldn't solve anything, and showing out would only make things worse. Besides, she needed to stay calm for Taylor's sake; she could still hear the child crying in the other room.

"Hey Bob, why don't you let me talk to her for a moment, while you and Karen talk to the little girl?"

Big Bad Bob shot a dirty look her way, as if he wanted her to try something. It took everything in her power not to stick her tongue out at him. Finally he gave up and left the room.

The remaining guard gave her a smile. "Sorry for that, ma'am," he said, his tone apologetic. "Bob takes his job very seriously."

"Bob needs to loosen the tie around his neck," she retorted. "The skin's turning red."

The guard cracked a hint of a smile. "Bob's got a problem seeing a black woman with a little white girl," he said, as if in explanation. "Especially when that girl's yelling that you're not her mother. So what's your story?"

"What do you mean, what's my story?"

He shifted closer to her, lowering his voice. "Come on, it's just you and me. Talk to me, and I'll vouch for you when the police come."

Maya could feel a jackhammer-like pain beginning at the back of her head. "Vouch for me."

"Of course." He smiled again. "I'm sure it's all a simple misunderstanding."

"Of course it is."

"Or maybe somebody put you up to it."

"Put me up to what?" She had a good idea what he meant, but she wanted to see if he actually had the audacity to say it.

"You know what I mean." He spread his hands, the picture of the helpful guy. "You or your man got into some trouble, needed to make some quick cash. He comes up with the idea of taking the little girl. Beautiful child like that, of course her parents are gonna pay to get her back."

He did have the audacity to say it. "You've been watching way too many cop shows, sir," she said, stressing his title. "Taylor isn't a kidnap victim."

He gave her a look that made her skin crawl. "Sure. So why was she trying to get away from you?"

Maya balled her hands into fists, fighting the urge to pop the arrogant son-of-a-bitch in his filthy mouth. "Because she's tired and grumpy and sick of shopping in this sorry excuse for a professional establishment. Can you get that through your head?"

His eyes sparked with anger. "Maybe you need to try again."

"And maybe I should use smaller words this time." Maya knew she should keep quiet, but anger pressed her forward.

He climbed to his feet, towering over her. "Look, I'm trying to make this easy for you. You wanna play hard ass, you go right ahead. Cute little thing like you will make a nice treat in lockup."

For the first time, fear replaced anger. "Are you threatening me?"

"I'm not threatening you, I'm just telling you what will happen if you don't cooperate," he said. "Nowadays, when it comes to kidnapped children, people act first and ask questions later. I'd hate for you to get all hurt up."

She felt her bravado draining out of her. "If you don't release me and Taylor right now, I'll—"

"You'll what?" the first security guard said as he reentered the room. "We have witnesses that saw you grab the child by the upper arm, heard her yell that you weren't her mother, and saw her try to get away from you." He gave her a slow measured look that made her want to take a shower. "I believe what my eyes tell me, and they tell me that you ain't that girl's mother."

"Of course I'm not her mother," Maya said clearly, though it hurt to get the words out. "I'm her next door neighbor. Her father and I are dating."

"A little 'jungle fever,' huh?"

Both security guards laughed. Maya folded her arms across her chest, fighting the urge to cry.

The police arrived at the same time as the manager. Maya bit her lip and sat silently as the two officers went through her purse, her pockets, and watched the security camera tape. Then she had to choke on humiliation as the female officer patted her down. "She's clean."

"Of course I am," she said, feeling anything but. "I'm not a kidnapper."

"The address on the license is next door to the address the girl gave us," the officer explained, all but rolled his eyes at the security guard. "She's got business cards with her name and information on them, two platinum credit cards, and her car key has an emblem for an upper level sedan. She probably makes three times what you do. Oh, and her cell phone has the father's office and pager numbers programmed into it."

"Hey it's not our fault she wouldn't let us check her purse," Bob sputtered.

"Good thing you didn't," the officer said. "Because if she had claimed anything missing, we'd be cuffing you right about now."

Maya would have smiled if she'd been capable, but she felt too eaten up inside. "Thank you, officer," she managed to say.

"Just doing my job, ma'am," he said. "I'd say these people owe you an apology, probably more than that if you want."

"What I want is to go home."

"You're free to go, ma'am," the officer said. "The girl's father is in the other office, waiting for you."

The cop stood back to let her out of the office. She looked up to see Nick standing toe to toe with the night manager. "If you think just an apology will suffice for the rude and unimaginable crap you've put my fiancée and daughter through, you are sadly mistaken."

"Dr. Whitfield—"

"You terrorized my daughter and you verbally abused my fiancée," Nick continued, his face a mask of fury. "There is nothing you can say that will make this better. And if you even dare say it was just a misunderstanding, I'm going to really get angry."

"But sir—"

"I'm sure your corporate office will be thrilled to hear how you harass customers, how your security guards make prejudiced, discriminatory assumptions."

"Nick."

He broke off his tirade, swinging around to face her. Taylor broke free of his grasp, running towards her.

"Maya!"

Taylor ran headlong into her, throwing her arms around Maya's waist. Maya froze, afraid for the first time to touch the little girl. Aware of people watching her, she carefully untangled the young girl.

"I'm sorry, Maya," the child cried, hysterical tears running down her face. "I tried to tell them that you were my new mommy and they didn't believe me and wouldn't let me see you!"

"It's okay, Taylor," she said gently. "Remember, princesses have to be strong. Go back to your father."

Nick came up to them. "Are you okay?" he asked, his eyes raking her face as he reached out to touch her.

She dropped her gaze, not wanting to meet his, or anyone else's, eyes. "Fine. I just want to go home."

An arm slipped around her waist. "You're shaking!"

"It's all right." Really, she couldn't feel it. She was too numb to feel much of anything.

"It's not all right!" Lifting Taylor into his arms, he turned back to the manager. "Expect to hear from my lawyer in the morning!"

Choking on embarrassment, Maya forced her chin up and pasted a neutral expression to her face and let herself be guided out of the store. Dusk had fallen, but not enough to obscure the faces of curious onlookers as the police followed them through the glass doors.

She took a deep breath, trying to get her bearing, trying to shake off the mortification and pain that tumbled inside her. "I…my car—Taylor's list…"

"We'll get school supplies somewhere else, and we'll come back for your car tomorrow," Nick said, guiding her through the parking lot. "Right now I just want to get both of you home."

"No." With her emotions tangled like a wind-blown kite caught in a tree, she couldn't sit in the car with Nick and Taylor. Couldn't be near them with the hurt and embarrassment and anger threatening to break free. She had to be alone. If only so that she could scream and cry in the relative privacy of her car.

"I can drive home."

He searched her eyes. If he looked for weakness, she'd be damned if she'd show any. Two minutes, just two more minutes…

"All right. We'll ride behind you."

"Fine." It took several precious seconds to find her keys, then she almost dropped them trying to thumb the unlock key. Without another word, she snatched open the door, got in, then slammed the door shut.

It took everything in her not to peel out of the parking lot. It took even more not to scream and cry in disappointment. Taylor had never acted out on her before, and she couldn't understand why she had done it then. Maybe there wasn't a logical reason, maybe the cold-hearted truth was that Taylor didn't consider her a replacement mother and probably never would.

Not that it had come to that anyway. Sure, she and Nick had revealed their feelings, but what did that mean in the scheme of things? He hadn't mentioned anything about moving in together, about getting engaged, about what a future together could be like. And if Taylor planned to pull that "you're not my mother" routine every time she didn't want to do what Maya asked of her, there would be no need to mention it anyway.

She'd never been that humiliated in public before. Not since her ex-husband had proclaimed her useless as woman had she felt so humiliated. Being treated as a kidnapper and a thief because of the color of her skin was something she'd never experienced, or ever expected to. It didn't matter how she dressed or how she spoke; all the people at the store saw was the color of her skin.

She'd told herself when she'd gotten serious with Nick that it wouldn't matter, that race wouldn't be an issue. She was wrong. Race and racism was an issue, and always would be one. Anytime she went out with Taylor it would be the same, with people wondering how she ended up with a little white girl calling her mother.

Of course, Taylor wouldn't call her mother. She knew that now. That hurt worse than what the security guards had done to her. Having Taylor snatch away from her and declare that Maya wasn't her mother tore the deepest part of Maya's heart. It was bad enough that her own body betrayed her by refusing to make her a mother. Having Taylor deny her, the child she'd lavished with love and attention, felt like as much of a betrayal as anything ever could.

Feeling beaten and disappointed, she pulled into her driveway, wanting nothing more than to curl up on the sofa with her pets and a good romance novel to take her mind off her own pain. Maybe a glass or three of wine would help, too.

Nothing would help, she knew. Nothing would ease the pain except forgetting, and that wouldn't happen for a long time.

TWENTY-FIVE

Nick struggled to control his temper on the ride home. He was outraged at the treatment Maya had received; outraged that she didn't seem more upset herself. His daughter still sniffled in the back seat.

"I didn't mean to cause trouble, Daddy," Taylor said in a small voice. "I just...Gamma said that Maya wasn't going to be my mother, that she could never be my mother and that I didn't have to do what Maya said."

He hit the brake, hard. "What?"

"Gammy said that Maya wasn't going to stay with us, so I didn't have to mind her or pretend that she's my mommy," Taylor said with a sniffle. "Why would Maya leave us?"

Dear old Mom. He should have known that his mother would fill Taylor's head with nonsense. He should have known something was wrong, considering the way Taylor had been acting since returning from Florida. This went way beyond meddling, however, and he intended to let his mother know exactly how little he appreciated it. That would have to wait, though, until he could take care of Taylor and Maya.

"Maya's not going anywhere, pumpkin," he said, hoping that it was still true. "She loves us, remember?"

He watched Maya pull into her driveway, then just sit there, engine idling, headlights still on. "Taylor, unlock the door and go into the house."

"I wanna talk to Maya."

"Sweetheart, you can talk to her in the morning, after I make sure she's okay," Nick said. "Right now, I need you to go get ready for bed. I'll be up in a few minutes."

Taylor ran for the house, and he knew more tears were on the way. He didn't want to punish her; the ordeal she'd been through had been punishment enough. But she had to understand that actions had consequences, some more terrible than others.

He crossed the short distance to Maya's car, having to tap on the window to get her attention.

She turned to face him slowly. "Yes?"

"We're home, sweetheart. You can get out of the car now."

She turned off the car and undid her seatbelt. He opened the door for her. "Ham and Harry are over at my house," he said, taking her hand in his. It was like ice, and he worried that she might be in shock.

He helped her inside, seating her on the couch. She moved automatically, her emotions tamped down so tight he wondered if he'd be able to reach her. She needed to talk about what happened. They needed to talk about what happened. A sense of panic blanketed him. He had a feeling that if he didn't talk to her tonight, if he couldn't get through to her, he'd never have the chance to again.

"I'll be right back, sweetheart," he said, wrapping the afghan about her shoulders. "I'm just going to check on Taylor and I'll be right back down. Okay?"

She didn't answer, but he really didn't expect her to. He trotted upstairs to Taylor's room. She lay crumpled on her bed, still in her clothes, a doll clutched in her arms. She'd cried herself to sleep.

His heart took another blow as he removed his daughter's shoes and pulled the comforter over her. The women he loved more than his life were both hurting, and he didn't know how to stop that hurt. He should have been with them, should have stopped it from happening.

Maya had tried to warn him that something like this would happen, but he'd blithely ignored her warnings. He couldn't ignore them anymore. Something like this could happen again. Someone would react to Taylor and Maya being together, someone in school would say something nasty to Taylor about Maya. What could he do? How could he protect them from stupid senseless bastards like the store guards?

His hands contracted into fists. Somehow, he'd protect them. Somehow he'd find a way. That's what he was supposed to do, shelter them and keep them from harm. And he'd do that. But first he'd have to soothe their souls.

After making sure Taylor still slept, he went back downstairs, fully expecting to find Maya gone. She wasn't. She sat on the couch, her head in her hands. Even before he reached her, he could tell by the silent shaking of her shoulders that she sobbed.

Anger evaporated in a rush of heartbreak. "Maya, sweetheart, talk to me," he said, kneeling in front of Her. "Please talk to me."

"I can't."

"Please try," he said, needing to reach her. "I love you, and I don't want to see you hurting like this. Let me share it with you."

She raised her head, tears streaking down her cheeks. "You can't share this with me," she said brokenly. "Nothing like this has happened to you. Nothing like this will *ever* happen to you."

"And you won't ever have to worry about someone entrusting you with their life, with their health, only to have them die," he said. "I shared that with you, because I know that it helps to talk it out, helps it hurt a little less. Let me return the favor."

"I don't know what to say." She stared straight ahead, her voice distant. "So many things are going on inside me right now that I can't really say what I feel. Mostly though, I just hurt."

She sighed, leaning back against the couch. "The store was crowded and we were both tired. My ankle was bothering me, and when Taylor started complaining, I grabbed her arm and told her to behave. She jerked away from me, screamed that I couldn't tell her what to do because I wasn't her mother. Apparently someone reported me to security. They were just doing their jobs."

"Just doing their jobs?" he echoed, fury rising in him again. "Accusing you of being a kidnapper is doing their jobs?"

"I don't look like Taylor, Nick. My mother's Vietnamese, but my father's black. That makes me black. That's what they saw. A black woman with her hand on a fussy little white girl's arm. They did what they thought was right."

"God, you're defending them?"

"Getting angry won't solve anything."

"Being complacent and just accepting it won't either!" he shot back. "People need to learn that this kind of behavior is unacceptable and won't be tolerated!"

He put his hands on her shoulders. "If you do nothing, those people will continue to bully and harass others. They need to learn that what they did was wrong. They need to be taught a lesson."

"I'm not that person, Nick," she said, her throat tight. "I wish I could be that person, but I'm not. All I want to do is find that little piece of this world where I can be happy and be loved. I don't want to change the world, I just want to find my place in it."

"And who are you going to let dictate where that place is?" he demanded. "People like those security guards?"

"They were right. And Taylor's right," Maya said, her voice heavy with weariness. "I'm not her mother. I've been living this fantasy, but it's time to face the truth. I'm never going to be Taylor's mother."

"Maya…"

"I tried to tell you, Nick," she insisted, wiping at her eyes. "Before we started dating I tried to tell you how it would be. That there would be some people who wouldn't understand or who would have a problem with us. Sometimes their opinions don't matter, but this time they obviously did."

She shook her head. "I had this stupid thought that we could be a family, that I would finally get my wish. Everything's been going so well, it was easy to believe…but we can't. Reality proved otherwise today."

"So you're going to accept that?" he asked. "You're going to let people who don't matter affect you like this? I thought you were stronger than that."

She pushed a shaky hand across her leaking eyes. "That's not me, Nick," she whispered, her throat tight. "You weren't there in that store, a store I've shopped in at least once a week for the last two years. You didn't see how people looked at me when Taylor pulled away and declared to everyone that I wasn't her mother and couldn't make her do anything. I know I'm not her mother, everyone there knew I wasn't her mother, but to say that I had abducted her and was shoplifting…"

She took a deep breath. "I'm sorry, Nick. This is really too painful for me to talk about right now."

"Okay, I understand. But you've got to understand, those people don't know us. We can't let them judge us."

"It wasn't us they were judging, Nick," she said quietly. "Just me."

"No, it wasn't just you. It was Taylor, and it was me, too. It was all of us they were judging, because we want to be together. Would you let them judge you as incompetent or unsuccessful? Would you let them call you cruel and violent? Then don't let them judge you in this. If you do, you let their idiocy win. You know your parents wouldn't do that, and neither should you."

She remained silent for a long moment, then stretched out her arms to him. He pulled her to her feet and into his arms, holding her close, as if holding her would shield her from the hurt and pain she felt. She held onto him tightly, her body trembling with emotion.

"I'll be your strength," he said. "Let me protect you this time. Let me give you that place in the world you want to be in."

"How?" she asked brokenly. "How can you do that for me?"

"We can create a place together, you, me, and Taylor." He said against her hair. "A place just for us, where the outside world doesn't matter. If you marry me, we can build that place together."

She stiffened in his arms. "You want me to marry you?"

"Of course I do. Why wouldn't I?"

"Why?" she asked, her voice strained. "Why would you want to? I'm not white. Your mother doesn't like me. I can't give you more children. Why do you want me?"

"Because, at the end of the day, I can't imagine being without you," he said, his voice quiet with intensity.

He reached into his pocket and pulled out a small velvet box. "Listen to me, Maya. Listen to my words, so you can know how I feel. I want you for you, because you're beautiful, smart, sexy, funny, and loving. And I want you for me, because you make me feel free and fulfilled, and worthy. I want you beside me every morning and I want you beside me every night. I want to try to make you as happy as you've made me and my little girl. I don't give a damn what other people think. All that matters to me is what you think and how you feel."

She wanted to believe him. God, how she wanted to believe him. "Nick."

"Do you think you could love me?" he asked, his voice rough.

"I don't have to think about it," she said. "I already do. But—"

"No buts," Nick cut in, putting a finger to her lips. "I love you, you love me, Taylor loves you, and you love Taylor. We all love each other. Make us a family, Maya. But more than that, be the better half of me that you already are."

He opened the box to reveal an exquisite round solitaire with two smaller stones set in the band on each side. "I was going to wait to do this, but now's the perfect time. If I could only have one wish, this is the one I'd make: that you'll say yes to me being your husband, lover, and companion for the rest of our lives."

Voiceless, Maya stared down at the ring. "Oh…"

"This isn't the way I wanted to propose to you," he said, dropping to one knee before her. "I wanted to take you back to Amora's Retreat, back to where we had our first date. I wanted to wine and dine you, and maybe even get you tipsy enough that you'd say yes even though I'm a flawed human being."

"You're not flawed," she managed to say. "You're perfect."

"No, I'm not," he said. "But I'll try to be perfect for you. I'll try to be worthy of you, if you'll have me." He held the ring up to her "Will you have me?"

"Oh my God."

"Does that mean yes in Vietnamese?"

She dropped to the floor beside him. "It does. It most certainly does."

TWENTY-SIX

It was the perfect day for an engagement party.

Early afternoon clouds had given way to a gorgeous sunset and relatively cool evening. Citronella candles and strings of lights had transformed Nick's backyard into a wonderland of food and frivolity.

Maya couldn't stop grinning as she darted looks at the ring she'd been wearing for the last two weeks. It was the happiest night of her life, especially when Taylor decided to start calling her "Mommy" then and there. With her friends and family gathered around her, Maya realized this it couldn't get any better.

"What the hell are you doing here?"

The harshness of Nick's voice cut through the party atmosphere like a buzz saw. Maya craned her neck to see to whom he was talking. She noticed a dark-haired woman standing next to him, actually trying to get past him.

Nick grabbed the woman by the arm and began pushing her toward the house. "Taylor, honey, stay here with Leila and Tamera, okay?" Maya said, then followed Nick into the house.

She found them just inside the kitchen. Nick still had his hand on the woman's arm. "What the hell are you doing here?" he demanded.

"I came to see Taylor."

"If you think I'm going to let you get near my daughter, you're out of your mind!"

"Nick? What's going on here?" Maya asked.

"Nothing's going on," he said, his face taut. "Our uninvited guest was just leaving."

The woman tried to wrench her arm out of Nick's grasp. "Not until I see Taylor!"

Realization hit Maya like a freezing rain. "You're Jessica, aren't you? You're Taylor's mother."

The woman turned, and Maya got her first good look at Nick's late—no, make that ex—wife. She was beautiful. Her hair was more auburn than brown, but the bright blue of her eyes reminded Maya of Taylor, leaving no doubt of the woman's identity.

"You're looking amazingly well for a dead woman," Maya said, turning her gaze to Nick. He flushed, whether from anger or embarrassment, she couldn't tell and didn't care.

"Dead?" Jessica echoed. She, too, turned to Nick. "You told everyone I was dead?"

"You might as well have been!" he retorted. "You walked out on me and Taylor when she was just a baby. You walked out and never once looked back. You were as good as dead."

"I was scared!" Jessica exclaimed. "I was just twenty-three. I didn't know the first thing about taking care of a baby. My life wasn't my own anymore. I felt trapped."

"So you decided to escape," Nick said, his voice heavy with sarcasm. "You left Taylor at my parents' house and just disappeared. I get a frantic call from them, thinking that you were in an accident or something. I get Taylor and come home to find all your things gone and a note that said 'I'm sorry.' "

He snorted with derision. "I'm sorry. Like that's supposed to make things all better. All you did was think about yourself. You never once thought about me, or Taylor. Never thought about the hell I went through trying to take care of a newborn and complete my residency. Did you?"

"You had your parents—"

"Who already had raised two children and didn't need to raise another at their age!" Nick yelled. "But yes, they helped me. Because unlike you, I wanted my child. I wasn't going to walk away from my responsibilities just because life got too damn tough."

"Of course not," Jessica said. "You're far too noble for that. I was constantly reminded of all the sacrifices you were making so that we could have a wonderful life. It was always you, you, you. What about me? Don't you think I made sacrifices, too? I should have been exploring the world and finding my future after graduating from college. Instead I was a bride at twenty-two and a mother at twenty-three. I didn't have a life anymore!"

"So being with me wasn't a life? Being married killed you?" Nick's expression hardened. "Why didn't you say no when I asked you to marry me?"

Tears glittered in Jessica's eyes. "Because I thought I loved you as much as you loved me."

Maya decided that this train wreck was too painful to continue witnessing. "I think I'm going to go back outside, tell everyone that the party's over. You two obviously have a lot to talk about, and you don't need me here."

"No," Nick said, stepping into her path. "I want you to stay. You need to know this."

"You haven't even told her the truth?" Jessica asked, her voice climbing an octave. "You're going to marry her and you didn't tell her about me?"

Good question. Maya wanted Nick to answer it, but not now, not in front of Jessica. She turned to Nick, whose expression couldn't have been more alien.

"You are no longer an important part of my life, Jessica," he said. "You made that perfectly clear eight years ago." He thrust a hand through his hair. "How did you know where we were? Why did you show up Today, of all days?"

"I called your sister, and once I told her what was going on, she told me where you live," Jessica answered. "I didn't know about the party."

"Caroline?" That one word sounded like glass being ground to bits. "Caroline knows that I don't want anything to do with you. She wouldn't have given you my information without a good reason. And she sure as hell wouldn't have told you to show up today of all days!"

"I didn't know about your engagement party, Nick. Please believe that. And I do have a good reason."

"Why should I believe you?" he wondered. "Why should I ever believe a word you say, ever again?"

"Because it's important," Jessica said, wringing her hands together. "It wasn't easy for me to come here, but I need to talk to you. And I want to see Taylor."

"And what in the hell makes you think that I'm going to let you near my daughter?"

"I'm her mother, Nick."

The look he gave her could have frozen hell. "You gave birth to her, but you'll never be her mother."

Maya couldn't stand the stricken look on Jessica's face. "Nick."

"It's true. You've been more of a mother to Taylor in the last five months than Jessica has in eight years," he insisted.

"Nick, please," Maya said. "Don't do this."

"You can't be on her side," Nick said, surprised.

"If I'm on anyone's side, it's Taylor's," Maya said. "She deserves to know the truth. She deserves to know that her mother's alive."

"I don't believe this!" Nick said, running his hand through his hair. "You honestly think I should let her see Taylor?"

"Do you honestly think Taylor will forgive you if you don't?" Maya shot back, her temper finally fraying. "Maybe you had a good reason to lie to me, but lying to your daughter about something like this is unconscionable, no matter how good your intentions."

"Thank you," Jessica said softly.

"Don't thank me," Maya said, her words bitter in her mouth. "Children are a precious gift, and you threw yours away. I don't think I can ever forgive that. But it's not my place to forgive or not. It's Taylor's, and she deserves the right to see you and decide for herself if she wants to get to know you."

Nick took Maya by the arm and put distance between them and Jessica. "After everything you've heard, how can you say that I should let Taylor near Jessie?" he asked, his voice low and anguished. "How can I do this to my little girl?"

"That's the question I want answered," Maya said, struggling to keep her voice down. "How dare you let your daughter think that her mother was dead?"

"What was I supposed to tell her?" Nick demanded. "Should I have said, 'Oh, honey, your mom didn't die. She just didn't want you' instead? How could that have been better?"

"I don't know," Maya said, flinging her arms wide. "But you can't tell me that this is better."

"This *is* better," Nick said. "Because I'm not letting her near Taylor. If she never sees Taylor, Taylor will never know."

"Yes, she will," Maya said, feeling the weight of her decision pressing down on her. "If you don't tell Taylor the truth, I will."

Nick stared at her in disbelief. "You would do that?" he asked, his voice hoarse. "You would go against my wishes concerning my daughter?"

Maya heard the emphasis loud and clear, and it broke her heart. "Yes," she all but whispered. "I can't keep the truth from Taylor. I won't."

"Fine," Nick spat. "If that's the way you want it, fine."

He stomped to the kitchen door, flung it open, then shouted across the yard. "The party's over, folks. Thanks for coming. Taylor, come here."

Holding open the door, he turned to face Maya. The look he gave her froze her heart in her chest. For whatever was about to happen, he already blamed her. In a way, he had a right to.

"Daddy?" Taylor's voice sounded hesitant as she stepped to the door. "What's wrong?"

"Nothing's wrong, pumpkin," he said in a false tone of voice. "I have a surprise for you."

Shutting the door behind her, he led her into the kitchen. When she saw Jessica she stopped, shooting Maya a questioning glance. Maya nodded and gave her a smile of encouragement. Jessica gasped and put her hands over her mouth, tears leaking down her cheeks.

Taylor turned to Nick. "She looks like me."

"I know," Nick said. "That's because she's your mother, Jessica."

"Hi, baby," Jessica said, taking a step towards Taylor.

Taylor backed up a step. "But…I thought my mommy was dead."

"That was a mistake," Nick said.

"I had to go away for a while," Jessica said through her tears. "But I'm back now, and I'd really love to get to know you."

Taylor's face scrunched up with the effort to understand. "But if she's my mommy does that mean that Maya can't be my mommy anymore?"

Maya had to close her eyes against a wave of pain that threatened to drive her to her knees. She forced her eyes open again, putting her hand on the child's shoulder. "You're going to always be my special girl. But that's your real mother. Don't you want to say hello?"

She hung back for a moment. "It's up to you, Taylor," Maya said into the charged silence. "No one will make you do what you don't want to do."

For a heartbeat, Taylor remained silent. Then she said one word, "Mom?"

"Yes, baby," Jessica said through her tears. "It's me."

One moment Taylor stood next to Maya, the next she was in her mother's arms, both of them crying. Maya turned away from the reunion, freezing when she caught sight of Nick's expression. All the anger had leached out of him, replaced by something she couldn't identify. Wonder, hope, happiness? She didn't know, and she didn't want to see anything more.

"I'm going back outside," she said to no one in particular, then turned for the door.

"Maya." Nick's voice made her pause, turn back. His expression was carefully blank. "We'll talk later, okay?"

Unable to speak, she simply nodded, then escaped into the early evening air. "I'm sorry everyone," she said, amazed at the steadiness of her voice. "Nick's had a family emergency. I'm afraid the party's over."

Brandt, her parents, and A.J. crowded closer. "What's going on, Maya?" her mother asked. "Who is that woman?"

"Oh, her?" Maya smiled, though it made her face hurt. "That's Jessica, Taylor's mother. Taylor's meeting her for the first time."

Gasps of shocked disbelief and anger filled the air, followed by a slew of questions. "Yes, I thought she was dead. No, this is as much a surprise to me as it is to you. No, I don't know what's going to happen next."

She pushed through her family heading for the relative safety of her house. "Mai?" her mother called. "Are you all right?"

"No, I'm not all right," she said, not slowing her stride. "All I know is that right now, I need to go home. I need to think."

She made it through the kitchen door and to the table, then put her head in her hands. "Damn him!" she burst out, slamming her hands against the table. "Damn him for doing this!"

The kitchen door opened, and Brandt stepped inside. He didn't say anything, just took the chair opposite her in silent support.

She shot to her feet, her sandals clicking on the tile floor. "He could have told me. All this time he let me believe that his wife was dead. And stupid, gullible me, I didn't question it."

She folded her arms across her chest. "But I'm more angry that he deceived Taylor all these years. Every night that little girl prayed to heaven, prayed to a mother she thought was dead. I can't begin to imagine what's going on in her mind."

"It can't be easy, and it wouldn't be even if she'd known that her mother had left them," Brandt said. "But what's Nick's take on this?"

"Besides anger?" Maya snorted, shaking with the force of her rage. "He didn't want to tell Taylor. His ex-wife was standing in his kitchen and he still didn't want to tell Taylor that her mother was alive. It was only when I threatened to tell Taylor myself that he relented and called her in."

She stopped in the middle of the kitchen, feeling a heavy weight pressing down on her. "You should have seen him, Brandt," she said, her voice thick. "Taylor just stood there, and then she looked at me, as if asking permission."

"What did you do?"

"What could I do?" she asked, wrapping her arms about herself. "I gave her a nod of encouragement, and she ran into her mother's arms. When Nick saw them together, his expression changed. I don't know how to explain it. He just…surrendered. He looked as if his heart had been broken all over again."

She returned to the table, slumping into her chair. "What should I do now, Brandt? I know Nick probably had a good reason to do what he did, but I can't understand it."

"Can you forgive him?"

"I don't know," she said, and her response scared her. "I honestly don't know."

She folded her arms across her chest, wondering if her heart would stop its racing. "It's not up to me to forgive him. It's up to Taylor, and even Jessica in a way. He and Jessica both have to ask Taylor for forgiveness. I don't think it's going to be easy for any of them."

"What do you want to do?"

"What do I want to do?" Maya stifled a half-laugh. "I want to turn back time. I want this to have never happened."

She wiped at her eyes. "I've gone through so much in the last couple of months. I dealt with his mother, other people's attitudes, and my own fear that I might not be good enough for him. Maybe this is a sign. Maybe fate or God or whatever has been trying to tell us all along that this wasn't meant to be, and we just didn't listen. Maybe I should be listening now."

She closed her eyes, but all she could see was the image of Nick's beautiful ex-wife standing in his kitchen, hugging her daughter as if she'd never let her go.

And why would she? an insidious part of Maya's mind whispered. It was obviously what she'd come back for—to reclaim her place in Taylor's life. And Nick had loved her once, loved her enough to get married. He was so affected by her leaving him that he'd convinced himself that she'd died. Love was a hard thing to exorcise from the heart. Maya knew firsthand that you never stopped loving people, you just hoped it faded enough to let you lead a normal life.

A normal life. Wasn't that what Nick said he wanted? A mother for Taylor, and a companion for himself. Why wouldn't he choose Jessica, who would be able to take Taylor out without someone thinking the girl had been kidnapped? Why wouldn't he choose the woman who'd given him a child—and could give him another?

"I can't compete against that," she whispered, and knew to the depths of her soul that it was true. As much as she wanted a child to love, she knew she could never come between Jessica and Taylor. She would never be able to give Nick a son. And even if that were different, Nick would do whatever was in Taylor's best interest. If Taylor wanted her birth mother, Taylor would have her. Soon Nick would remember the good times he'd had with Jessica, remember why he'd fallen in love with her. And where would Maya be?

"Can't compete with what?" Brandt asked.

She stared down at the ring on her left hand. "Wishes," she whispered. "So many wishes."

Nick's wish and Taylor's were still the same: someone for Nick to love, and someone to be a mother to Taylor. Jessica fit that wish perfectly, being Taylor's mother and the love of Nick's life all rolled into one. How could Maya's wish measure up to that? They could be a family again. At the very least, Maya thought, they deserved the opportunity to try.

She pulled the ring off her finger, then placed the glittering jewel on the table. A good thing that she hadn't had time to get used to it. But how would she get used to living next door to the man and child she'd thought she'd have forever?

Brandt reached over, picking up the ring. "You know I'm not the relationship expert in the family. But if you want some advice from me, I'd tell you not to make any decision now, while you're emotional."

He handed the ring back to her "Talk to him, try to find some way to deal with this, but don't make a rash decision that you'll regret later."

"I won't," she promised. She told the truth. Her decision wasn't rash, it was one that she'd made a long time ago.

"I think I'll take a little drive around the Perimeter," Brandt announced, getting to his feet. "If you need me, just give me a call."

She hugged him tightly, thankful for his support, knowing that he'd stand by her no matter what. "Thanks."

TWENTY-SEVEN

Five minutes after her brother left, the doorbell rang. Her heart in her throat, she crossed the room to the foyer, opened the door, then turned away. She didn't need to see Nick to know that he stood there.

She sat on the couch, waiting, while he shut the door. It made her feel slightly better to see the worry and fatigue on his face, but only slightly.

Nick knew he had an uphill battle as soon as he saw Maya's face. Anger, maybe even tears, he could have dealt with. But this silent, withdrawn Maya disturbed him, as if she had already built a wall between them. He shoved his hands in his pockets. "You have every right to be furious with me," he said into the quiet. "But I hope you'll give me a chance to explain."

"How's Taylor?"

The question startled him, and he didn't think to check his words. "Jessie's with her. She's still upset, but she's getting used to it."

Maya nodded, as if they were talking about the weather instead of the return of his supposedly dead wife. "How about you? Are you used to it already?"

"What do you mean?"

She raised her face, her skin pale in the dim light. "Are you used to having *Jessie* around already?"

Too late he realized his mistake. "That's what I called her when we were married."

She nodded again, and he could have kicked himself. "I'm sorry, Maya. This whole thing has knocked me for a loop. I don't know where to begin."

Her expression could have been set in stone. "How about starting with the fact that you lied to me?"

No anger, no tears, just a coldness Nick had no idea how to counteract. "It wasn't my intention to lie to you."

"The road to hell is paved with intentions," she said with the same eerie calmness. "What did you intend to do? When did you intend to tell me? After Taylor graduated from college?"

"No, I just—I don't know."

"Uh-hunh. You were going to let this lie of yours play out as long and as far as you could, weren't you?"

"I didn't lie to you, Maya. I never said that Taylor's mother was dead."

"You didn't lie." She spat the words as if they were venom. "You told your daughter that her mother died right after Taylor was born. That's what Taylor told me, and when I talked to you about it, you just went right along. You don't think that was a lie?"

"I know I should have told you."

"Yes, you should have," she replied, no heat in her voice. "But you can tell me now. I want to hear it, hear all of it."

Nick slumped into the empty chair with a sigh. "We were young," he began. "I was young enough and naïve enough to believe in love at first sight and happily-ever-after. I thought Jessica felt the same. She told me she felt the same, and I believed her

"We didn't plan to have children right away. Jessica wanted to go into grad school and I was just starting my residency. It was just one of those things, but we were both thrilled at the thought of having a child."

He sighed again. "I know I left a lot on her, and on my parents. My residency was anything but easy but I still did my best—went to parenting classes, Lamaze, shopped for things, everything I could fit into my schedule. My mother helped out a lot, spending a great deal of time with Jessie. If she noticed something wrong, she never told me.

"After Taylor was born, though, Jessie started to change. I thought it was just that the delivery took a lot out of her, or maybe it was just post-partum depression. I tried to spend as much time with her and Taylor as I could, or look after Taylor while Jessica went to lunch with friends or just got out of the apartment. But one day she apparently decided that enough was enough. She dropped Taylor off at my parents' house before noon one morning, and disappeared. I didn't know anything was wrong until my mother called me about six that evening, asking if I'd seen Jessie. I hadn't. I got to my parents' about ten that night, and they still hadn't seen her. I was getting frantic, wondering what had happened to her. I started calling around to other hospitals, checking with her friends, but I came up empty. Finally I gathered Taylor and went home. And that's when I discovered the truth."

His jaw tightened. "All her things were gone, and so was the extra money we'd stashed away. I found a note explaining that she felt like she was suffocating, that she'd given up her life and she wanted it back. Two months later, I was served with divorce papers in which she promised to give up all parental rights if I didn't contest.

"I loved her," he admitted, his shoulders scrunched with discomfort. "I loved her and I would have done anything for her. Anything. But I never got the chance."

But there's a chance now, a small voice in Maya's heart whispered. A chance to rekindle the love he'd had with Jessica. And, most importantly, a chance to put his family back together, to reunite mother and daughter. Maya knew she didn't have a chance against that, no matter how much she might wish it otherwise.

All at once she became angry. Angry at Nick for lying to her, even if it was a lie by omission. Angry at Jessica for picking today to re-enter his life. Mostly she was angry with herself, for believing that Nick and his daughter could make her wishes come true.

"Do you want the chance now?" she surprised herself by asking.

Nick looked just as surprised. "What?"

"Is that why you never told me the truth?" she demanded, rising to her feet. "Were you hoping all along that she would return so that you could get another chance?"

"Of course that's not why I didn't tell you!" he shot back.

"Then why?" she asked flinging her arms wide. "Why did you keep this from me? Why did I have to find out like this? You let me open myself up to you, tell you my deepest secret, and you didn't even have the decency to return the favor!"

"I wanted to tell you. I tried to tell you, several times."

"And people in hell want ice water," she said coldly. Coldness was much better than the sadness and defeat that she'd experienced earlier. "All that matters is that you didn't tell me. Obviously you didn't trust me enough. Or love me enough."

"I do love you, Maya. You know I do."

She smiled bitterly. "You loved Jessica, too. And you just said you would have done anything for her. Me, you couldn't even tell the truth."

"What do you want from me?" he exclaimed, crossing the floor to stand before her. "What do you want me to say or do to make this right?"

"Can you honestly tell me that you don't still love her?" she asked. "Can you tell me that you don't have feelings for the mother of your child?"

He remained silent. A stabbing anger filled her. If she'd had anything in her hands, she would have thrown it at him. As it was, she had to fold her arms across her chest, hoping to hold the rage in, hoping to keep the pain at bay.

"I love you, Maya," he said at last. "I never planned on seeing Jessie again. I was prepared to send her on her way, but you were right, Taylor at least deserved to see her." He sighed. "Things just got real complicated real fast. I don't know what I feel for her besides anger. But I know what I feel for you. That hasn't changed. I want you and I'll do whatever it takes to make this right."

"There's only one thing you can do to make this right," she said, her anger leaving her. "You need to give Taylor time to get to know her mother. Whether Jessica deserves that or not, I can't say. But Taylor should know her mother."

"Why?" he wondered. "She walked out on me and Taylor less than a month after Taylor was born." Disgust filled his features. "She left me struggling to complete med school and my residency and raise a newborn. After she sent me the divorce papers, I never heard from her. Never once has she tried to contact me or any member of my family in the last seven years. Not even to ask how her own child was doing. If it was just post-partum depression, I could've forgiven that—or at least I would have tried. But she just wiped her hands and walked away. She obviously didn't care."

"Except that she came back," Maya pointed out. "So what does that mean?"

"It means one of Jessica's kids is sick, and she wants to test Taylor's bone marrow."

"No," she whispered, horrified. Her heart welled with sympathy for a child she didn't know, and for a mother's desperation that would drive her to the one place she wasn't welcomed. "What are you going to do?"

"I don't know, Maya. I just don't know. But that doesn't mean that things have changed between us."

Pain twisted in Maya's stomach, sharp and bitter, and she had to force her words out. "Things have changed between us, Nick. Surely you can see that."

"No, I don't see that. We can still get married, we can still be a family."

She stared at him in disbelief. "Do you really think I can pretend that this never happened? Do you really believe I can accept that you lied to me? And even if I did accept you being dishonest with me, I can't accept that you lied to your own daughter!"

"I had no choice!"

"There's always a choice. You just took the easy way out!"

"Easy? You think this was easy?"

"Yes, it was easy—for you. You had a hell of a lot fewer questions to answer by telling Taylor her mother was dead than if you'd told her the truth about her mother leaving you." She spun away from him. "Do you have any idea what Taylor's going through right now?"

"I know she's understandably upset—"

"*Understandably upset?* Nick, your daughter spent the first seven years of her life thinking that her mother died when she was born—because she was born. And now she's thinking, 'Oh, my mother didn't die because I was born, she left me because I was born.' And you're making her go through that!"

"All right. I took the easy way out. Is that what you want to hear? Jessica walked out on our child and me and left me to juggle my residency and a newborn. I nearly killed myself trying to look after Taylor and become a doctor. Don't I deserve some slack for that?"

"Oh that's rich! You think you deserve some sort of commendation just because you've managed to raise Taylor and get banked as a doctor?" She clapped her hands, a staccato, angry sound. "Whoopdee-freakin'-doo!"

"I don't want commendations. I want you to understand." Nick's face tightened with anger. "I had every intention of telling Taylor the truth, to leave it to her if she wanted to contact her mother or not. I just wanted to wait until she was old enough to handle it."

"Old enough to handle it? Nick, you've let your seven-year-old daughter believe her mother was dead. How do you think she handled that?"

"What makes you the expert? It's not like you ever had a child!"

Nick's eyes widened as he realized what he'd just shouted. Maya lifted a hand to her cheek, as if he'd slapped her "Maya, I'm sorry—"

"No, you're right." Her voice grew wooden. "I can't possibly know what a parent would do in that situation. I don't know why you didn't tell Taylor the truth, and I don't know why your ex-wife walked away. And I don't know why you made me open up, confess all my fears to you, and you didn't have the balls to extend the same courtesy to me. Maybe that just proves that this isn't right. *We* aren't right." She took a deep breath. "I think you should leave now."

"Maya, don't throw me out. Not like this."

"We're a mistake, Nick. Everything that's happened was pointing this way. Your mother, that incident in the store, now this…maybe life has been trying to tell us something and we haven't been listening."

"So what does that mean?" he asked, fear and anger churning inside him. "When things get hard we should just roll over and take our lumps? Are we not supposed to fight for what we want? Are we not supposed to even try?"

"We've tried, Nick, don't you see that?" she asked, throwing her arms wide. "We've been trying for months. Each time we move forward, something happens to slap us two steps backward."

"So you want to give up? Don't you believe in us?"

"I did believe in us, Nick. But what I believed was a lie." She took a deep breath. "Don't you see, Nick? You need to take time to sort this out, to deal with Jessica and her request. All of you need to sit down and talk this through. Having me around will just muddy the waters."

"That's not true," Nick insisted. "We need you, Maya. I need you."

"And Taylor needs to know her mother. At least, she needs the chance to get to know her. Maybe a family therapist can help all of you deal with this.

Who knows? Taylor and Jessica may bond with each other." *And I can't watch that happen.*

Her hand touched the door before his voice stopped her. "Maya, look at me. Tell me you still love me. Tell me we still have a future together."

She wouldn't lie to him, not about that. "I do love you, Nick." It was all she could say, would say.

His eyes roamed her face, searching, hoping. The longing and pain in his eyes almost made her relent. Almost.

"Go home, Nick," she urged, her voice gentle. "Go to your daughter. You've always said that you would put Taylor's needs above everything else. I know you can't do anything less."

"You're right," he said, sounding defeated. "I have to think about Taylor. I have to make sure she's going to be okay. But I need you to do something for me."

"What?"

"Remember when we started dating, you warned me how difficult it would be. You gave me a chance to think about it and make up my mind."

He took her hands in his. "Now that you know everything, and I swear, you do know everything, I want you to take some time to think about it. Think about whether love is worth fighting for. Think about the moments of pure happiness we've had. After all that, then make up your mind."

He kissed her once, hard, then headed out the door. Maya closed the door behind him, then sank to the floor as the dam that held back her tears finally broke. She didn't have to make up her mind. She'd already cut herself free.

She just hoped she wouldn't spend the rest of her life in regret.

TWENTY-EIGHT

She hadn't thought it could get much worse, but it did.

She couldn't bear to be next door to Nick and Taylor. Couldn't bear the thought of accidentally catching them and Jessica going on some outing that she would have been a part of. Couldn't bear the thought of seeing them as a family, seeing them happy. So she took Brandt up on his offer to switch places, crashing at his apartment while he looked after her house.

Working dulled the pain, and Maya threw herself into her job, actually putting in more time at the office instead of working from home. Roger noticed. "Are you going to tell me what's going on?"

Maya's hands paused on the keyboard. "Nothing's changed."

"I guessed as much," her boss said, entering her office and shutting the door behind him. "That's why I want to know what's going on."

"Everything's fine, Roger, really," Maya said. She was getting better and better at the lie. Maybe she should head for Hollywood. "There's been utter silence from the other side, and that's just fine with me. My only issue has to do with making this program do what I want it to."

"All right." He paused. "If you want to discuss business, fine. Travis was supposed to handle Shipman in San Francisco, but he's out sick."

"I can do it." It would be great to get away. Not that she was escaping or anything. It was for work, and she needed to hold up her end regarding out of town jobs.

"You haven't heard the details yet," Roger said.

"I can coordinate with Whitehorse through my laptop, or I can pass it to Samantha if need be," Maya pointed out. "I know Shipman is going to be important for us, and if that means having someone on-site, I can do that as well as Travis."

"I'm not doubting that for a minute. In fact, I'd say you're better at onsite than he is-not that he needs to know that," her boss added. "It should only be for a couple of days, but it may require more."

"No problem. When was Travis supposed to head out?" she asked.

"Tomorrow morning," Roger said. "It's short notice, and I hate to ask you while you're in the middle of personal things, but—"

"But I can do this. Besides, I haven't done my obligatory visit to my West Coast geeks this year. It's my time to go."

Six days. Maybe a week away would keep her from picking up he phone to dial Nick's number, keep her from driving past her neighborhood, too afraid of what she might see if she actually drove down her street.

She shared the news with Brandt as she met him at her house. His response was pure Brandt: straight to the point.

"Good. I think you should get away."

"What? Why?"

"I'm not blind, Maya. I see what this is doing to you. You were dreading making the drive back home. Why else would you have called?"

"I wanted to see if you were here," she answered. Truth was, she wanted to make sure that Nick and his family weren't.

"Yeah, right." Brandt clearly didn't believe her, not that she'd expected him to anyway. "So get away. Don't put yourself through it. Clear your head."

"I'm going out there to work, Brandt, not to run away from my issues."

Brandt sorted. "Who do you think you're talking to? I know what you're feeling, sis. I know you want to give up. Believe me, I know you want to give up. I know it's not easy. But we weren't put here for easy. We were put here to learn something, to make a difference. At least, I have to believe there a reason. If there isn't, and this is all some cosmic joke…" He cleared his throat. "Anyway, I know it may seem like the question of the ages, but it's really very simple."

"Simple? How can you say this is simple?"

"Because it is," he insisted. "Do you still love the man?"

She wanted to lie. She tried to lie, but words wouldn't come. Instead, she pulled her knees against her chest to rest her forehead, trying to hold back tears.

"I'll take that as a yes," Brandt said quietly. She felt him lay one beefy hand on her shoulder. "What makes you think that Nick doesn't feel the same way?"

"Did you get a good look at Jessica?" she asked, lifting her head. "She's beautiful. He told me that he would have done anything for her, he loved her that much. They have a history together. They have a child together. And she can give him another."

"And you really believe he'll throw you over for some woman who abandoned him and their child eight years ago."

"Why wouldn't he?" she asked, dashing her hand across her suddenly leaking eyes. "She's everything I'm not: white, fertile, Taylor's mother, and she's a widow, too. It's not a hard decision to make. I always said that I'd walk away if he wanted another child, if we couldn't deal with being a blended family."

"Do you really think the guy you fell in love with could think that way?"

"I fell in love with Russell," she reminded him. "And he betrayed me and went back to a woman who'd already given him a child." Her eyes widened with shock. "Oh, God," she whispered. "I let history repeat itself."

"No. No you didn't. Nick isn't anything like Russell."

"Isn't he?" she asked bitterly. "Didn't he do the exact same thing?"

"What? Mentally abuse you?" Brandt shifted in his chair. "Nick lied to you. I know it was a big lie, but I also know the man loves you."

Maya shook her head, tired of the whole argument. "I've been around and round this for the last two weeks," she said softly. "I've examined everything that happened, and I always get the same conclusion. Sometimes wishes just don't come true, no matter how badly we want them to."

TWENTY-NINE

Nick sat at the kitchen table, an untouched cup of coffee before him. He rested his forehead in his hands, eyes scrunched shut to stave off the headache and heartache that had dogged him for days.

Maya wasn't coming back.

The moment to face reality had come. Because he'd tried to protect his daughter, because he'd tried to do the right thing, he'd lost the one woman perfect for him and his daughter. His daughter punished him with silence, talking only to Nana Henderson. She didn't even talk to Jessica, and refused every bribe his ex-wife had offered the three times she'd visited. Despite that, she'd agreed to help the half-brother she didn't know, and had her bone marrow tested.

"Daddy?"

Nick looked up to see his daughter standing by the kitchen door, the Asian Barbie clutched in her arms. As happy as he was that his daughter had come to him, the sadness on her face tore at his heart. "Hey, pumpkin. What's up?"

She inched further into the room. "Why did Maya go away?"

Taking a deep breath, Nick decided to tell the truth. "Because Daddy messed up. I should have told both of you about your mother a long time ago, but I didn't know how."

"When is she coming back?"

"I don't know, sweetheart," he admitted, his breath shaky. "She wanted us to take some time to get to know your mother, to spend some time together as a family."

Taylor's face crumpled. "But we're not a family," she pointed out. "My real mommy left, just like Maya did."

"No, sweetheart, no." Nick moved out of the chair so fast it tumbled to the floor. He dropped to his knees before his daughter and hugged her tight. "Jessica had to go home, to be with your half-brother. And Maya loves you. I know she does."

"Then why won't she come back? Why doesn't she want to be my mommy?"

"Listen to me, sweetheart," Nick said, puffing her onto his lap. "Did Maya ever tell you that she didn't want to be your mom?"

"No."

"Of course not. She wouldn't say that because she loves you."

"Then why isn't she here?" she asked.

"Because she has a problem with me, and I have to make it right." His jaw clenched with determination. Somehow he had to make it right.

―⁓―

"Where's Maya?"

Brandt folded his arms across his chest. "San Francisco."

A chill crept into Nick's chest. "San Francisco? Did she want to get away from me that badly?"

"Don't flatter yourself," Brandt said. "She's out there for work."

"Permanently?"

"What if she was?"

"Then I'd have to book a flight," Nick said. "I need to see her. I have to talk to her and convince her that I love her, only her, and always will."

"Sure," her brother said. "You love my sister so much you threw her over for your ex-wife."

"That's not true!" Nick all but shouted. "Maya knows that isn't true."

"Does she?" Brandt asked, his voice ruthless. "She seemed to think that you'd rather have Taylor's mother instead of her. Especially since you already had one child with your ex, and Maya can't give you another."

"Why would she think a ridiculous thing…oh my God." A sick feeling lodged in the pit of his stomach.

"Maya's ex-husband did that, leaving her for his former lover and the son he'd had. That left a pretty damn deep scar, and as much as she liked to pretend it wasn't there, something like that never really heals."

"I told her that didn't matter," Nick said, heartsick. "Over and over I told her. When she first told me about it, I told her she was all woman to me. Why wouldn't she believe me?"

"I don't know," Brandt said heavily. "Maybe she was afraid to believe it. Hell, maybe she sensed something with you and she didn't want to fully commit to you until you fully committed to her."

Nick curled his hands into fists, choking on his guilt. "I was wrong not to tell her about Jessica. I was wrong not to tell Taylor. But she's wrong if she thinks I would choose my ex-wife over her."

"I believe you," Brandt said. "For what it's worth, I tried to tell her that."

"You did?" Nick asked, surprised. If anyone would be against him, he'd thought Brandt would be the one.

"Yeah, not that it made any difference. She seemed convinced that her life with you was over."

"She's wrong," Nick declared. "Jessica and I took Taylor to therapy for two weeks. Taylor's marrow isn't a match either. Now Jessica's returned to her life, and I want mine back."

"I think Maya's going to be out there for a while longer," Brandt said. "She was only supposed to be out there for a couple of days, but the job's causing more trouble than expected."

"What hotel is she staying in?" Nick asked. He'd go out west and camp out in the hotel lobby if he had to.

Brandt gave Nick the information. "I assume you're going to get out there as soon as you can?"

"You're damn right I am. Do you think Dina would mind looking after Taylor for a couple of days?"

"I don't think she'd mind at all," Brandt said, giving one of his rare smiles. "But she does expect to be the first to know when everything's settled."

"Trust me, if everything gets settled you'll be able to hear it all the way from San Francisco."

"Room service."

Groaning, Maya pulled the blankets off her head to stare at the clock on the nightstand beside her. Four thirty-three. She didn't know if that was a.m. or p.m., and she didn't care. Thanks to her co-worker Travis or the San Francisco Bay, she had the worst case of stomach flu she'd ever had. Who knew you needed a vaccine to travel to the West Coast?

The first three days had gone by like a breeze, smooth and easy. A prototype was agreed upon and she began the storyboards the fourth day, they decided to scrap everything and start over. Already feeling the effects of her flu, Maya had lost her religion on the fifth day, telling her startled clients that they had two days to come up with an acceptable concept or she'd be on the next plane to better health.

As far as she knew, that had been a day ago. She'd ordered flu medicine and orange juice to be delivered to her room and hadn't left it since. In fact, the most movement she'd done was from the bed to the bathroom, alternating between vomiting and other less savory uses for a commode.

The knock at the door came again. "I didn't order anything," she called, wanting nothing more than to go back to sleep. Sleep was her friend.

"The concierge found a doctor for you, ma'am," the voice called through the door. "He agreed to see you."

Really? That caught her fatigued interest. Her boss had insisted that she stay at this particular hotel. She'd initially thought it too swanky for her hearth-and-home tastes, but she had to admit the customer service blew her away.

"Ma'am?"

"Just a moment." She crawled out of bed, clawing her hair into some semblance of style. After shrugging into her robe, she found a couple of wrinkled bills in her purse. She crumpled them into her palm, wondering if she should put some antibacterial hand cleaner on them. Would that count as money laundering?

With a weak smile, she wiped the sleep from her eyes, shuffling her way to the door of the suite. She thumbed off the security bolt, then opened the door. "Thanks so much for coming to see me," she said, looking first to the hotel employee to give him the tip. She caught sight of the doctor from the corner of her eye, noting his height, the color of his hair. His cologne.

She couldn't believe it. "Nick?"

"Hi," he said quietly, his eyes searching her face. "Can I come in?"

Completely unnerved, she stepped back. The world suddenly began to spin and she found herself slipping with no way to catch herself. Strong arms caught her, lifting her up and holding her close. She closed her eyes.

"I'll take it from here," she heard him tell the bellman. "Thank you."

She heard the door close, then Nick carried her across the room and back to bed. She didn't open her eyes again until the covers were tucked under her chin. Nick leaned over her, his beautiful blue eyes dark with worry. "I didn't know you were ill, or I would have come sooner."

"How did you know I was here?" she asked, watching him go into the bathroom and return with a damp cloth.

"Brandt told me," he said, wiping her face gently. "I left Taylor with Nadine and took the first flight out. What happened to you?"

"I was fine a couple of days ago," she said, trying to come to terms with him being there. "Then I started feeling queasy and hot and tired. I think it's a combination of working too much, eating too much seafood, and some sort of bug."

"And being put through the wringer by me and my issues," he said, and she could see remorse bright and stark in his eyes.

She couldn't deny the truth of his words. Instead, she asked the question she most wanted an answer to. "Why did you come all the way out here, Nick? You could have just called."

"Because you're here," he answered simply. "And I want to be with you."

Hope flared in her chest, burning away a portion of her misery. But after the pain and uncertainty of the past two weeks—the past two years—she didn't dare believe just yet. "What about Jessica?"

"My ex-wife is still my ex-wife," he said. "We spent two weeks in family therapy just like you suggested. We made some headway, not a lot. Taylor volunteered to have her bone marrow tested."

"She did?"

"Yeah." Nick blinked rapidly. "Said she'd learned from you how important brothers and sisters are, and she wanted to help if she could. She wasn't a match, but I think it helped Taylor some, which is the important thing. Then Jessica hopped on a plane back to her children in Milwaukee."

"That's where she lives? Milwaukee?" It seemed a safe distance away.

He nodded. "I told Taylor that she could go visit whenever she wants, if she wants. It's her choice if she wants to see Jessica and her half-siblings. I'm not going to push her either way. But I don't want to talk about that."

"Wh-what do you want to talk about?" she asked, half-dreading, half-anticipating his answer.

He knelt on the floor beside her. "I want to talk about you, and how much I love you and need you," he said, his voice rough. "I want to talk about me, and how my world isn't complete without you in it. And I want to talk about us, about being a family."

Maya closed her eyes against a flood of emotion. She wanted so desperately to believe him, to be with him. But she had to know if he really and truly wanted her.

She opened her eyes as he clasped her hand in his. "I'm not Russell, sweetheart," he said softly, his eyes bright. "I'd rather die than hurt you like that. I love you for you, not for what you can or can't do. I love you for who you are, I love you for loving my daughter. I love you because when we're with you—"

He broke off, then started again. "I love you because when we're with you, I understand what family really means. You give us that, Maya. Only you."

Tears ran unchecked down her face, making it difficult to see his gorgeous face. "Nick," she whispered brokenly, throwing her arms around his neck. "Oh, Nick."

She sat back from him, reaching over to open the drawer on the nightstand. With trembling fingers, she removed a small velvet box. "I didn't want to give it back," she said in a shaky voice, opening the lid to reveal the glittering ring. "I didn't want to give up hope that everything would work out the way I hoped and prayed and wished it would. I didn't want to believe that you'd stop loving me, because I didn't stop loving you."

He took the ring from her, his trembling fingers almost dropping it before putting it where it belonged. "Say you'll come back with me," he said hoarsely. "Say you'll let me love you. Say you'll grant our wish, and let us be a family."

"I will," she swore. "I'll come back with you. I'll love you. I'll make us a family."

EPILOGUE

The next night, Nick turned down the bed of their magnificent honeymoon suite, waiting patiently for Maya to appear. Correction, waiting patiently for his wife to appear. She'd been in the bathroom a good ten minutes. He didn't want to disturb her. After all, they had the rest of their lives to be together.

Her suggestion that they elope had surprised and delighted him. Vegas was only one state away, a very short plane ride. He found himself wanting to make their love official as much as she did.

He smiled as he remembered the calls they'd placed after they were pronounced man and wife. Taylor had been excited, chanting, "I got a mommy, I got a mommy" over and over. Maya's reassurance that she'd be home the next night to tuck her new daughter in made his heart swell with love all over again.

Maya's parents had been thrilled with the news that they'd reconciled, and mildly upset that they'd decided to elope. Once her parents were reassured that they intended to have a formal wedding in Atlanta, they calmed down. Well, Carson Hughes had calmed down. Loan had worked herself into a fury of wedding planning.

The call to his parents was somewhat different. He'd already exchanged words with his mother about Taylor's stay in Florida, and informed them of Jessica's visit and its outcome. His mother had surprised him by accepting the news of his marriage, then immediately demanding a big wedding. He gave her Loan Hughes' phone number. They'd either hate each other or become the best of friends. Nick had a feeling it would be the latter. His mother definitely needed to loosen up a bit, and Loan Hughes was the person to do it.

"Nick!"

Maya's cry had him leaping off the bed, running into the bathroom. "What? What happened?"

She turned to face him, tears running down her cheeks, holding a plastic stick out to him. "It's blue!"

"What's blue?" He took a closer look at what she held. His heart seized up in his chest. "Maya?"

"I started to wonder about it last night, after we made up, because we haven't used protection since I broke my ankle," she managed through her tears. "I didn't want to say anything, in case I was wrong, but it's blue. It's blue!"

Two and two added up in his brain. "We're going to have a baby?" he dared to ask. She nodded. "We're going to have a baby!"

With a whoop of laughter, he scooped her in his arms, spinning her around until they were both breathless. "A baby! We're going to have a baby!"

"All this time, I thought the problem was with me," she said, wiping ecstatic tears from her cheeks. "I believed Russell, and all this time he was the one with the problem, not me."

"There was never a problem with you, sweetheart," Nick said. "As far as I'm concerned, you always were and always will be perfect."

He stopped suddenly, holding her close, his heart so full he thought it'd break. "You do realize what this means, don't you, love?"

"No. What?"

He smiled down at her "It means that our three wishes have come true."

2008 Reprint Mass Market Titles

January

Cautious Heart
Cheris F. Hodges
ISBN-13: 978-1-58571-301-1
ISBN-10: 1-58571-301-5
$6.99

Suddenly You
Crystal Hubbard
ISBN-13: 978-1-58571-302-8
ISBN-10: 1-58571-302-3
$6.99

February

Passion
T. T. Henderson
ISBN-13: 978-1-58571-303-5
ISBN-10: 1-58571-303-1
$6.99

Whispers in the Sand
LaFlorya Gauthier
ISBN-13: 978-1-58571-304-2
ISBN-10: 1-58571-304-x
$6.99

March

Life Is Never As It Seems
J. J. Michael
ISBN-13: 978-1-58571-305-9
ISBN-10: 1-58571-305-8
$6.99

Beyond the Rapture
Beverly Clark
ISBN-13: 978-1-58571-306-6
ISBN-10: 1-58571-306-6
$6.99

April

A Heart's Awakening
Veronica Parker
ISBN-13: 978-1-58571-307-3
ISBN-10: 1-58571-307-4
$6.99

Breeze
Robin Lynette Hampton
ISBN-13: 978-1-58571-308-0
ISBN-10: 1-58571-308-2
$6.99

May

I'll Be Your Shelter
Giselle Carmichael
ISBN-13: 978-1-58571-309-7
ISBN-10: 1-58571-309-0
$6.99

Careless Whispers
Rochelle Alers
ISBN-13: 978-1-58571-310-3
ISBN-10: 1-58571-310-4
$6.99

June

Sin
Crystal Rhodes
ISBN-13: 978-1-58571-311-0
ISBN-10: 1-58571-311-2
$6.99

Dark Storm Rising
Chinelu Moore
ISBN-13: 978-1-58571-312-7
ISBN-10: 1-58571-312-0
$6.99

2008 Reprint Mass Market Titles (continued)

July

Object of His Desire
A.C. Arthur
ISBN-13: 978-1-58571-313-4
ISBN-10: 1-58571-313-9
$6.99

Angel's Paradise
Janice Angelique
ISBN-13: 978-1-58571-314-1
ISBN-10: 1-58571-314-7
$6.99

August

Unbreak My Heart
Dar Tomlinson
ISBN-13: 978-1-58571-315-8
ISBN-10: 1-58571-315-5
$6.99

All I Ask
Barbara Keaton
ISBN-13: 978-1-58571-316-5
ISBN-10: 1-58571-316-3
$6.99

September

Icie
Pamela Leigh Starr
ISBN-13: 978-1-58571-275-5
ISBN-10: 1-58571-275-2
$6.99

At Last
Lisa Riley
ISBN-13: 978-1-58571-276-2
ISBN-10: 1-58571-276-0
$6.99

October

Everlastin' Love
Gay G. Gunn
ISBN-13: 978-1-58571-277-9
ISBN-10: 1-58571-277-9
$6.99

Three Wishes
Seressia Glass
ISBN-13: 978-1-58571-278-6
ISBN-10: 1-58571-278-7
$6.99

November

Yesterday Is Gone
Beverly Clark
ISBN-13: 978-1-58571-279-3
ISBN-10: 1-58571-279-5
$6.99

Again My Love
Kayla Perrin
ISBN-13: 978-1-58571-280-9
ISBN-10: 1-58571-280-9
$6.99

December

Office Policy
A.C. Arthur
ISBN-13: 978-1-58571-281-6
ISBN-10: 1-58571-281-7
$6.99

Rendezvous With Fate
Jeanne Sumerix
ISBN-13: 978-1-58571-283-3
ISBN-10: 1-58571-283-3
$6.99

2008 New Mass Market Titles

January

Where I Want To Be
Maryam Diaab
ISBN-13: 978-1-58571-268-7
ISBN-10: 1-58571-268-X
$6.99

Never Say Never
Michele Cameron
ISBN-13: 978-1-58571-269-4
ISBN-10: 1-58571-269-8
$6.99

February

Stolen Memories
Michele Sudler
ISBN-13: 978-1-58571-270-0
ISBN-10: 1-58571-270-1
$6.99

Dawn's Harbor
Kymberly Hunt
ISBN-13: 978-1-58571-271-7
ISBN-10: 1-58571-271-X
$6.99

March

Undying Love
Renee Alexis
ISBN-13: 978-1-58571-272-4
ISBN-10: 1-58571-272-8
$6.99

Blame It On Paradise
Crystal Hubbard
ISBN-13: 978-1-58571-273-1
ISBN-10: 1-58571-273-6
$6.99

April

When A Man Loves A Woman
La Connie Taylor-Jones
ISBN-13: 978-1-58571-274-8
ISBN-10: 1-58571-274-4
$6.99

Choices
Tammy Williams
ISBN-13: 978-1-58571-300-4
ISBN-10: 1-58571-300-7
$6.99

May

Dream Runner
Gail McFarland
ISBN-13: 978-1-58571-317-2
ISBN-10: 1-58571-317-1
$6.99

Southern Fried Standards
S.R. Maddox
ISBN-13: 978-1-58571-318-9
ISBN-10: 1-58571-318-X
$6.99

June

Looking for Lily
Africa Fine
ISBN-13: 978-1-58571-319-6
ISBN-10: 1-58571-319-8
$6.99

Bliss, Inc.
Chamein Canton
ISBN-13: 978-1-58571-325-7
ISBN-10: 1-58571-325-2
$6.99

2008 New Mass Market Titles (continued)

July

Love's Secrets
Yolanda McVey
ISBN-13: 978-1-58571-321-9
ISBN-10: 1-58571-321-X
$6.99

Things Forbidden
Maryam Diaab
ISBN-13: 978-1-58571-327-1
ISBN-10: 1-58571-327-9
$6.99

August

Storm
Pamela Leigh Starr
ISBN-13: 978-1-58571-323-3
ISBN-10: 1-58571-323-6
$6.99

Passion's Furies
AlTonya Washington
ISBN-13: 978-1-58571-324-0
ISBN-10: 1-58571-324-4
$6.99

September

Three Doors Down
Michele Sudler
ISBN-13: 978-1-58571-332-5
ISBN-10: 1-58571-332-5
$6.99

Mr Fix-It
Crystal Hubbard
ISBN-13: 978-1-58571-326-4
ISBN-10: 1-58571-326-0
$6.99

October

Moments of Clarity
Michele Cameron
ISBN-13: 978-1-58571-330-1
ISBN-10: 1-58571-330-9
$6.99

Lady Preacher
K.T. Richey
ISBN-13: 978-1-58571-333-2
ISBN-10: 1-58571-333-3
$6.99

November

This Life Isn't Perfect Holla
Sandra Foy
ISBN: 978-1-58571-331-8
ISBN-10: 1-58571-331-7
$6.99

Promises Made
Bernice Layton
ISBN-13: 978-1-58571-334-9
ISBN-10: 1-58571-334-1
$6.99

December

A Voice Behind Thunder
Carrie Elizabeth Greene
ISBN-13: 978-1-58571-329-5
ISBN-10: 1-58571-329-5
$6.99

The More Things Change
Chamein Canton
ISBN-13: 978-1-58571-328-8
ISBN-10: 1-58571-328-7
$6.99

Other Genesis Press, Inc. Titles

Other Genesis Press, Inc. Titles (continued)

Bodyguard	Andrea Jackson	$9.95
Boss of Me	Diana Nyad	$8.95
Bound by Love	Beverly Clark	$8.95
Breeze	Robin Hampton Allen	$10.95
Broken	Dar Tomlinson	$24.95
By Design	Barbara Keaton	$8.95
Cajun Heat	Charlene Berry	$8.95
Careless Whispers	Rochelle Alers	$8.95
Cats & Other Tales	Marilyn Wagner	$8.95
Caught in a Trap	Andre Michelle	$8.95
Caught Up In the Rapture	Lisa G. Riley	$9.95
Cautious Heart	Cheris F Hodges	$8.95
Chances	Pamela Leigh Starr	$8.95
Cherish the Flame	Beverly Clark	$8.95
Class Reunion	Irma Jenkins/	
	John Brown	$12.95
Code Name: Diva	J.M. Jeffries	$9.95
Conquering Dr. Wexler's Heart	Kimberley White	$9.95
Corporate Seduction	A.C. Arthur	$9.95
Crossing Paths, Tempting Memories	Dorothy Elizabeth Love	$9.95
Crush	Crystal Hubbard	$9.95
Cypress Whisperings	Phyllis Hamilton	$8.95
Dark Embrace	Crystal Wilson Harris	$8.95
Dark Storm Rising	Chinelu Moore	$10.95
Daughter of the Wind	Joan Xian	$8.95
Deadly Sacrifice	Jack Kean	$22.95
Designer Passion	Dar Tomlinson	$8.95
	Diana Richeaux	
Do Over	Celya Bowers	$9.95
Dreamtective	Liz Swados	$5.95

Other Genesis Press, Inc. Titles (continued)

Other Genesis Press, Inc. Titles (continued)

I Married a Reclining Chair	Lisa M. Fuhs	$8.95
I'll Be Your Shelter	Giselle Carmichael	$8.95
I'll Paint a Sun	A.J. Garrotto	$9.95
Icie	Pamela Leigh Starr	$8.95
Illusions	Pamela Leigh Starr	$8.95
Indigo After Dark Vol. I	Nia Dixon/Angelique	$10.95
Indigo After Dark Vol. II	Dolores Bundy/ Cole Riley	$10.95
Indigo After Dark Vol. III	Montana Blue/ Coco Morena	$10.95
Indigo After Dark Vol. IV	Cassandra Colt/	$14.95
Indigo After Dark Vol. V	Delilah Dawson	$14.95
Indiscretions	Donna Hill	$8.95
Intentional Mistakes	Michele Sudler	$9.95
Interlude	Donna Hill	$8.95
Intimate Intentions	Angie Daniels	$8.95
It's Not Over Yet	J.J. Michael	$9.95
Jolie's Surrender	Edwina Martin-Arnold	$8.95
Kiss or Keep	Debra Phillips	$8.95
Lace	Giselle Carmichael	$9.95
Last Train to Memphis	Elsa Cook	$12.95
Lasting Valor	Ken Olsen	$24.95
Let Us Prey	Hunter Lundy	$25.95
Lies Too Long	Pamela Ridley	$13.95
Life Is Never As It Seems	J.J. Michael	$12.95
Lighter Shade of Brown	Vicki Andrews	$8.95
Love Always	Mildred E. Riley	$10.95
Love Doesn't Come Easy	Charlyne Dickerson	$8.95
Love Unveiled	Gloria Greene	$10.95
Love's Deception	Charlene Berry	$10.95
Love's Destiny	M. Loui Quezada	$8.95
Mae's Promise	Melody Walcott	$8.95

Other Genesis Press, Inc. Titles (continued)

Other Genesis Press, Inc. Titles (continued)

Path of Fire	T.T. Henderson	$8.95
Path of Thorns	Annetta P. Lee	$9.95
Peace Be Still	Colette Haywood	$12.95
Picture Perfect	Reon Carter	$8.95
Playing for Keeps	Stephanie Salinas	$8.95
Pride & Joi	Gay G. Gunn	$8.95
Promises to Keep	Alicia Wiggins	$8.95
Quiet Storm	Donna Hill	$10.95
Reckless Surrender	Rochelle Alers	$6.95
Red Polka Dot in a World of Plaid	Varian Johnson	$12.95
Reluctant Captive	Joyce Jackson	$8.95
Rendezvous with Fate	Jeanne Sumerix	$8.95
Revelations	Cheris F. Hodges	$8.95
Rivers of the Soul	Leslie Esdaile	$8.95
Rocky Mountain Romance	Kathleen Suzanne	$8.95
Rooms of the Heart	Donna Hill	$8.95
Rough on Rats and Tough on Cats	Chris Parker	$12.95
Secret Library Vol. 1	Nina Sheridan	$18.95
Secret Library Vol. 2	Cassandra Colt	$8.95
Secret Thunder	Annetta P. Lee	$9.95
Shades of Brown	Denise Becker	$8.95
Shades of Desire	Monica White	$8.95
Shadows in the Moonlight	Jeanne Sumerix	$8.95
Sin	Crystal Rhodes	$8.95
Small Whispers	Annetta P. Lee	$6.99
So Amazing	Sinclair LeBeau	$8.95
Somebody's Someone	Sinclair LeBeau	$8.95
Someone to Love	Alicia Wiggins	$8.95
Song in the Park	Martin Brant	$15.95
Soul Eyes	Wayne L. Wilson	$12.95

Other Genesis Press, Inc. Titles (continued)

Soul to Soul	Donna Hill	$8.95
Southern Comfort	J.M. Jeffries	$8.95
Still the Storm	Sharon Robinson	$8.95
Still Waters Run Deep	Leslie Esdaile	$8.95
Stolen Kisses	Dominiqua Douglas	$9.95
Stories to Excite You	Anna Forrest/Divine	$14.95
Subtle Secrets	Wanda Y. Thomas	$8.95
Suddenly You	Crystal Hubbard	$9.95
Sweet Repercussions	Kimberley White	$9.95
Sweet Sensations	Gwendolyn Bolton	$9.95
Sweet Tomorrows	Kimberly White	$8.95
Taken by You	Dorothy Elizabeth Love	$9.95
Tattooed Tears	T. T. Henderson	$8.95
The Color Line	Lizzette Grayson Carter	$9.95
The Color of Trouble	Dyanne Davis	$8.95
The Disappearance of Allison Jones	Kayla Perrin	$5.95
The Fires Within	Beverly Clark	$9.95
The Foursome	Celya Bowers	$6.99
The Honey Dipper's Legacy	Pannell-Allen	$14.95
The Joker's Love Tune	Sidney Rickman	$15.95
The Little Pretender	Barbara Cartland	$10.95
The Love We Had	Natalie Dunbar	$8.95
The Man Who Could Fly	Bob & Milana Beamon	$18.95
The Missing Link	Charlyne Dickerson	$8.95
The Mission	Pamela Leigh Starr	$6.99
The Perfect Frame	Beverly Clark	$9.95
The Price of Love	Sinclair LeBeau	$8.95
The Smoking Life	Ilene Barth	$29.95
The Words of the Pitcher	Kei Swanson	$8.95
Three Wishes	Seressia Glass	$8.95
Ties That Bind	Kathleen Suzanne	$8.95

Other Genesis Press, Inc. Titles (continued)

Tiger Woods	Libby Hughes	$5.95
Time is of the Essence	Angie Daniels	$9.95
Timeless Devotion	Bella McFarland	$9.95
Tomorrow's Promise	Leslie Esdaile	$8.95
Truly Inseparable	Wanda Y. Thomas	$8.95
Two Sides to Every Story	Dyanne Davis	$9.95
Unbreak My Heart	Dar Tomlinson	$8.95
Uncommon Prayer	Kenneth Swanson	$9.95
Unconditional Love	Alicia Wiggins	$8.95
Unconditional	A.C. Arthur	$9.95
Until Death Do Us Part	Susan Paul	$8.95
Vows of Passion	Bella McFarland	$9.95
Wedding Gown	Dyanne Davis	$8.95
What's Under Benjamin's Bed	Sandra Schaffer	$8.95
When Dreams Float	Dorothy Elizabeth Love	$8.95
When I'm With You	LaConnie Taylor-Jones	$6.99
Whispers in the Night	Dorothy Elizabeth Love	$8.95
Whispers in the Sand	LaFlorya Gauthier	$10.95
Who's That Lady?	Andrea Jackson	$9.95
Wild Ravens	Altonya Washington	$9.95
Yesterday Is Gone	Beverly Clark	$10.95
Yesterday's Dreams, Tomorrow's Promises	Reon Laudat	$8.95
Your Precious Love	Sinclair LeBeau	$8.95

Dull, Drab, Love Life?

Passion Going Nowhere?

Tired Of Being Alone?

Does Every Direction You Look For Love

Lead You Astray?

Genesis Press presents
The launching of our new website!

RecaptureTheRomance.Com

Ignite
The Flame!

Order Form

Mail to: Genesis Press, Inc.
P.O. Box 101
Columbus, MS 39703

Name _____

Address _____

City/State _____ Zip _____

Telephone _____

Ship to (if different from above)

Name _____

Address _____

City/State _____ Zip _____

Telephone _____

Credit Card Information

Credit Card # _____ ☐ Visa   ☐ Mastercard

Expiration Date (mm/yy) _____ ☐ AmEx   ☐ Discover

Qty.	Author	Title	Price	Total

Use this order form, or call 1-888-INDIGO-1	
Total for books	_____
Shipping and handling: **$5 first two books,** **$1 each additional book**	_____
Total S & H	_____
Total amount enclosed	_____
Mississippi residents add 7% sales tax	